The Keeping-Room

BOOKS BY BETTY LEVIN

The Forespoken
A Griffon's Nest
The Keeping-Room
Landfall
The Sword of Culann
The Zoo Conspiracy

The Keeping-Room

by Betty Levin

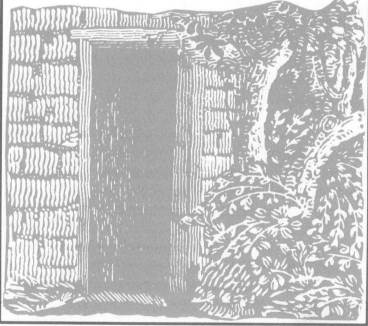

 Greenwillow Books, New York

Library of Congress Cataloging in Publication Data
Levin, Betty.   The keeping-room.
Summary: When Hal explores the Titcomb farm for
a school project, he learns the truth behind the
Candlewood curse.   [1. Mystery and detective stories]
I. Title. PZ7.L5759Ke [Fic] 80-23931
ISBN 0-688-80300-8

*For Jonathan
and for Sarah*

I am no more lonely than a single mullein or dandelion in a pasture, or a bean-leaf, or sorrel, or a horse-fly, or a bumble-bee. I am no more lonely than the Mill Brook, or a weathercock, or the North Star, or the south wind, or an April shower, or a January thaw, or the first spider in a new house.

—HENRY DAVID THOREAU, *Walden*

1

Hal Woodruff peered down Nutters Hill Road. No sign of the bus yet. If he counted on its being late, that would be the one morning it came on time. Then he'd have a three-mile walk to school. And trouble.

He didn't need trouble. Not now. Cars whisked past him on their way to Boston or its outlying industries. He stepped back onto the shoulder, avoiding the poison ivy that hugged the oak stump left from when they straightened the curve.

Facing the morning commuters, Hal found himself drawn toward the Titcombs' driveway. A few days ago it was just part of the landscape of this lonely bus stop. A few days ago the Titcombs and the Candlewood curse were something you could laugh at. Old Miss Titcomb maintaining she was well rid of her eighty acres of backland, telling all her concerned neighbors that it had some curse on it.

When had Hal stopped laughing? When the new Social Studies teacher, who also happened to be Hal's neighbor, told him he should take on the Candlewood back lot for his class project? Every kid in class was supposed to choose some nearby place, their own home if it was old, and find out what it was like before paved roads and cars and electricity. They'd all laughed when their teacher, Lew Rifkin, had mentioned the Candlewood curse.

Hal heard the bus before he saw it, and made his way back to the stop. Two eighth-grade girls were sitting together up front. Hal picked his usual seat way back and

1

waited for his friends, Josh Rosinus and Bill Sparkman. The bus lurched past the Titcombs' driveway, where yesterday afternoon Lew Rifkin had taken some of the neighbors to have a look at the old foundation that no one had known was there.

Twisting around, Hal had a brief glimpse of the Titcomb house and the small barn across from it. You'd never have guessed how much there was up there beyond those buildings, up behind the orchard, where they had walked along an old walled lane that led to the wooded hilltop. There was even a meadow, nearly consumed by blackberry canes, overgrown with goldenrod, but still suffused with the late September sun like a tiny open sea.

The bus stopped twice for groups of kids before Josh and Bill got on. "How was it?" they asked him right off, meaning Candlewood Farm and the outing with Lew Rifkin.

"Everyone was very impressed."

"You mean about the old farm foundation?" said Bill, whose parents had been there too.

"Even Mr. Atherton." Hal grinned, recalling the way Bliss Atherton, the local authority, had launched into a grand explanation about how easy it was to confuse granite outcroppings with laid stones, while Lew Rifkin, down on his hands and knees and looking like a frog or toad that belonged there, had spread apart the wiry sheep laurel, flattened the shiny green leaves, and revealed the stones nearly hidden by leafmold and lichens. You had to lower yourself to see the line of them, barely visible, yet straight and true and squared at the corner. "Poor Mr. Atherton had to discover something too, so he said that the big dead tree on top of the hill was probably planted when the farm

2

was built, maybe even before the Revolution." They'd all craned their necks to view the trunk jutting up through the greenery like a giant bleached bone.

"So what's wrong with the place?" asked Josh.

"The dump?" suggested Bill. "My parents weren't too happy about all that junk."

"Yes, well, Lew says there's probably a lot of history buried there. He dug in and pulled out some rusty sort of clamps with a chain connecting them and said they were to keep a cow from kicking. His kid put them around her neck. That's when he got me . . . when he asked me to take care of her." Hal shook his head. He'd been thinking the dump had real possibilities, hundreds of things down in there you could use or trade, when suddenly he understood what Lew was driving at. On Wednesday afternoons in Westwick the kids were free, but not the teachers. "He said I could take her with me exploring the back lot and trying to get old Miss Titcomb to talk about the past."

"Doesn't sound too bad, if he pays you," said Bill. "You'll be earning money while you're working on your project."

"You don't know what it's like there. And that kid." Hal couldn't begin to explain. Everyone trooping up to see the foundation and then staring bleakly at the beer cans and the blown-out tires that spilled over the hillside. When Lew had remarked that farm dumps were valuable records of human interaction with the environment, everyone had just looked away. They had gazed with relief at the swamp maples blazing scarlet through all the green of the lowland and concluded regretfully that this wasn't a likely site for historic preservation.

"So what's the matter with her?"

"She doesn't have any sense. She just wanders off. Lew

3

didn't even notice at first. Then he assumed I had her with me. I hadn't even agreed to take her on Wednesdays. It was getting dark too. Then my mother saw her, halfway down to the pond. Lew called and we waited. My mother says you can't leave five-year-olds, not for a minute, not in a place like that."

Bill shrugged that off. "No one watched Karen when she was five."

"Karen's nothing like this kid. Nothing." Hal could see Lew's child trudging upward through the gloom. "You know what she told her father? She'd been following the pigs. That's what she said."

Josh hooted. "What did he say?"

"Nothing. My mother called her an imaginative child, but then she's not being stuck with her." Hal's voice rose. The bus was full of jabbering kids now, and it was harder to talk. "So what am I going to do with a loony kid like that?"

"Tell him you're not qualified," suggested Josh.

"Bring her to my house," Bill offered. "Let her play with Karen and we'll split the money. How much is he paying?"

"Maybe he'll pay in grades," put in Josh. "A's all around."

"But seriously—"

"Seriously." Josh made his voice go hollow. "The curse of Candlewood has struck. In the shape of . . . What's her name?"

"Emily," said Hal glumly.

"Emily, who is not all she seems to be. When darkness falls—"

"Where's her mother?" asked Bill. "I haven't heard anything about a mother."

4

Hal only knew that Lew was divorced, that he'd moved to Westwick because he believed he should live in the community where he taught. He could only afford something like the Thayer house down the road from the Woodruffs. Some of the neighbors called it a commune because the tenants there weren't a family but just shared the house. They had goats for milk too, and hens and bees. An ideal set-up for Lew, what with built-in baby-sitters. Only none of the tenants was available on weekday afternoons.

Hal looked from one friend to the other. "How can I refuse him?"

His friends were silent. They had run out of ideas, out of jokes.

The trouble was that a little kid on Second Hill Road couldn't go off on her own to find friends that might be across one of the bad roads or just plain too far. Nobody knew that better than Hal, whose parents had often worried about raising an only child in such isolation, especially when they both worked in Boston.

When Hal was little they used to invite other kids to come over on Saturdays, but mostly he was by himself. There were swimming lessons or trips to the Science Museum, encouragement in interests like stamps and insects and dinosaurs. When he got interested in bees and started to spend a lot of time at the Thayer house, his parents said, "Why don't you call up Josh? Or someone else from school?" *Someone your own age,* is what he understood them to be saying. They bought him a bike that was so good it was stolen the first time he left it in Josh's garage. And for his tenth birthday they got him an antique telephone, an upright one like the kind you see in really old movies, but it never got around to being installed.

5

These days everyone knew that even though Westwick looked like a village on a Christmas card, that was only part of the picture. Commuter traffic could be deadly, and so could hitch-hiking. Last spring a man followed Andy Greenfield's little sister from the school bus and nearly got her in his car. The police chief had come to school to talk to all the kids, even the youngest, warning them to watch out for each other and to report anything suspicious.

So how could Hal refuse? There was going to be what's-her-name Emily waiting for him every Wednesday at noon, and probably hungry and cranky and expecting a real lunch when they got home. And there was Candlewood Farm to be seen to, with that little kid in tow.

"Come on," said Josh. "Face the music." The bus was almost empty, Josh and Bill in the aisle and edging toward the door.

Hal swung up out of the seat. "Face the curse," he amended, trying lamely to revive the joke.

Turning back for his notebook, which had slid to the floor, he froze for an instant, caught by this gesture in a replay of yesterday afternoon. Everyone else had gone on ahead when something had made him stop and turn. What had compelled him to face the lowland from which the the child had emerged? Hardly anything was visible anymore; yet he had to stare and stare. Even the swamp maples were extinguished in the dusk. Nothing could be seen but a section of the pond glinting dully like a sightless eye.

2

Wednesday at noon, just before bus time, one of the kindergarten teachers dropped off Emily at Hal's school. On the bus Josh and Bill hung over the back of the seat in front of Hal and Emily. Curious about Lew Rifkin, they asked her what her father gave her for breakfast, what time she went to bed, which television shows she wasn't allowed to watch.

"Do you know Andy's sister?" Josh finally asked. "She's in first grade, but she'd be on the early bus with you. Her name's Muffy Greenfield."

Emily shook her head. She stared out the window.

Josh cast Hal a pitying look. "What're you doing this afternoon?"

Hal shrugged. "Go up to the Candlewood lot first off. Since the bus stop's so close." He sighed. "Play it by ear, I guess."

"No lunch?"

"Afterwards. So we don't have to go all the way home and then back again."

Josh looked doubtful. "I bet she's hungry."

"Are you?" asked Hal. "Are you very hungry, Emily?"

Still looking away, Emily shook her head once more.

After Bill and Josh got off at their stop on Great Road, there was a turn and then a stretch on Nutters Hill Road before the bus stopped at the fork to Second Hill Road. Hal and Emily only had to walk back a few yards to the Titcomb driveway. When they got to the house, Hal told Emily he had to get permission to explore. "You can wait here," he said, indicating the old glider on the porch beside the front door, which seemed to be sealed for good. The

7

porch continued along the front and around the corner to the door that faced the calf barn. "Stay right there," Hal ordered, as he left Emily sitting on the edge of the glider and picking at colored flakes from its disintegrating cover. "All right?" Emily never even looked up. She separated the colors, green on one knee, orange on the other.

As soon as Miss Titcomb opened the door, Hal tried to get through all the necessary explanations and requests. It wasn't that simple, though.

"You'd better step in a moment."

"Well, I have a . . . There's this little—"

The glider creaked, and then Emily came up to them. Miss Titcomb peered at her. "Who is this?"

"What I was trying to say. My nextdoor neighbor's daughter. He's also my Social Studies teacher that I told you about. Her name's Emily."

"A girl, is she?" Harriet Titcomb surveyed the short, curly hair, the patched pants. "You're not taking her up back, are you?"

"It's all right. Her father—"

Harriet Titcomb shook her head. "You'd better keep a sharp eye on her, then. We don't need another child lost up back."

"Another? Did you lose one?"

Emily sniffed. "I smell something good. I'm hungry," she declared.

"You'd better step in."

A few minutes later Hal and Emily were seated at the kitchen table spooning up hot, fragrant gingerbread while Harriet Titcomb went to fetch her brother from the front room. Hal noticed, as he ate, that the old things around him, like the cast-iron skillet and the rocking chair, looked really used, not decorative. He supposed you could call the salt and pepper shakers ornamental; they were ceramic, shaped like cows standing on a little platform that said: FRYEBERG FAIR. Not what you were likely to see in Westwick houses.

"Harvey," shouted Harriet Titcomb, wheeling her brother into the kitchen, "here's our two young visitors!"

Harvey Titcomb propped his chin on his bony hand and examined Hal with interest.

Hal stood up, but was afraid to extend his hand, afraid that if Mr. Titcomb let go of his chin it would drop to his chest. Brother and sister were both thin, but Harvey seemed all curves, Harriet angles. Harvey's long hair made him look like Father Time; Harriet's, pulled back to a straggly knot, gave an impression of severity more than of age. Their eyes were alike, though, deep set, and with the color almost washed out of them.

"Wants to know about the back lot!" she yelled at her brother. "For school!" She gestured Hal to his chair and lifted another square of gingerbread from the pan.

"Time was," allowed Harvey Titcomb, "we had all those fields the other side of the road."

Emily shoved her plate toward Harriet, who served her another helping too.

"I'm not doing that part," Hal told him. "I'm doing the back woods. The hill and the pond."

"No good back there," said Harvey.

"I already told him it wasn't anything to speak of."

"But that doesn't matter," Hal insisted. "I have to know about when people lived and worked there. And Mr. Atherton says it was in your family from before the Revolution."

9

"Mr. Atherton!" Harriet sucked in her breath. "Was it him sent you?"

"No, no." Hal started all over. "It's for school. All the kids are doing this. Only I'm luckier, because you're still alive. I mean, in some parts of town there's just new houses, not old farms, old roads, and foundations. That's what I'm to look into."

"Well." Harriet digested all of this, but Harvey muttered something about the Athertons interfering in other people's business.

"That's all right, Harve," his sister said consolingly. "This boy's just doing his homework, that's all." She looked around her. "I guess I can tell you something about this kitchen anyway. It was built onto the house when I was ten years old. I can remember my father and mother arguing about whether to have the milk room here or across at the barn."

There was a pause. Emily ate with concentration. Hal wondered if he could just come right out and ask about the child that had been lost. Harriet offered him more gingerbread and, when he declined, told him that when Harvey was his age he could eat a whole panful, if they let him. "With hot applesauce," she added. "From the best trees that ever were. We never get but a handful anymore, just blossoms. This you've been eating is from an old recipe. My grandmother's. Yes, and hers before that."

Hal pulled out a pad and pencil. "I'm supposed to have dates."

Harriet gazed at the blank sheet of paper. "Well, let's see. The kitchen. That was when I was ten, and I was born in 1892. So it was 1902. Wasn't it, Harvey?"

Harvey shrugged. "What I remember," he began, then

10

faltered. "What I remember . . ." He drifted off into his memories.

Lew had told the class that if they found older residents to talk to, they should listen carefully for what they might be saying under the surface of things. Hal was finding it hard enough just getting the things themselves.

"The back lot," Harvey reflected. He really did seem to be trying. After a moment he said, "We took ice."

"From the pond," Harriet filled in. "But you couldn't bring it over the hill. You had to haul it around by the road, which wasn't a real road then, just a track through the woods. The brook was still there. Ragged Brook. There weren't any houses on the way, none at all." She stopped. "That the sort of thing you want to hear about?"

"Yes, and how it was done. And who you sold it to."

"Well, of course there wasn't much call for ice after the electricity came."

This statement brought the subject of ice to a close. Give them plenty of time, Lew had advised. Hal had a vision of himself spending every afternoon waiting for the Titcombs to release one single gem from their storehouse of memories. Without meaning to, he blurted, "Then why is it bad luck? What was the curse?"

There was a long silence. Emily swiveled away from the table; she sat swinging her feet and kicking the rung of her chair. Harvey Titcomb rubbed his stubbly chin; it sounded like something being grated. Harriet picked up the cow pepper shaker, stared hard at it, then set it down. She said, "It was the first farm. It burned down. There were bad . . . It was full of misfortune."

Hal said, "Please, Miss Titcomb, will you tell me about it?"

"Sometime, maybe." She stacked the plates. "Isn't that right, Harve?" Her voice rose. "Harvey, we might look for some of those things of Gran's."

"No one's business," Harvey muttered.

"Why, Gran wanted all the world to know. That's why she wrote those stories and had them put in the magazines."

Hal had a feeling Harriet was gearing up to something important. Maybe he'd get so much information now that he could finish his report ahead of everyone else and have no homework for weeks and weeks. "Is there something in the library?" he asked. "That I could look up?"

They didn't know. Those stories were from long ago. They were around the house somewhere.

"Oh, and the letters," Harriet exclaimed. "Harvey, where did we put those old letters of Gran's?"

Hal supposed the polite thing to do was to thank the Titcombs and leave them in peace, but he couldn't tear himself away, not even though Emily grew more restless with every minute. If only he could keep Miss Titcomb talking, she might suddenly remember where the stories or letters were; she might even talk about the curse. "This house," he said gropingly, "the main part before the kitchen, when was it built?"

Emily jumped down from the chair and sighed with impatience.

"The house, let's see. Mid-1840's, I think. No, a little earlier. My grandfather built it."

Hal reached down to pick up Emily's jacket from the floor. "Why didn't he build where the old foundation is?" He slung the jacket over the back of his own chair, hoping Miss Titcomb would answer him before there was nothing left to do but face her.

12

"Too much grief in that place," came her prompt reply.

Don't press people, Lew had cautioned. Give them elbow room. Ask about specific things that might jog their memories. "Grief because of the fire?" he asked lamely. And then, fed up with the proper methods of inquiry, "I mean, that can't be all. Not if it was someone's fault."

Harriet Titcomb shook her head. "It was a simpleton set the fire, a fellow they'd taken on to help with the heavy work in return for feeding and sheltering him. They'd got him from the Overseer of the Poor. My Gran said he was just a muddled hulk of boy who could only do just what you showed him."

"What happened to him?"

"Happened? Why, nothing." Harriet Titcomb fixed Hal with a look. "Wasn't his fault, poor soul. It was just something that was . . . bound to be. At least, that's how my Gran saw it."

"And that's part of the curse," he pressed. "The fire, right? The guy that set it?"

"Is that what you think?"

Hal's glance fell on Emily, who was standing close to Harvey and running her fingers along the spokes of his wheelchair. "I don't know what I think," he answered, suddenly uncomfortable. "Someone was lost too. Someone like . . . Emily?"

Harriet nodded.

"Who was it?"

"Hannah. Gran's sister. It's in the stories."

"Hannah!" Emily repeated the name, plucking on a spoke as if to play it.

"Yes, Hannah. She was the grief that came to the back farm. That's why Gran wouldn't live there again. I guess,"

13

she added, "if a thing can cause grief in a person for nearly eighty years, you can figure there's a curse to it."

"But I don't understand. Did Hannah die, or what?"

"That's just it. They never knew. Never were to know. Not ever."

"Hannah," Emily echoed softly.

Harriet tilted her head at Emily. "You mind that child," she warned Hal. "You'd better mind her well if you're walking our back lot."

Harvey cleared his throat, coughed, and tried again to clear it. Emily, retreating from him, reached for her jacket. Hal got up to go, but didn't quite know how to do it. Harriet was taken up with Harvey, who looked like someone on television who's been shot in the stomach. Would he die? He was awfully old.

Harriet wheeled him through the door to the front room. When she returned to the kitchen, she was wiping her hands on her skirt. "Time for you to go now," she told Hal. "Come back again. I'll see what I can find for you." She dismissed him with a curt nod.

"Will Mr. Titcomb be all right?" he asked.

She gave him a steady, slightly unnerving look. "All right?"

He couldn't think how else to put it.

"All right," she muttered. She wasn't really thinking about him, he guessed. She just wanted him to take Emily and go.

It was a relief to get outside. Emily raced ahead of him, and then he caught up, thinking of Harriet's warning, not quite sure it was the kind of thing a sensible person paid attention to. At the dump, though, it seemed perfectly

14

natural to caution Emily: she was to start next to him, look for things to save, watch out for glass.

Emily collected broken plates and metal levers, which she used as spoons. She didn't interfere with Hal at all, though when he pointed out that one lever was really part of his tractor—a pedal, as she ought plainly to see—she had her own ideas about it. "It's a masher," she informed him. "It's mine."

"I even have the part it matches." He showed her the curved parallel grips that would attach to it with a bolt.

"You're teasing. It doesn't mash that."

"What do you think it matches?"

"Potatoes!" She turned, dragging it off with her.

"Where are you going?" he called after her. "I won't take it away from you. Don't go near the pond."

"I won't," was all she said, but she established her digging area some distance from his.

Some time later Hal sat back to examine the afternoon's gleanings. This was the time to empty out pockets and lighten his book bag. Dump-foraging was like beach-combing. First you picked up everything that caught your eye; then you discarded all but the most precious. He set aside bits of an old cast-iron stove, then hesitated over an eggbeater. The gears could be taken apart, cleaned, and made to work again.

"Emily," he called, holding up the eggbeater. "Want this?"

Emily had moved downhill again. She was squatting, leaning over something.

Swinging the eggbeater above his head, he stomped down to her. "Want to trade it for the potato masher?" As he

15

picked his way over the junk, something white fluttered past him, then plummeted to the ground. He gasped. A dove? No, a small white duck. There it lay, thrashing helplessly.

Emily said, "You scared it."

"I didn't mean to."

Beating its wings, the duck struggled to break free.

"It's hurt," Hall whispered. "Let's catch it." He made Emily veer off to the farther side. The duck hurtled toward her and was drawn up short, its head caught in one of the holes of a plastic six-pack container that was pinned under a wheel. The bright orange bill opened and closed, and then, as Hal and Emily reached down to it, the duck thrust itself deeper into the tangled junk.

Hal had to use a broken fence post as a lever to get it free. "Hold on to it," he commanded, but Emily needed no orders. She had a firm grasp on the duck and was already tucking it inside her jacket when he let down the wheel.

"It's bloody," she told him. "Its behind's all gucky." But she didn't seem to mind holding it against her all the way home.

The pedal, or masher, was left behind. So was the egg-beater. The duck was put in a chicken crate and left with water and mash for Lew to take care of when he got home from school. "Because," Emily informed Hal, "he's my daddy. And it's my duck."

3

At dinner that evening Hal told his parents about the duck.

His mother said, "White? Really? Maybe it's a mutant."

"Is that some special kind?"

"It's a genetic abnormality," Hal's father informed him.

"Like an albino," she supplied.

"Does that make it rare?" Hal stirred butter into his potato.

His mother shrugged. "We could ask the Audubon Society. More likely it's just someone's lost duck. You'd better report it to the police after supper."

Hal's heart sank. If it was wild and rare, the Audubon Society would get it. If it was a domestic duck, it would be returned to its owner. "Either way," he mused, "it's a dead duck."

"What do you mean?"

"Lew said he'd keep it till it was well. He put purple stuff on its chewed-up rear end. If he has to give it back now, it'll probably be neglected and die. Anyhow," he added, "it's not up to us. Emily found it. It's hers." Even with his eyes on his last forkful of potato, he knew his parents were exchanging glances about him. Later he would hear them discussing him in undertones.

Then his father declared that, strictly speaking, it was up to the Titcombs, whose permission Hal should have for taking ducks or, for that matter, digging around in their back lot. Before Hal could explain that he had permission, his mother had gone off on a tangent: "Everyone in Westwick walks and skis in the woods. What's left of them. I just wish we'd all been wider awake when the Titcombs decided to carve theirs up into house lots."

"Wouldn't have done any good, though. Not at their price. Anyhow, Westwick can't afford any more conservation land for a while."

"Maybe," Hal remarked, "it's theirs."

His parents gazed at him. "Of course it is. But there's such a thing as concern for future generations. The land—"

"I mean the duck," said Hal.

"Oh, yes—well, maybe."

"I'll ask them tomorrow," he went on, feeling better already.

"I'm not sure you'll get a clear answer out of them," Hal's father warned. "I understand they're rather hard to talk to. Not surprising at their age. Off in their own world."

Hal thought of the steaming gingerbread made from a recipe at least two hundred years old. "Their own world," he ventured, "goes back a long way."

He saw his parents smiling at each other. He hated it when they were amused at something he hadn't meant to be funny. "What's wrong with that?"

"Nothing, dear," said his mother.

His father said, "It's just that some of Lew Rifkin is rubbing off on you. All that reverence for the past."

Hal could feel his ears begin to heat up.

"I wonder," added his father, "if Lew could be as effective with an old-fashioned textbook on American history."

"We're not doing history all by itself," Hal informed him. He pushed back his chair and got up to clear the table. "I'm learning a lot already," he mumbled on his way to the sink.

His parents, who never liked to end a discussion on a note of discord, asked him what he had learned.

Hal thought a moment. "They made ice on the pond."

He paused. "There was a man that was given to Miss Titcomb's grandmother. No, her great-grandmother. I think it was a little like being a slave. He was given to her by someone called the Overseer of the Poor. This guy that was given to her was retarded. He was supposed to do the hard work around the farm for no money, just his food and clothes and a place to sleep. He burned down the old farm."

"I shouldn't wonder," remarked Hal's father. "Then what?"

"They don't know. That's all they know about him. But don't you think it's . . . interesting that people were taken care of that way back then?"

"Back when?" demanded his father.

"In the olden times," Hal replied.

"That's what I mean," his father pointed out. "You don't even know the date or the decade. How about the century?"

"I think he's doing pretty well so far," Hal's mother put in. "He's only just begun this project."

Hal was calculating from the date of the kitchen addition, when Harriet was ten and Harvey was thirteen. He wanted so much to be able to snap back with an exact year, but he floundered among the dates of the 1800's. Just wait, he vowed. He'd get so familiar with those times that it would be like saying his own age.

The next day after school he sat by the pond. Lew had mentioned that ducks usually paired in the fall. If the injured duck's mate was looking for it, this was the obvious place to wait.

He sat for what seemed a long time. Once the tranquility was broken by two dogs nosing their way along a scent trail on the opposite bank. One of them raised its head for

19

a moment, gazed in his direction, stiffened, then disappeared into the underbrush. A jay shrilled; a squirrel took off, scolding and chattering. After a moment Hal heard branches breaking, footsteps. Someone appeared a good distance off, disappearing and then emerging again between trees and in the brambly clearings. For some reason Hal remained still. The walker stopped once, then tramped on. Was the person looking for a lost duck?

When the footsteps died away, Hal stood up and surveyed the calm, darkening surface of the pond. Then something crackled. It wasn't as loud as the walker; it wasn't as sudden as the squirrel scuttling over the ground. But the pond seemed to heave as though a great ladle had been dipped into it. A plopping splash. Was it the duck's mate alighting?

It was too dark to tell. Hal stepped toward the water. He heard dripping, saw something white at the far edge of the pond. A white splotch that didn't look very ducklike. But it had to be the drake; it couldn't be anything else.

Leaning out over the water, Hal peered into the thick dusk. The patch of white seemed to rise from the surface of the pond. Yet it wasn't flying away. There it was, almost without shape and awfully large for a small duck.

He felt his foot sinking. Liquid mud oozed up around his ankles. His arm flailed for balance, striking at a slender branch before clutching it. On the opposite bank the white patch shot up, then held for an instant. He couldn't believe what it looked like; it was a trick of the dusk. The sinking darkness had transformed the fleeing duck into the face of a cow or bull or something.

He was too muddy to stop at the Titcombs'. Instead he made his way to the Thayer house. Leaving his shoes and socks in the woodshed, he padded into the kitchen, where Lew and Peggy, another Thayer house tenant, were making dinner.

"I think I just saw the duck's mate."

"Now?" Lew turned from the sink. "You saw him in the dark?"

"I was down by the pond. I saw something white. Actually, it looked like . . ." But Hal felt too silly saying what it looked like. "It must have been the drake. It was white."

Emily sidled up to Lew, who was peeling carrots, and took one away into the living room.

Peggy remarked that the duck was a lot livelier today. They'd have trouble keeping her with the hens if they didn't clip her wings.

Lew said, "We'll have to have a house vote on that."

Hal couldn't tell whether he was kidding or not. They had house votes on all kinds of things. He said, "My parents think it has to be set free. I mean, if no one claims it. The police will tell us if they get any calls. They said it wasn't their business; so did the dog officer."

"What this town needs is a fowl officer," declared Lew. "For when people run afoul of the law. Right?"

Peggy jabbed him with her elbow, then asked Hal, "Why'd you call the police? I mean, isn't that sort of looking for trouble?"

"My parents made me." Quickly changing the subject, he added, "I'll go look again. Tomorrow. When I see the Titcombs." For the first time in his life he wished his parents were not lawyers. Or anyhow not so extremely law-abiding.

21

4

Hal noticed the Athertons' Land Rover as he came barreling up to his door. He'd run all the way home from the Titcombs', but now, carefully tucking the envelope inside his jacket, he walked in slowly. He didn't bang the door.

The Athertons were standing in the hall with his parents. Hal greeted them as politely as he could, then slipped past them. In the kitchen he opened his jacket, placed the envelope on the counter.

"No," he heard Bliss Atherton proclaim, "I'm afraid that paunchy young man, well-intentioned though he may be . . ."

Hal's mother spoke in an undertone.

"Oh, sure. Admirable, a young fellow like that, a small child."

Mumble mumble mumble.

"Divorced!" A pause. "She didn't take the child?"

Hal's parents' voices mingled in reply.

"Well, look, he's *your* neighbor."

Mumble mumble "duck."

Quickly Hal returned to the hall. "The duck's fine," he announced. "I talked to the Titcombs. They're semi-wild."

Gertrude Atherton laughed. "Oh, I don't know if I'd go *that* far."

"I mean the ducks. Miss Titcomb says they're call-ducks. They used to winter over with the barnyard ducks and geese. The Titcombs thought they'd started migrating. Anyway, it's all right. And we—I mean, Lew—can keep the duck till it's well. And we're going to—" We're going to catch the drake, he had almost blurted. No point pushing his luck with the Athertons, who might raise some objection.

In another moment the door was closed and he was dragging his parents into the kitchen. He pulled the folded letters from the envelope. "They're awfully brittle," he said. Slowly he unfolded the paper and spread it out on the counter. "You have to be careful." One of the letters had been taped together some time ago. The tape was yellow and raised like dead skin; some of the writing was pulled right off with it.

"Miss Titcomb said I could borrow them because her eyes aren't good enough, and I just can't make out all the script. One's from her grandmother to *her* mother. And the torn one . . . it's from Hannah. That's Miss Titcomb's grandmother's sister."

"Look at this!" exclaimed Hal's mother. " '8 September 1838.' " She began to read:

" 'My dear Mother—I have spoken with Mr. Handy, my overseer, who assures me there will be a place for Hannah in the Corporation. She will have to begin as a bobbin girl, a doffer, at two dollars a week, but in time may advance to frame-tending and higher wages, but even as a start it will help with the tax payments. The Corporation requires children to attend school three months each year, but as Hannah has had schooling in Westwick, she may be put to work at once. I hope that you can manage alone with Nathaniel until spring.

" 'I have begun arrangements at the boarding house. Mrs. Keeler will make an excellent home for Hannah. Of course I shall keep her by my side whenever possible. As you know, there are three beds for the six in our room.

Hannah will share mine as soon as Dorcas can find another bedmate.

" 'I thought to fetch Hannah at the time of the Moodys' husking bee.' "

Hal's mother broke off. "The Moodys. That would be the old Moody place she's referring to. Where the Athertons live."

"Go on," said Hal. Then he asked, "What's a bobbin girl?"

"Something to do with spinning," said his father.

"In a mill," added his mother. She read on:

" 'The occasion might distract her. Dorcas suggests I take Hannah on the canal boat if the day is fair. All the excitement may keep her from fretting. She should have a warm cloak for the winter when she must go to and from work in full darkness, also one merino shawl if possible. I am bringing you real rubber overshoes from Merrimack Street. I am eager for the sweetness of your embrace. Your devoted daughter, Eliza.' "

"I wonder how old she was," mused Hal's mother.

"I know. Miss Titcomb told me. Her grandmother Eliza was born in 1821. And that means she was . . . was seventeen." There, he thought: my first hard fact.

"And the little sister?" asked his father.

"Hannah was . . ." Hal faltered. "I don't exactly know. Miss Titcomb doesn't like to talk about her. She said she'd show me a story, but she can't find it. There's a lot of unhappiness about Hannah."

"Oh, come on, Hal. That's a hundred and fifty years ago. No unhappiness lasts that long. Anyway, the girl's dead and buried."

Hal didn't answer.

His mother turned over the letter with great care. "Look," she said, "here's more writing on the back of it. Well . . ." She read silently, then looked up. "This is a different letter. And it's harder to make out. The ink's faded. But look at the date. 'September 19.' It's from Eliza's mother, and it's a reply." She showed Hal and his father the uneven script, more like that of a young child than Eliza's. Haltingly she began to read aloud:

" 'Dear Daughter I paid some of the debt with the last money you sent, but must look to winter needs, and though we have excellent turnips the early frost hit the squash and pumpkins. I thought to sell Brindle while she had her summer fat only Hannah wept so. The gentleman from Mallets Mr. Lum Hamlin came with money in hand. Hannah led Brindle to the woods claiming she had promised her father she would not let one of the kind go. She has worked . . .'

"I can't make out that line," Hal's mother told them. "Something something 'seems to have her father's way of fancying great results from singular efforts. I must break this news to her bit by bit. I fear her gingham is in a sad state, but I will have her good brown frock ready in time for the husking bee, which is the first Saturday in October, and I will tell Mr. Lum Hamlin that he may come for Brindle as soon as ever you and Hannah depart for Lowell. Your . . .' I guess that's 'Mother,' and then, 'Patience,' I think, Patience Something."

Hal's father reached for the other letter, which was in even worse condition.

"The writing's clearer," said Hal's mother. "More . . . more adult, don't you think?"

All three peered at it. Then Hal gathered up the folded

pieces. "I think I want to try reading this one myself," he told them.

"Your mother's done pretty well so far."

But this was Hannah's letter. Harriet Titcomb had told him as she handed it over that it was the last word anyone had had from her. "I'll come for help if I need it," he said. "It's part of what we're supposed to be doing." He could hear his father telling him: The girl's dead and buried. Only Hal knew that Harriet and Harvey Titcomb didn't feel that way. Not exactly, anyway. If you thought she was dead and buried, her letter was just history. But if there was something else to it, something not quite right, maybe Hannah's letter was important, even if it was nearly a hundred and fifty years old.

In his room Hal kicked the door shut. He spread the pieces of Hannah's letter on his unmade bed, meaning to clear the top of his desk. Then he surveyed the stuff to be moved; making space was easier said than done. He started to read the spread-out letter right on his bed.

"Dear Eliza," it began. "I hope you understood my note and were not too vexed at my decision. I intend to return to Lowell . . ."

Wait a minute, thought Hal. She's talking about returning, so she's already been there. He examined the date: September 12, 18 . . . He slid his hands under the square of brittle paper and held it to the light. "1839." This letter was written a whole year later than those his mother had read. He went on, squinting, finding that if he tilted the paper, it was easier to make out the small, faint writing.

"Our home is a sorry sight. I am glad you are spared seeing its charred remains. Mr. Hinckley says I must settle

26

myself before long as I am yet a child without means, or else I shall be placed like poor Nathaniel. Yet I proved I have means, for I paid over ten dollars of our tax bill, and I have informed Mr. Hinckley that I mean to establish our continued right to Candlewood. I am seeking the stock that escaped burning and may have avoided the pound. A few hens are roosting in the trees. It is a miracle that Grandfather's beech was not destroyed, and many good hickories have survived along with oak, maple, and pine. The gander appeared once, but now is gone. Perhaps he was caught and sold.

"Eliza, I implore you to send money to reclaim Bestor before he too is auctioned. He would be hard to replace, and we cannot do without an ox. I have left my good frock and my linen stockings and slippers, which you might be able to sell. I have the cowhide shoes and footings for winter wear, but at present am barefoot, though not yet with my former ease. I also have my *Pilgrim's Progress* and the little volume by Mrs. Sherwood that Dorcas gave me. I bought two copy books for letters and to keep a journal. You will see I left you the Reader in the hope that you will consider Daniel Webster's dedication to the 'distant regions of futurity.' Father often told me that he believed, with Mr. Webster, that we must leave 'for the consideration of those who shall occupy our places, some proof that we hold the blessings transmitted from our fathers in just estimation.' It is with this conviction, dear Eliza, that I have returned to Candlewood, so that when future generations look back, 'they shall know at least that we possessed affections, which, running backward, and warming with gratitude for what our ancestors have done for our happiness, run forward also to our posterity, and meet them with cordial salutation, ere yet they have arrived on the shore of Being.'

"As you see, I have committed my favorite lesson to memory. I ask you to open your heart to it.

"I inquired at the ropewalk for employment, but they would not have me. I may seek employment in Boston or some place close enough to visit Candlewood as the law dictates to hold our title to the land. Yet if I am forced to this, what will become of the stock? There is still no sign of the cows, and I dare not inquire too closely lest I be presented with another unpaid charge. But I grieve for Brindle, as she was raised by me. I shall let you know what course I take and you must tell Mother when she is well enough to understand. Your loving sister, Hannah.

"Since writing, I overheard the rakers in the cranberry bog speak of John T., sent by you to fetch me back to Lowell. I will not allow this. Leaving you was very hard, but I managed and shall continue. From the first, I learned about concealing myself. A kindly lock-tender, who gave me cheese and pie, warned me from the open tow-path along the canal. I met him tending the lock for two brothers on an excursion in such an odd boat of their own making. Any lock-tender could have refused to set them through on the Sabbath, but not he who took me in and sent them on their way to the Merrimack River. Listening to the brothers tell of their first night in a meadow alongside the Concord River gave me courage to sleep alone in wild thickets. And though I lost my way a number of times, I was not daunted, nor found, nor turned back from home.

"Now Eliza I hope you will heed me. I shall not write

28

again if I learn that your John continues his search of me. Hannah."

Hal sat for a while surrounded by the pieces of this letter. The house was intensely still. "Hannah." He spoke the name out loud, just as Emily had done. Cursed? What was the curse? What had happened to sour Eliza on the Candlewood backland? Were there more letters? He craved answers. He wanted to know everything about the year between Eliza's letter and Hannah's. He needed to find out whether Hannah ever found her Brindle, or whether Hannah's mother had actually sold the cow as she planned.

Leaving the pieces in their separate order, he backed off the bed. "Mom!" he shouted, opening his door. "Dad?"

They were in the living room going over some work together.

"What's up? Did you decipher the letter?"

"What does it say?"

"It's long. It was a year later. I'm going over to the Titcombs' to see if they have any more, because it leaves out everything. I have to find out what happened."

"Wait a minute, Hal. You can't just charge in—"

"It's all right. They won't mind." Hal was already getting his jacket on. Then he was out of the house, out and down the driveway, around Second Hill to Nutters Hill Road.

But at the Titcombs' door he faltered. When Harriet asked him in, his queries were about the old farm, about whether her grandmother had ever shown her where things had stood and what they had looked out on. Then, still standing, still with his jacket on, he asked for and received permission to mend the broken letter.

29

When he left, he could hear Harriet calling to her brother. "He came all the way," she was explaining, "just to thank us for letting him have a look at Gran's old letters. What do you think of that, Harve?"

Had he actually thanked her? Walking along, taking his time now, he doubted whether the words themselves were what mattered most to Harriet Titcomb.

5

Oak leaves like copper scales glinted in the filtered light. The few remaining birch leaves stood out from the oak like flakes of sun. It was so warm that Emily peeled off shoes and socks to go padding about at the edge of the pond while Hal and Lew settled the chicken crate with the duck in it. Yet the buttonbushes were withered now, and not one scarlet leaf remained on the swamp maple.

The duck started to squawk and shriek.

Hal said, "The drake must be near."

"Or else it's the pond she wants," answered Lew.

"Can't we let her swim? I mean, she still can't fly, but wouldn't she be safe in the pond?"

Lew opened the crate. The duck screamed at him and drew back until he had withdrawn. Then she fluttered out, hit the water, and shot back and forth ecstatically. They watched her cavorting, diving, dipping sideways, splashing. After a while she came close to Emily, who was squatting on a tussock. The duck tilted her head as though to size up the child, then began to graze among the flooded marsh grass.

Emily, with outstretched arm, dropped a fistful of mud. Like a dog retrieving a stick, the duck submerged, then came up with blackened head. Emily studied the effect with some interest before resuming her digging and stirring in the mud.

Lew said, "We can't expect the mate to come while we're this close." He called to Emily. "We're going up the hill."

On the upland farm site Hal found himself trying to place Hannah here. How much had been open, how much wooded? Behind him the silver beech commanded all the ridge and the surrounding slope. When had it died? How many years could a dead beech stand?

He looked down toward the pond, thinking that if the land here had once been cleared, it would have made a terrific place to slide, especially if you landed on the frozen pond.

"Could girls go sliding then?" he asked Lew. "I mean, in the olden days, with skirts."

"I suppose it depended on local customs."

But Hal was already recalling what Hannah's mother had written about Hannah working and the sad state of her dress. "I bet she did," he said almost to himself. "I bet she went sledding right where we're standing. On this spot." He turned to Lew, who was patiently allowing Emily to tie her sneaker laces by herself. "What do you think?"

"I think," declared Lew, "that we should pay a call on Miss Titcomb and see if we can lure her out here on this rare, balmy day."

"I'm coming too," said Emily. "I like her."

"You like her gingerbread," muttered Hal.

31

Kicking her loosely tied sneakers through the leaves, Emily deliberated. "I *love* her gingerbread," she corrected him finally. "I *like* her."

Harriet and Harvey Titcomb were having their dinner. Lew apologized for interrupting, but Harriet said it was all right, they were nearly done. Emily sidled up to the table to get a look at Harvey Titcomb's teeth lying beside his soup spoon. Hal expected Lew to remind her of her manners, but Lew was busy inviting Harriet to go for a stroll in the back lot. Hal stood by awkwardly, waiting.

Harvey took up the round spoon, dipped it in the bowl, and inserted it into his diminished mouth. Suddenly he turned, catching Hal staring. Hal wished he could shrink to Emily's size, but Harvey only wheezed out a kind of laugh and mumbled something. He looked as though he were sharing a joke. He pointed with his spoon at Emily.

"Put your teeth in, Harvey!" Harriet shouted at him. "Hal can't make out what you're saying!"

Under Emily's rapturous gaze, Harvey clawed up the teeth, did something magical with his twiglike fingers, and inserted the teeth into the slot of his mouth. At once he was transformed. He grinned at Hal, at Emily, who grinned back.

"I wish I could do that," she confided.

Harriet shuffled out to the pantry and, returning with her coat, told Harvey she was going out for a bit.

"To the pond," announced Emily in Harvey's ear.

"Not that far," Harriet protested. "Up the lane if I can make it."

"Where?" asked Harvey.

"The old place. The woods."

He stared up at her, open-mouthed.

32

"How long since you've been back there?" Lew inquired as he helped her down the porch steps.

"The contractor who's developing the lot for us took me in, but it was the other way, and in a machine. Where we used to have a track, only the trees came up since. Now they're starting to clear it again. For the subdivision road." She was silent awhile, concentrating on her footing, reaching out for support and taking Lew's arm.

At the upper end of the orchard she had to rest; to get her breath, she said. "Berries." She waved her hand in the direction of the meadow. "Berries in the summer, nuts in the fall, sugaring in March. They're what brought us back here when we were growing up. But we always hurried past the ridge. We'd race away home as soon as we could."

They continued on to the old foundation. Harriet looked up at the dead beech, over to the dump, and below to the pond. "Even now," she told them, "I'd never come here alone. I suppose it was my grandmother always insisting that her little sister would appear one day. 'I know that girl,' she'd tell us, 'as well as I know myself.' That's what my Gran used to say when we were young and she was so old only half her mind was here and the other half lost in the days of her own childhood."

Emily planted herself in front of Harriet. "Girl?" she asked.

"That's what she called Hannah, even though by then Hannah would have been an old woman too. But Gran said Hannah would be hoeing the potatoes and pulling turnips and fetching the cattle back from the brook till she dropped dead."

"Ragged Brook you told me about?" said Hal. "Where is it?"

Harriet scanned the forest swamp beyond the pond. "Gone. Dried up. Vanished like Hannah."

"But how can a brook vanish?" Hal exclaimed.

"That's what you're supposed to be discovering," Lew reminded him. "How the land changes. What happens to it when we build reservoirs and eight-lane highways and shopping centers and factories."

Hal turned back to Harriet. "But if you made ice and maple sugar and everything, I should think that's where the farm would've been rebuilt."

"Well, it wasn't us, don't forget. Our grandparents built it after they'd acquired the land across the road where the big barn is now. I mean the Sturgis place—that was our barn. Besides, Gran looked on the old farm as cursed. I keep telling you that. You can't change the past and you can't change people that live in it. There! There's a lesson for your learning."

A sudden clamor from the pond made them all turn and stare downhill. The duck swam into view; Hal thought she had gone crazy, the way she circled and screamed. Then he realized there were two ducks chasing each other round and round.

"The drake!" Hal exclaimed.

"Is that the duck you asked me about?" Harriet wanted to know.

"The one with the blue stuff on its tail. The other's her mate. We think."

But Harriet couldn't see well enough to distinguish one from the other. She could only tell what they were because they sounded and behaved like the little white call-ducks that had always been there.

34

She looked around her. "It's different now. All different. Except," she added, nodding toward the dump, "that. We always burned what we could and threw the rest over the ridge. My father found something once, wouldn't ever say what it was, only that it was out in the woods, and my grandfather made him chuck it in the fire right under the pot with the maple sap boiling in it so my Gran wouldn't ever see it. Because she'd have taken on something awful if she'd known. For that thing was Hannah's, I don't know what." She paused. "It's not so dark with the leaves gone. You don't get the feeling so strong. . . ." Her voice trailed off.

"What feeling?"

"You know. Of Hannah here."

Hal sighed. "I wish there was a picture from that time."

Harriet nodded. "There was a story," she began haltingly. "My Gran would tell it, how my great-great-grandfather, who was the first of this family to settle here—how he lived in the hill like a woodchuck or a mole."

"In the ground?"

"Well, it was a story she told. She herself was born and raised in the house he finally built, the one that was burned; but she seldom spoke of it."

"She must have told you *some* things, though," pressed Hal.

"Why should she? A lot of money and work has gone into building Candlewood since then. The house we live in now, the big barn across the road, and all the cows we milked. When we had our dispersal sale, people came from all over to bid on our herd. The ones that kept on dairying after us, the Moodys and Duncans and Donatellis, they

35

never had production records like ours. If you ask me, that's what you should be studying, not this old place with its old grief."

At the pond one duck flew up, circled, and alighted again, kicking up a splash. Emily's head appeared beyond a boulder on the far side.

"Don't bother the ducks," Lew called to her. "We're going to have to catch the hurt one later."

She called back something and disappeared behind the rock.

"Come on now. We're taking Miss Titcomb home."

Emily emerged, heading not up the hill but toward the water.

"Emily!" yelled Lew. "Right now, or I'll leave you home when I get the duck."

Shouting back something that sounded more indignant than defiant, Emily retreated from the water, made her way around the pond, and began to climb the steep slope. At last she arrived, but she was Emily with a difference. All of the front of her was smeared greeny brown. The unmistakable odor of cow manure wafted up from her. And there she stood, arms out, legs slightly parted, everything slick and soaked.

"I told you I should wash first," she finally said to them.

"But how—" Lew stopped, then started again. "Where were you?"

"That's cow flop," said Harriet. "Fresh."

"But what's it doing here?" exclaimed Lew.

Harriet shrugged. "Someone's cow got out."

"But there aren't any—" Lew fell silent. Then, in another tone, he said, "See many cows around here, do you?"

Harriet eyed him. "No," she answered shortly, adding,

"Only now and then." She regarded him a moment. "There's plenty of fodder. Acorns make a fine meal for a cow or a pig or suchlike."

"You'd think people would see it."

"They do. Don't you read the police notices in the paper? Now that I don't read much anymore, Sadie Duncan tells me the news. There's been reports of a cow over her way. Of course, the Duncans don't keep cows anymore either. What are you going to do about this child?"

Lew made Emily keep her distance while they took Miss Titcomb home. It was slow going. Emily dawdled, sulked, and, at the door, warned away from the porch, glared at Miss Titcomb and charged, "I bet you're not going to let me in."

Lew said, *"I'm* not going to let you."

"Come back, though," Harriet told her.

"When?" demanded Emily.

"Next time," Harriet replied. She looked and sounded tired. She went in and closed the door firmly behind her.

"Now what?" asked Hal. "Back for the duck?"

"Home first," Lew declared. "Emily. The washing machine."

Emily giggled. She began to twirl. "I'll go round and round."

Hal said he'd stay. Maybe he'd see the cow again.

That brought Lew up short. "Again? You never said anything about a cow before."

"I didn't think . . . I thought it was the drake."

Lew nodded thoughtfully. "Let me see. You saw a small white cow swimming in the pond."

"I saw something white. I was looking for the drake, so I assumed . . ."

"That's the trouble with expectations."

"Yes," said Hal. He felt kind of foolish. "But a cow! It didn't seem possible. Besides," he added, "I don't believe in ghosts."

"Well," Lew concluded, "you certainly couldn't believe this cow was a ghost if you were Emily. Or even Emily's father." He set off down the driveway. Emily, her arms held stiffly like a wooden soldier, trailed behind.

6

The kids were giving their first progress reports on their projects. Some hadn't even got started. Lew didn't say they were lazy or anything; he just asked others for suggestions to get the slow ones going. Kim Spurling said anyone who lived in an old house could look for the gravestones of people who lived there before and make rubbings. In the eighteenth century all the S's were F's.

"I bet she got help," Bill whispered.

Lew heard him. "Why not? If your family can't help, try someone in the Historical Society. Try asking at the Town Hall. Try asking me. You'll find lots of interest in your project."

All the same, Lew had warned Hal to keep quiet about the cow. There was always some nut with a gun. "Let's hope," Lew had said, "the cow will go home when it runs out of grass and acorns."

Home where? Hal had wondered. Why wouldn't the owners come for it? He thought of the Titcomb dairy barn on the other side of Nutters Hill Road. The barn was a house now with solar panels on the roof. Even with the Sturgis pony and the horses in the field behind, it didn't look like a real farm.

When it was Josh's turn to report, he held up a plastic bag with a few dark berries in it. He wondered why there were so few cranberries, and Lew talked about second-growth woods replacing cultivated land and attracting birds that ate the fruit that had once been harvested.

The reports went on. Soon it would be Hal's turn. He didn't even want to draw attention to the back lot.

"Hal?"

"I've been talking to the Titcombs," he began. "They're very old. Their pond used to be bigger when they were kids, and there was a brook too, Ragged Brook, but it's gone now."

"Ragged Brook," Amy Thorne broke in. "I've got a Ragged Brook too. Dr. Meltzer says his house was once a mill and the brook came down right past him. He says it's in the deeds where his boundaries are."

"A gristmill?" asked Lew. "You'll need to find out. Which reminds me. Anyone come across a tannery? A ropewalk?"

Hal almost answered, almost told about Hannah's letter, but he wasn't ready yet. There was so much he still didn't know. But he said, "What's a ropewalk?"

"Anyone know?"

"A circus act," Josh offered.

Lew shook his head. "It's where ropes were made. First it was done with people walking backward and twisting the fibers. Then machinery took over."

Half listening, Hal considered the kind of job Hannah

had asked for. He couldn't picture her twisting stuff and walking backward. Instead, he found himself picturing Emily. She'd walk backward, all right. Backward into a cow flop. He had her on his hands again today too. What would she get into this time? He wished he wasn't about to find out.

As soon as they got off the bus, Emily took charge. "Let's go to your house."

"Later."

"I'm hungry. What's for lunch at your house?"

What was for lunch was cold leftover meatloaf and a lot of very good Brie cheese, which Emily had never tasted before.

"I don't think you should eat so much of this," Hal said. It was usually spread sparingly on crackers.

"Is it bad for you?" Emily helped herself to another slice. The soft inside bulged and oozed when she pressed the knife down. "It's a sandwich all by itself," she said. "You don't even need bread."

"That's enough," Hal told her, returning what was left of the cheese to its wrapper.

Emily pushed back her chair. "What's for dessert?"

"Cookies?" suggested Hal.

"Let's go see Miss Titcomb."

"Later. We did what you wanted first, so now we do what I want second, which is to feed the ducks."

While Emily went to the bathroom, Hal filled an empty coffee can with cracked corn that his parents kept for the pheasants. Then he thought about the cow. He pulled open the cupboard door and examined all the cans and boxes of food. Finally he selected a round container of oatmeal and an airtight jar of raisins. Then, recalling a television

40

show on animals surviving in winter, he poured some salt into the oatmeal and stirred it around.

Meanwhile Emily had found her way to his room. "What's this?" she asked as Hal came in to get her. She raised the receiver of his old-fashioned telephone, almost as if she already knew what it was for. "It looks like one of those flowers. The yellow ones."

He saw what she meant. "Yes, daffodils. It's an old telephone."

Emily put the receiver to her ear.

"You can play with it when we come back. You can call anywhere."

That was what he had said to his parents when they gave it to him. He didn't need it installed. He could pretend to call anywhere in the world, or even into space, or back into another time.

"But it's to use," his mother had pointed out. "You don't need to pretend."

"Can't get your own number in the book," his father had told him, "till the phone's hooked up."

"It's all right. I can make one up."

His parents had exchanged one of their looks, and the installation question had been allowed to lapse.

Emily replaced the receiver. "Will you play with me too? Will you answer when I call?"

Hal said yes, but they'd better get started now before it was too late.

They went the long way, partly because they would reach the pond first, but also because they would bypass the Titcomb house.

"This isn't the way," Emily objected as he led her along the road and then into the woods where the trees had been cleared and there were wheel marks leading in. But soon they were in thick woods. Hal veered off, heading toward the meadow to avoid a swampy area, and suddenly they found themselves in a glade. Here the brush was flattened and all the low branches of surrounding trees were bent and stripped of bark.

"That's cow shit," said Emily, pointing to the drying cakes of manure. "They look hard, but they're not underneath. Like that cheese," she added.

Hal thought that was a pretty gross comparison, but he refrained from saying so. He said, "We'd better be quiet. The cow might be right around here somewhere. We don't want to scare it away."

"What are we going to do with it?"

A good question, thought Hal, but he said, "Feed it, for one thing. Try to keep it here where it's safe." He deposited a little pile of salted oatmeal where the cow had obviously bedded down. "Now," he whispered, "let's go find the duck."

"Talk," Emily demanded.

He shook his head. "We don't want to scare the cow."

"Well, you scare me when you whisper."

"Why?" he asked in his normal voice.

"It's what they do in caves," she told him. "And in the dark. I don't like it."

"Okay. But keep your voice down. Don't go that way. The pond's over here." But he noted where the cow path forked to the left and wondered whether it would lead to the meadow.

The ducks were like porcelain figures against the gray water and sky. The drake, of course, was the more graceful of the two; its tailfeathers swept up into a single curl.

42

Hal and Emily walked along the edge of the pond, trying to avoid the black slime. At last they reached the thick tussocks. As they approached, the ducks swam smoothly off. Hal poured cracked corn on a fallen tree that lay rotting, half submerged. As he backed away, the female duck approached the tree.

"Don't move," he whispered.

Emily said loudly, "Don't whisper."

The duck disregarded the voice. Flapping her wings, she gained a purchase on the slippery trunk and thrust her orange bill into the tiny heap of corn, spilling most of the kernels into the water. Then she slithered back into the pond and deftly scooped these up.

Emily wanted a turn feeding the duck. Scattering most of the corn Hal gave her, she straddled the log. "The water's coming into my boot," she informed him.

"Pick it up, then," said Hal.

"I can't. It's too heavy."

Hal watched the duck dabbing at Emily's hand. There would be no problem catching that one, but what about the drake? Lew had said it would have to be caged or there would be no breeding pair, no ducklings in the spring, and probably no drake either. The duck had finished with Emily, who was rocking back and forth and humming.

"I have to go to the dump now," Hal told her. "To look for things."

Emily twisted around. "I'll stay here."

"You can't, Emily. You might fall in."

"I won't fall in. Anyhow, I can swim."

"You can't even lift your boot," he pointed out.

Emily shimmied back along the log and climbed off backward. Her seat was smeared with rotted bark and

43

moss. Collapsing on the ground, she extended her leg. "I'm hurt. My boot's full of water and that's the blood. You'll have to carry me."

"I'm not carrying you anywhere. You're not a baby." He pulled off the boot and held it upside down while mud and water plopped and ran from it.

"I know I'm not a baby. I'm a duck and that's my wing."

Promising to play with her after he'd spent a while at the dump, he pretended to dab her leg with purple stuff from a bottle. But he made sure that she came with him.

Even so, it was easy to lose himself in the layered discoveries awaiting his excavation. This part of the dump was beginning to speak to him. All around and higher up was the debris from recent accumulation, while right down here Hal was reaching into the life of Candlewood, or anyhow its not too distant past. Thinking hard, he sat back on his heels. Maybe he could use some of his finds to prod the memories of the old people. He'd pick something to show the Titcombs, then ask questions and take notes.

He sighed. Taking notes was the part that never seemed to come off. As soon as you got interested, the last thing you were going to do was pull out a pencil and a pad and start jotting things down. It was only afterward that you thought of it, when it was too late.

He hauled out an odd-looking slab that seemed to be made of corrugated glass framed in splintered wood. But it was kind of big to carry if he had to fuss with Emily and bring the oatmeal container and raisins. Maybe the brown bottle would do. Ruthie Nettleton said you could get a lot of money for old bottles; her mother collected them.

"When do we play?" Emily had come up behind him

44

so quietly he jumped and dropped the bottle. "What did you do that for?" She frowned at the broken glass.

He wheeled around. "What did *I* do? Why did you creep up on me like that?"

"Because," she said, "I found somebody."

"What do you mean?"

"In there."

"Here in the dump?"

She nodded. "Upside down." She led Hal to her digging place and pointed to a boot sticking up through the rubble. She was quite right about it being upside down. He stooped to pull it out, but the boot wasn't empty; it was attached to something. Somebody? Some body?

Emily said, "I don't like it."

"It's just an old boot," Hal tried to assure her, but he couldn't utter a sound. He felt hot all over; his hands were clammy and his fingers refused to grab hold of the boot's heel. Then he remembered Emily's mud-filled boot and understood the association for her. He said, "It's just an old boot," and pulled hard at it. It came away with a chair leg in it, wrenched from the seat to which it had been attached. "See?" he said to Emily. He tossed the boot back on the heap.

"When are we going to play?" Emily answered.

"Right now," said Hal. "On the way to the Titcombs'." He gave her a nudge in the small of her back. "Go on," he told her. "You're Hannah."

"No," Emily countered. "I'm the cow."

"Okay. You're the cow. Your name is Brindle."

Emily tried out the name. "Brindle." She lowered her head and walked with a swinging gait.

Suddenly remembering the oatmeal and raisins, Hal

45

said, "It's time to feed you. Where did we leave the round box with the oats?"

"The box turned into a boat."

Hal stopped. "Are you serious?"

"A boat, a floating duck house."

"Emily, it was full of oatmeal. It was for the cow."

"I already fed the cow."

He looked at her suspiciously. "You mean you ate it?"

Emily met his stare. "I ate the raisins." She pointed to the empty jar perched on the low stone wall. "I went for a walk. The cow ate the oatmeal." She paused. "Then I came back."

It was too much pretending for Hal.

Emily seemed to sense his resistance. Approaching, she offered him the imaginary contents of her hands. Then, in the middle of this charade, she dropped them to her sides. "You're Brindle, see? You lean down and blow at me and rough me with your tongue."

Hal shook his head and grinned. This kid had such a vivid imagination she needed actors to play with. He'd better get her home, let her loose in his room with the telephone and the dried-up ant farm and the dinosaur models. Get her going on something real.

7

Over the weekend Lew mentioned he was considering a class field trip to Candlewood. Hal sat in the Thayer house kitchen on Saturday morning and mustered every possible argument against it.

"The kids might hear about those bobcats; then you'd get it from the parents."

"Bobcats!" exclaimed Sherry from the sink.

"Uh-huh," grunted Mac, another Thayer house tenant, who was trying to wake up slowly. "Didn't you hear that the old lady told Hal there were bobcats back there?"

"One bobcat," Hal amended. "And actually she only said they heard it."

Mac snickered, Sherry laughed, Lew shook his head, and Emily brushed cat fur onto the butter.

Hal remembered thinking that probably Harriet was mixed up about long ago and recently. Like with that glass thing from the dump she called a washboard. She'd insisted she only threw it away a little while ago.

"You don't believe me about the bobcat, do you?" she'd charged. And Hal, at a loss to answer both truthfully and politely, could only listen to her story about their last bobcat kill. "I guess I'd know that screech anywhere. Our nephew Carl was here that time. They're coming for Christmas, all the way from California. You can ask him yourself."

She'd gone on about Carl and Marjorie and how a person's land is their own. Somehow she ended up with a tirade against Mr. Atherton, who'd been there to talk to her about her responsibilities. "I guess I know my responsibilities," she'd declared fiercely, while Emily slurped her cocoa and a blast of music issued from the front room. In the deepening dusk, the only light came from the blue television glare in the doorway.

Hal had tried to steal away, but Emily had to be pried from her chair. When he finally got her limping off to find her soaked boot, he had turned back to Harriet, wanting to say something pleasant, like how nice to have family come at Christmas, without sounding phony. Harriet had never moved a muscle. Hal had gone over to help Emily with her boot.

Emily had leaned over his shoulder, grabbing a fistful of his hair to steady herself. "Is she asleep?"

"Sort of. Look, we'll leave the raisin jar. It'll be a present." Sooner or later there would have to be an accounting, what with brie and raisins and handsome glass jars disappearing every Wednesday. Quietly he had shut the door behind them.

"Will she stay there all night?" Emily had wanted to know. "What if she forgets to go to bed?"

Hal had thought of Harvey stuck in his chair in front of that blaring box, and Harriet sunk in her angry memories.

"How does he go to the bathroom?" Emily had asked.

"Oh, for God's sake," Hal had snapped. "How do I know?"

"But what if he has to?"

"Well, they have a system. People work out systems for that kind of thing. They have to, so they do."

"System," Emily had muttered to herself. "System."

"System," she murmured now as she brushed the cat. Hal could tell the word was meaningless to her; it had probably come into her head when she heard bobcats mentioned again. Were all kids that much apart? He couldn't remember about being five. It suddenly seemed to him all wrong, like blindness or deafness, that being five could be so vivid for a time and then be swept away by six and seven and so on.

Sherry spoke up without turning. "If your field trip's next weekend, count me out for sitting. I've got plans."

"No, it's on school time. Don't worry about Emily."

Mac slumped over his coffee and rubbed his eyes. "Ought to team up with the Science teacher, kill two birds with one stone."

Emily said, "I won't go if you kill birds."

"That's not what he means," Hal started to tell her, but Emily didn't seem to be listening anymore. Here at the Thayer house she acted like a child with a whole lot of different parents. It was only when she felt crummy that you noticed who came first; then she would lean up against Lew or climb into his lap to be babied. And listen to the grownup conversation with her eyes closed.

"No Science department," Lew stated with feeling. "They're super-organized."

Hal said, "You know what's going to happen, don't you, if you have the field trip at Candlewood? Cow manure."

Lew considered that, then groaned in acknowledgment.

"Think of Ruthie Nettleton all splattered . . ." But Hal didn't have to go on. He'd won his case.

In the last Social Studies class before Thanksgiving, Lew talked about important New England holidays. When he mentioned that people used to bake special cakes on Election Day, Amy said it sounded like a foreign country—she'd never heard of Election Day cakes.

"So go visit that country, even if it is in your own backyard," Lew said, dismissing them. "Learn some of its customs. See what was going on when your grandparents were growing up. Better still, *their* grandparents."

Going home on the bus was wonderful. It was Hal's first free Wednesday, and four full days stretched ahead.

"Come on home with us," Josh invited.

49

"Yeah, with me," said Bill.

Hal liked wading through the toys and kittens and noise of the Sparkmans' kitchen. One sister was beating something in a bowl. The middle one, Karen, was modeling clay, or maybe it was dough. The baby, its rump in the air and its thumb in its mouth, was fingering the ear of the mother cat. Like one of the kittens, thought Hal. And Mike was playing records in the next room.

Bill opened the refrigerator. "Where's Ma?"

"Watch out," warned his sister. "Everything's for tomorrow. Get out of there."

Bill grabbed apples, gummy leftover pizza, a dish with rice and something else in it, and left Josh and Hal to bring whatever appealed to them. Hal turned to the cupboard and fished a handful of crackers from a carton without even bothering to read the label. He was thinking: When Candlewood Acres has all its houses, it'll be something like this. Like this after school every day. Like a sit-com neighborhood. A disaster? That's what right-minded people believed. But secretly Hal couldn't help wondering how it would feel to have more kids around and other houses to visit.

Josh took the stairs three steps at a time. Hal started to follow, then found himself resisting. He leaned against the banister. The music screamed through the house and shook the mirror by the front door. Slowly, with a determined effort to pace himself to a different beat, Hal started up to join his friends. By the time he reached the landing, he could hear them already roaring with laughter. Before he turned the corner into Bill's room, Hal was laughing too.

That day and the next, Thanksgiving, were so full that it was nearly dark when Hal thought of taking some cranberry-orange relish over to the Titcombs. His mother was doubtful about the timing. Also about his deserting his young cousins, who were visiting for the day, all of them sprawled in front of the tube.

Uncle Frank said, "Don't you want to watch that Special too?"

Hal spooned relish into a freezer carton. "Not really. And it's part of my school project to find out about old-fashioned Thanksgiving customs."

It was clear that Harriet Titcomb wasn't expecting a caller. "Who is it?" she wanted to know from the other side of the door.

"Hal." Then, after no response, "I brought some cranberry relish."

After another delay the door opened. Harriet was wearing a wrapper. She had a small scarf on her hair and knotted under her chin. Hal could see bony ankles above the untied shoes.

"I hope I'm not too late for your dinner." By now he was in the kitchen and could see no sign of dinner at all. He noted the darkness in the front room and the absence of Thanksgiving cooking smells. An empty cup and saucer were the only things on the table.

Harriet's tone was less than cordial. "Television's broken," she informed him. "Harvey keeps telling me to turn it on." She went on standing, so Hal did too. "I tried to call the man. Nothing answers, nothing works. Not the man, not the television."

Hal was beginning to feel out of his depth. How could she get so worked up over a busted tube? "The television repair places wouldn't be open today."

"Why not? It isn't Sunday."

51

"It's Thanksgiving." He averted his eyes, but not before catching a glimmer of her confusion.

After a moment she retorted, "Oh, is that it?"

He nodded.

"Then I suppose that's why the chicken. Steve brought us a chicken this week in our things from the store."

Hal wanted to get her mind off forgetting the day. "Years ago," he blurted, "did you have chicken or turkey? Do you know how your grandmother celebrated Thanksgiving?"

"Certainly. They had pies." Harriet drew her wrapper around herself and pulled out a chair. "They may have killed the rooster the way we used to. Though I can remember one old turkey gobbler I'd've killed with my own hands if I'd dared."

"Why?"

"Used to lie in wait for me. Tormented me. I was to get the eggs out of the hen house. That gobbler would light out after me. My legs were black and blue. I hated him."

"Did you finally kill him?"

Harriet Titcomb turned the empty cup in its saucer. "I suppose. Someone must have. Unless a fox got him. Though I'd bet on that gobbler against any fox. I don't recall eating the bird. Probably he was too tough."

"Maybe you could make a Thanksgiving dinner tomorrow and have this relish with it."

Harriet shook her head, but she reached for the carton and pried up the lid. "I cooked up the chicken already. Some still in the pot in the icebox." Then, noticing his concern, she added, "It doesn't matter. There's Christmas coming, and all the doing for that with our nephew and his wife here. First time in years. We'll be busy enough with that." She took the spoon from her saucer and dipped

52

it into the relish. "That's good," she told him, tasting it. "I'll take some to Harvey. He could eat that very nicely, and it'll make him forget how mad he is about the television."

She got up and shuffled over to the cupboard, where she found three dishes.

Hal said, "Oh, none for me, thanks. I've just had a big dinner." It was hard to keep in mind that he was supposed to be interviewing her and taking notes. He looked at her spooning out the brilliant berries, all crushed and oozing their wonderful juices. He said, "I bet you had squash and pumpkin pies too," and felt ashamed when she paused thoughtfully, the crimson spoon upraised.

She smiled. "And apple too. Not the kind you get now, though. Real apples."

"What do you mean?" he asked, feeling for his pencil in his jacket pocket.

"Baldwins. They're the best. And the Ben Davis. Those old kinds held their shape and taste. Nowadays they're white and soft and hardly keep. Why, Harvey can even mash them without his teeth. That's what your apples are today."

Hal followed Harriet to the front room, but stayed in the doorway while she fumbled with the lamp switch. Even when the light went on, the room stayed dim. The nondescript furniture was dark—a huge chair and footstool in front of the television, a glass-fronted bookcase, a desk, and a bed against the wall, where Harvey Titcomb lay blinking up at the ceiling.

"Harvey, just think of it!" Harriet shouted down at him. She set one dish on the wheelchair seat and leaned over to haul her brother up.

53

Hal started forward to help, then held back. He might do something wrong, might hurt the old man.

Harriet was telling Harvey about the surprise. And explaining why the television repair man hadn't answered her call. And asking Harvey if he could remember some of the good old times when they went to pick the berries, down past the pond.

"So that part wasn't cursed? I thought you didn't like it there."

Harriet straightened and sent Hal a stabbing glance. "Lift the pillow for me," she told him. "Lay it right there." She raised Harvey so that he was almost sitting, picked up the dish, and seated herself in the wheelchair next to the bed.

Hal backed away from the sight and smell of the old man. He couldn't help wondering how often Harvey got washed or the sheets got changed. Everything, including Harvey's breath, was sour.

"I never said I didn't like the place," Harriet said. "You can't dislike what can't be helped. It's the place that never liked *us*. My grandmother used to say it was determined to rid itself of plowlands and mowing fields, house and barns. Ever since *her* grandfather set himself down there and brought his bride home to the hill." She pointed her spoon at her brother's chin. "Watch the juice, Harve."

"Do you know exactly when that was?" asked Hal.

Harriet shook her head. "Only that my great-great-grandfather set up housekeeping right inside a cleft in the granite he quarried to make the foundation of the first proper house, if you could call it that. Gran used to say it was scarcely more than a keeping-room and a loft. She had no affection for that house. Said the place itself kept them

54

from what was fair and right, hidden back in the woods like that. When her brother died of consumption, it was two days before any neighbor knew of it. Or so she said."

Harvey mumbled something, spraying pinkish bubbles.

"No," she shouted, "I'm not talking about him!" She turned to Hal. "Harvey thought I was talking about our grandmother's father. Died and left his wife with a distant son and two daughters and farm debts and little more."

"Is that when Nathaniel went there to work for them?"

"I'm not sure. Yes, that was his name. I think Gran was away in Lowell when her father died. They sent for the son out in Ohio, but he was killed, and that left everything in bad shape at home. It's not like now with the Social Security."

Hal said, "Do you think you could have another look for that story your grandmother wrote?"

Harriet took Harvey's bowl and leaned back in the wheelchair. "I imagine it's in the attic. It's hard for me to get up there these days."

"But *I* could," Hal volunteered. "You could tell me where to look for it, and maybe I could get some other things down for you."

"Well, that's an idea."

"I could come tomorrow."

Harvey began to work at clearing the phlegm from his throat.

"The attic's pretty dark," Harriet told Hal, "even when the light works."

"I'll bring a fresh bulb." Hal backed toward the kitchen. He couldn't stand the gurgling in Harvey's throat. The thought of the red juices made him feel sick to his stomach. "I'll see you tomorrow," he said.

Harriet was helping her brother cough up mucus. From the kitchen door Hal heard her yell, "Tomorrow!" as she thumped Harvey's back.

Thinking she was answering him, Hal called back, "Fine."

Then he heard her go on. "Tomorrow," she was assuring her brother. "I'll get the man to come tomorrow. I told you, Harve. I can't turn it on. It's broken. No. I couldn't get it fixed today because it's Thanksgiving."

8

But Lew had other ideas about Friday. The pond had a thin sheet of ice across it. Soon it would thicken. If they didn't get the injured duck, a raccoon or fox or weasel surely would. So down they went with the cage, Lew and Hal deliberating strategy for catching the duck, and Emily tramping on ahead of them. Then they heard splashing; from the duck they heard, "Wrauck," or something that sounded like that. "Shall I catch her or what?" yelled Emily, and by the time they reached her she had it firmly in her grasp.

Lew let the duck go inside the cage and rigged a screen to keep it at one end. He set the trap door for the drake. "We'll leave them now," he said, but Emily objected. "The father duck's different," he explained patiently. "See, our purple duck got used to us. Used to being caged. Our best chance for getting both home safe and sound is to get away from them now."

Emily lagged behind, declaring that it wasn't fair. "I caught the duck. It's mine."

Hal said, "I'll never be a father."

Lew laughed. "You and me and lots of other guys."

Hal heard himself asking, "How come Emily's mother—" He broke off.

Lew nodded. "It's hard to explain. She was sick. Couldn't handle a baby. Afterwards, after she came out of the hospital, all she wanted was to start over. She's never seen Emily, never even asked."

"Do you still . . . hope?"

Lew shook his head. "Linda and I were never a family. Emily and I *are*. Anyway, Linda's married again."

Hal thought maybe Lew regarded Peggy and Sherry as substitute mothers for Emily, but it wasn't something he could ask about.

Lew scanned the area around them. "What the hell," he muttered. "Where's she off to now?"

"She's got the corn," Hal said. "Maybe she stayed back to feed the ducks. She's—" He gasped. Not more than two school-bus lengths away on the southwest slope stood Emily. She looked like a squirrel standing up to a St. Bernard. Only the animal she was speaking to wasn't a dog; it was an enormous cow, reddish brown with a white face. The cow's broad muzzle spaded downward; the great tongue slapped out over Emily's hands, withdrew, emerged once more, then reached to its damp pink nostrils. It blew rolls of white vapor into the frosty air.

"Emily." Lew cleared his throat, but kept his voice level. "Emily, just throw the rest of the corn on the ground." He walked toward her. "The cow can get it there." As he

57

drew closer, the cow rolled its eyes, snorted, then, lowering its head, turned from Emily.

"See what you've done?" She was furious. "First the duck. Now my cow."

"Emily," Hal declared, "you don't know anything about that cow. It might . . . might . . ." Then he remembered playing Brindle with her.

"I do so."

Lew had Emily in his arms now. He said, "It could step on you. By accident." The cow stood off, looking tense and watchful. "Cow!" screamed Emily, struggling. "Cow!" She dove at Lew's hand. He winced. "Jesus," he breathed, and Hal said, "You know, Lew, maybe it's tame. If it is, could we catch it?"

Lew was sitting, still holding his furious child, but rubbing his hand. From below came the screech of the caged duck. The din was a distraction for Emily, who fell silent.

"It's pretty big," Lew finally answered. "Too big, I think."

"To catch or to keep?"

Lew shrugged.

Emily said, "Anyway, it's mine." She picked up Lew's hand and examined it. Hal was shocked to see toothmarks on it.

"It hurts," Lew told her very quietly. "It hurts a lot."

Emily rubbed the skin with her grubby fingers, then flung herself against him.

"Let's go now," he said, rising and pulling her up with him.

Emily said, "I want to say goodbye." She pulled back, but Lew didn't release her.

"Say goodbye from here."

"But where is he?" Emily demanded.

The cow had disappeared. There was only a sprinkling of yellow corn on the slick mat of leaves and blackened holes for hoofprints.

She gave her father a long, reproachful look, which made him shrug again. "You're the one that howled. Scared it away. *Her* away." Emily swung off, yanking him after her, and marched along the stone-lined road to the Titcombs' orchard. After that she ran ahead of them, was already ensconced at the kitchen table by the time they reached the house.

They stayed awhile with the Titcombs, speculating about the cow. Harvey was more talkative than usual. It seemed there was an established ritual for dealing with stray farm critters. "Nobody would be fool enough to claim one before being sure there was no damage. Take your pigs, now," Harvey expanded. "Loose pigs can do a sight of harm."

"What about cows?" prompted Hal.

Lew signaled him to let the old man talk, but Hal knew they could spend the entire day there without learning a thing.

"Usually they come home on their own," Harvey responded. "A cow likes to get away while she drops her calf. Or the young bulls break out. One goes, and usually the rest follow. We used to put them up back in the rough pasture. Didn't matter too much if they got out. They'd clean up the woodlot. I remember one winter—"

"Could they make it through the winter?" pressed Hal.

"Who's that?"

"A lost cow."

"Don't know as I ever knew of one staying out that

long." Harvey sucked on his teeth and pondered Hal's question. "Depends, I guess. Depends how bad the winter gets, and what kind of cow, how old, all that. Like the deer. Some years you get a lot of starving deer. Dogs run them down."

Lew said, "The cow in your back lot, Hal means. I don't think it's a dairy cow."

"Beef? Watch out for that kind. We had one a few years back, one of those Black Angus steers from over to Donatelli's. Meanest thing I ever saw."

"This one's not black, though," Hal put in. "It's reddish brown with a white face and legs."

"A Hereford," said Harriet. "Haven't seen many of them around."

"Well," asked Hal eagerly, "would a Hereford be easier to handle?"

"Makes no difference," Harvey told him, "once they go wild."

"I think," said Lew, "I'll stick to goats."

Hal leaned toward Harvey. "It was eating out of Emily's hand." He raised his voice. "We saw it. The cow eating from Emily's hand."

Harvey said, "I hear you." He shook his head slowly. "Listen. Some animals are all right no matter what happens. Some take to the woods, and that's it. There's something in them. Why, even those little white ducks that used to come to the pond would never tame down like your barnyard duck. Never."

Hal drew back. "So what do we do about this cow, then?"

"I just told you. Leave it be."

"Won't it starve?"

"It seems in fine shape now," Lew remarked. "Probably it's learned to take care of itself."

"Don't let it go too long if you're planning to take it," Harvey advised.

That threw Hal. "I thought you just said not to."

"Shoot it, not keep it. Only you never want a living soul to know you've killed one of those lost critters. There'd be a dozen owners of lost cows at the barn claiming it."

"That's not exactly what we had in mind," Lew said mildly.

"Anyway," Emily announced, "it's *my* cow and I won't let you."

"We're not going to shoot it," Lew assured her.

"Well," chimed in Harriet, "it won't do anyone any good if the police do."

They sat awhile longer, the conversation drifting in other directions. Harvey told about the horses he used to raise in the days before tractors. He'd bred some of the finest teams anywhere.

Harriet sighed. "Broke his heart when Prince couldn't haul the wood anymore. Prince was the last we kept. How old was he, Harve?"

Harvey shook his head. "Damn sight better than any tractor."

"Harvey likes looking across the road now and seeing the Sturgis horses there." She walked to the window. "Not too many years ago it was Prince and Molly pulling the hay wagon, stop and go, stop and go, and the cows to the other side moving down from the north hill. Drifting toward the barnyard for the milking."

Lew said, "A lot of people feel it's a shame to lose all that. That's why they're trying to save some of the old land in Westwick."

"It can't be saved," Harriet retorted. "Look at that field. Even with those horses it's not the same. Red cedar already. Those people, the conservation people, they think all you got to do is hold it. They don't think of the plowing and harrowing and manure-spreading and clipping. You take an old farm and leave it, and nothing's going to stay the same. Nothing. You think we don't mind?"

Lew said, "The thing is, once you put the roads in and the houses, it's too late."

Harriet dug her fists into her pockets. "You talk like Mr. Atherton. People like that want it all for themselves. Well," she went on, "he didn't want it bad enough to make us an offer, did he?"

"I don't think that's really—"

But she wouldn't let him finish. "At least it's going to be used. It's waited a long time for that. And the new people won't know anything about the old curse. They're going to build houses and plant shrubs and mow their lawns. And Harvey and me can finish our lives here without a worry."

Lew stood up, nodding through the last of this tirade. All he said was, "I can't blame you for feeling that way."

"No?" Harriet snorted. "Well, Mr. Atherton did."

Lew started to smile, then covered his mouth. "I believe you," he said through his fingers.

Harriet grabbed at his hand; she peered at the toothmarks. "What's that?" she demanded.

"Oh, nothing." Lew dropped his hand.

"Something got you there," she observed. "I expect you tried to pick up a wild thing."

"That's right." Lew's grin was broad, unchecked.

But Harriet was all stirred up by now and could only scowl and compress her lips and whisk some bread crumbs from the table as though she were swinging a scythe.

Later, at lunch in the Thayer house kitchen, Lew declared that the only way he could take on the cow was if they had an understanding with the police.

"What kind of understanding?" asked Hal.

"That we can keep it under wraps."

Sherry burst out laughing. "A cow in this neighborhood and not have people know?"

"I mean, just keep a low profile."

Hal thought of that immense animal and began to laugh too.

Lew just smiled. "Anyway," he pointed out, "we're counting our cows before they're caught. First things first."

He talked Sherry into keeping Emily, who was already upstairs playing in her room. In town they stopped at the general store, where they picked up 100-watt bulbs for the Titcombs, raisins to replace those Hal's parents hadn't yet missed, and a length of Dacron rope.

Hal looked at it doubtfully. "Are you going to lassoo her?"

Lew didn't know what he was going to do. He just wanted to have it in case.

Chief Durand was genial and easy-going when Lew started talking about the cow. Yes, he told Lew, they'd had quite a few calls about a cow last summer, again in September. Then it sort of faded from the scene. "Actually," he said, "we can't be sure it's all the same cow. If it started over on the southwest side of town last July, it's had to cross two major highways to get to the Nutters Hill area." He drew a long breath. "However, if it did, and it keeps moving and crosses the town line without causing any accidents, we're home free. The trouble is there's a lot of traffic coming out of the Industrial Park. I wouldn't want to see the mess a cow could make down there if a car hits it."

"What if we caught her and took her to our place?" suggested Lew. "What if we fixed up the old fence and put her there, or in the barn . . . ?"

Chief Durand smiled. "You'd want one of those cow-catchers from up country. Beef critters revert to the wild, you know. I've heard stories. They'll go right through a barn wall."

Hal and Lew exchanged glances. "What if we get some-one to tranquilize it?"

"Listen," said Chief Durand, "don't let me stop you. I just don't want anyone hurt."

"But if we get her into the barn, would we have to advertise or just notify you or—"

"There's been plenty of notification. This cow's been wandering around town for five, maybe six months. If someone takes it out of a humane concern or worry over the damage it could inflict on a car and its passengers, I'm not going to go looking for complications."

Someone knocked on the chief's door. He stood up, and Hal and Lew rose too.

"One thing," Lew added, "and then we'll be going. Have you had any calls about the cow recently?"

"Hold on. I'll check." The chief left them standing in

his office, then reappeared, leaning around the door jamb. "Two calls this past week. Looks like things are stirring again. I guess something's going to have to be done, one way or another."

"Could you give us a week or so before you . . . do anything?"

"If nothing serious crops up. Leave your numbers at the desk and we'll pass on any calls we get."

"Oh, thanks," said Hal fervently.

"Don't thank me yet." The chief waved and was gone.

All the way home Hal was full of ideas for fixing up the fence and barn, but he had promised Harriet Titcomb to hunt for her grandmother's story in the attic, so Lew let him out at the bottom of the Titcomb driveway. He didn't feel like poking around dusty old furniture, not when he was about to become part owner of a magnificent Hereford cow. He slammed the car door. Lew said he'd be along later for the ducks. Hal nodded, then watched the car pull away.

Trudging up the driveway, he gazed ahead, beyond the house on the right and the small barn on the left, on through the old apple trees to the pines and hardwoods that screened the interior world of Candlewood, all eighty acres of it, from the people who lived along Nutters Hill Road and the Great Road to the north. In there, somewhere between the pond and the meadow and the high ridge that dropped to the southeast swamp, protected by thickets of bramble and blueberry bushes, sheltered under hoods of poison ivy and grapevine, honeysuckle and the tentacled bittersweet, a cow went browsing on the twigs where next spring's hickory and oak should bud. One lost cow feeding on hummocks and unearthing the acorns already hidden by troops of squirrels.

Sooner or later there would be another encounter. Next time, Hal vowed, it would be he who held the corn out and felt the hot breath, the rasping tongue.

Something crossed his mind. That must have been what Hannah had told herself when she returned alone to Candlewood, hoping, believing that if she kept looking, if she stayed long enough, her Brindle cow would come home.

9

Harriet Titcomb eyed the light bulbs critically. "We've got bulbs."

"These are hundred-watt ones."

"Wasteful."

"It'll be more cheerful," Hal said, screwing one of the light bulbs into the lamp socket.

"And who's going to pay for them?" demanded Harriet.

Hal thought of the raisins and the jar. "They're a present," he declared.

"What about electricity bills?"

"Oh." Did it make that much difference? He said, "By the time you've sold all of Candlewood Acres—"

"Yes," snapped Harriet, "everyone thinks we're rich now."

He mumbled, "I just wanted to brighten things up."

Harriet picked up the forty-watt bulb he had removed from the lamp. "Well, you can use this one in the attic," she informed him. "No one's up there hardly at all."

He took the bulb and followed her to the stairs. She pointed the way, saying she only climbed to her bedroom once a day if she could help it.

He came up the attic stairs into a low roofed space with a small window at each end. A light string dangled from the peak of the ceiling, but when he pulled, the string came off in his hand. He fumbled around boxes and a rolled rug till he found a way of reaching the short chain, which he pulled without effect. Then he retied the string to the chain and replaced the bulb. This time, when he pulled the light string, the attic space was transformed, full of packages and trunks and sacks, with dead wasps everywhere and roofing nails sticking through overhead like porcupine quills, and basins and jugs and jars of every size and shape.

For a moment he just took it all in, thinking how he could spend the winter here exploring. It was like an indoor dump, full of mystery and life.

The chest that Harriet had told him to look in was against the wall where the roof sloped so low that he had to crouch while he fiddled with the clasp. Then he found that all he had to do was lift the top, clasp and all. Inside were a few old books and papers. He picked up the first book he touched. It started to come apart in his hands, its cover flapping wide and hanging by a thread. Crawling toward the light, Hal read the title page: *The American First Class Book; or Exercise in Reading and Recitation, Selected Principally from Modern Authors of Great Britain and America and Designed for the use of the Highest Class in Publick and Private Schools. By John Pierpont. Boston, 1826.* It was the longest title he'd ever seen.

The brittle pages were brown at the edges like overbaked cookies, but the type was quite legible. Could this have been Eliza's schoolbook? Hannah's? He set the book aside and returned to the chest.

Now he came to envelopes and papers, even newspapers. When he reached the bottom of the printed material, he sat back, suddenly discouraged. Then he started over again. Even if he didn't find the story, he would have that Reader to look at. He could find out what kids in school were reading more than a hundred and fifty years ago. Still, he had another look through the papers, spreading his fingers and sliding them underneath each batch, and sifting through every set of pages that seemed connected.

When the yellow cover faced him on the pile, he couldn't imagine how he had missed it the first time through. There it was, *The Lowell Offering, A Repository of Original Articles on Various Subjects, Written by Factory Operatives. No. 1. Price 6¼ cts. This Number Wholly Written by Females Employed in the Mills.* Then came the contents. Which was Eliza's story? His eyes swept over the names of the pieces: "The Hemlock Broom," "Recollections of an Old Maid," "The Garden of Science," "Old Bachelor's Friend" . . . Harriet would have to show him.

He closed the chest lid, gathered up the magazine and the book, and then, with a final glance around the attic before turning off the light, couldn't resist the wooden scoop that was just within reach on an overturned tub. With his loot clasped against him, he backed into the stairwell. It was only after he was halfway down, his head level with the rough attic floor, that he caught a glimpse of an animal lying under the window. A rat? A squirrel? He couldn't tell. It was on its back with its paws drawn up to its chest; it didn't even smell. For some reason that small, lonely, dead thing sent a shiver of pity, or maybe dread, through him.

He came down to Harriet waving the wooden scoop, questions tumbling out of him.

Harriet more or less wiped at the dust that clung to it like a coat of fur. What was it for? She shrugged. Harvey said for apples.

"Use your nose," he advised. "I'm bound you'll find the apples on it."

But all Hal could smell was attic mustiness.

Harriet took the magazine to the light and studied the table of contents. "Come over here, Hal. What does that say?" She pointed with her bony finger.

Hal read out loud, " 'The Tomb of Washington, page 9.' "

"No, no. The next one."

" 'Knowledge in Heaven.' "

Harriet shook her head. "It's here somewhere. I think it's called 'Daughter of . . .' Daughter of Something."

Hal looked. "It's not here." Turning the pages at random, he came to another title page, another issue. Then his eye caught "The Last Daughter." He turned to the page indicated and read the title out loud.

"That's it! That's the one my grandmother wrote."

He didn't try to read it then. Lew was just coming, and anyway Hal wanted to go through it when he was by himself in his own room.

Lew had already checked on the ducks. The drake was hanging back. Maybe it would work its way into the cage during the night.

Hal picked up the magazines and the book. He felt as

if he had been away in another place.

Lew glanced at the things as they went out to the car. "How did you make out this afternoon?"

"Fine. All right." Hal tried to keep his voice easy. "I've got some stories to look at," he said.

As soon as he got home, he made for his room. He swept everything from his desk and opened the magazine. Too hurriedly. One of the pages tore as he thumbed it. But there was "The Last Daughter." He began to read.

"Picture a hilltop not far from Boston as the stage travels, not far as the farm cart trundles its sheep to market, but set apart by a dense wood as well as by a spirit of independence that tends to make an island of the hill. Indians may have sheltered in the rocky cleft that became this family's first dwelling. The family's first settler also dwelt like a savage, with only a roof of pine boughs and thatch to cover him. He cleared the summit of the hill, forming field fences out of the stumps of oak, but sparing the great sugar maples and hickory trees that grew there in profusion.

"He planted a beech tree high on the hill, but by the time he brought his bride to live there, he still had only the earthen cellar hole carved from the rock in that hill. Its roof was made from the straw of his first oat crop and supported by timber and stone. In that crude dwelling, called by him a keeping-room, an infant son was born. The child lay on the stone shelf where later cheese and tallow and apples and roots would be stored.

"The following summer a simple house was built on the hillside not far from the stone and earthen cellar. This new dwelling was little more than a true keeping-room, but it had space and light, its floors were well sanded, and its

70

great fireplace was the heart of the farm. Here the family worked and gathered; here was food prepared and eaten, wool spun and woven, the Bible read by the light of flickering candles made from tallow stored inside the old stone cellar where the firstborn began his life.

"Like his father, the son grew to be a man of vision, perhaps too much vision for the sake of his wife and children. Until his strength gave out, he worked as hard as his ox, but not always to useful purpose. While he dreamed of diverting the brook and building a tannery, the village tannery prospered. All that came of his effort was the destruction of an entire grove of oak, which glutted the local market with tanbark and cost him all his profit. Next he conceived the notion of starting a spinning wheel manufactory. By the time he was ready to commence construction, spinning mills had risen all around Boston.

"By the time his own strength was drained he had already buried three sons. The oldest son, long away in the west, had never shown interest in the home farm, but he was summoned home at the final hour. There were also two daughters, the eldest grown to responsible years. The other, the last daughter, was but ten years old.

"We shall call the child Anna. Her father begrudges her time at school, but will sit with her of an evening while her mother and older sister, Alice, ply their needles through the shirting or homespun cloth. With his last daughter he recites his sons' lessons from their school reader. Anna also reads the Sabbath School books like *The Dying Experiences of Mary Ann* and *An Epitome of Polite Literature*, and so she is made ready for the visit of the school supervisor.

"Little Anna trudges home from the school examination.

71

She climbs the rugged cowpath with her slippers in her hand to save them from the stones and dust. She goes to join her father, to drive the great slow ox, and while they work her father teaches her all the secrets of the woods and fields his father taught him and his remaining son should learn.

"Attacked by lung fever, he falls behind his payments of the taxes. Unable to carry out his portion of the town work, the road below the farm lies rutted and nearly washed away. Because of his wife, who still takes her place in the Women's Foreign Missionary Society and in the village sewing bees, kind neighbors offer to help with the harvest. But he prefers to let his own child swing the hook that cuts the corn. He sells a cow. He hires a man to take his sheep to Boston, and three are lost on the way to the road. And he, as feverish with dreams as with illness, instills in his last daughter the same devotion to the hill, till she would believe it Paradise or Robinson Crusoe's island. . . ."

Hal paused, thinking, Well, some things don't change. You could still feel cut off when you were up on the hill amid all those trees. It wasn't hard to imagine the last daughter growing attached to it. But it was disconcerting to find himself thinking of her as alive in the place he knew.

She and her sister were certainly different, he discovered as he resumed his reading. The older one, Alice, had friends she talked with at the Sabbath noonings. That was how she learned about employment of respectable girls in the cotton mills of Lowell. It grieved her that her little sister must labor in the woods to cut candlewood because they could barely afford candles. She looked to the world outside for an answer, and chose a life for herself in a world that was

72

not an island but a thoroughfare with many roads, many possibilities. In Lowell she grew accustomed to long hours indoors, to the racket of machinery. And when her father died of lung fever, she was so caught up in her new life, with its evening lessons and lectures, its companionship and comforts, that she was convinced her mother and sister should join her in Lowell.

But Anna stuck to the promise her father had extracted from her on his deathbed: to hold the land and farm it as it was meant to be. So arrangements had to be made between Alice and her mother. When Alice arrived home to fetch her little sister away to Lowell, it was "a bitter thing to see the child working beside the loutish fellow given over to their mother for his keep and the work she could get from him. Little Anna drives him as though he were an ox. She is never far behind, her bare feet and legs stained by soil and dung and tanning fluid. To Alice's astonishment, the child has continued to peel the bark from the felled oaks; strips lie in hollow logs or dry like hides across the whitened trunks. Only the twin oak where Anna and her youngest brother used to keep their playthings and Anna's rag babies is spared. And at night, while her mother sews and knits, little Anna sits with skirts drawn, rubbing at a muskrat skin, for she has taken to curing pelts and selling them to a neighbor who sells them again at his own considerable profit."

Here the story turned a corner. With something like relief, Hal read about the Moodys' husking bee, at which all the young people in the neighborhood came together. It was there in the Moody barn that Alice was reacquainted with a young law apprentice who had left the village before Alice had. When she husked an ear of corn with red kernels, the young man, already attentive, snatched it from her and hid it so that no one else would see it and claim its due, a kiss from her. There in the flickering lantern light they spoke together, shared the refreshment of cider and doughnuts, and kept to themselves. But when he walked her home, Anna watched him every second of the way, and he never managed to exchange the red ear for a single kiss.

Though Alice wasn't to see him again for many months, that night of simple reunion with childhood friends marked an important beginning in her life. "But this development," concluded the installment, "and the sisters' life together as mill girls is another chapter in the story of the last daughter and will presently be offered to the reader."

Hal sat for a long time, not trying to visualize the "island" home described, just letting all the impressions of its people surround him with imagined voices and motions. He didn't realize how dark it had grown until the ringing telephone pierced the late-afternoon silence. Were his parents resting? He knew they were going out to dinner tonight. Now his father's voice came through, for a moment raised, then subdued again. Anyway, they were home.

Hal switched on the light. There before him was the magazine with the story he had devoured so hungrily. His father was on the phone talking to someone real, someone now. For an instant Hal could feel himself suspended between this time and the time of the story, between fiction and fact. And then he caught himself. It was as though he had lurched off balance. Now, backed by his father's voice, he returned to reason. He knew better than to believe everything he read. Who could vouch for the accuracy of that story except queer old Harriet Titcomb? And Harvey. Hal wasn't about to go into school with a nineteenth-cen-

74

tury soap opera and present it as history. Even the author's name was questionable—"Alice," not "Eliza." If the story was true, why bother to change the names? If it was true.

He flipped back to the magazine's cover, stared at it, then pushed it aside. No one in his class would ever have to know how he'd been taken in by that story. He let his eyes run down the page. Here was an advertisement for "Feathers, Blankets, Comforters, Quilts, Damasks, Hair-Cloth," whatever that was. Here were doctors and dentists, one proclaiming, "All operations warranted to be of the first order. The most beautiful porcelain or incorruptible Teeth, set, on pivot or gold plate, in a style which, in respect to imitation of nature, firmness, durability, and elegance, is not surpassed in any of the American or European cities. Children's teeth regulated. Charges reasonable." Now, that was something for his class: some kids wore braces even in those days.

He skimmed over other items on the page: bonnets and dresses, carpenters' tools, cakes and fancy goods, boots and shoes, even a writing academy conducted by a Professor of Penmanship. All this would be good for a laugh, so it wasn't a waste, *The Lowell Offering*. Just a disappointment.

Handling the flimsy magazine with care, he took it over to the bookshelf and set it down next to the upright telephone that Emily had perched there for her own use. Absently he picked up the receiver. The way he felt, it was a good thing the phone wasn't connected, or he'd give Harriet a call and tell her what he thought of her grandmother's soppy story. Only maybe Harriet was honestly muddled. Maybe she actually believed it was a true account. She'd certainly sounded as if she did. Either way, he was going to watch his step from now on. It was one thing having to

75

entertain Emily on Wednesdays, and quite another—altogether too much—to play "let's pretend" with Harriet Titcomb.

"Hal!" His father was calling. "Hal, could you come here when you get a minute?"

Hal slammed down the receiver. "I've got a minute right now," he muttered. "I'm not wasting any more of my time on all this stuff."

He found his father in the study looking at the regular phone as though someone had made it up too.

"What's wrong, Dad?"

"A very odd call."

Hal's mother joined them. "We thought maybe you might know something about it."

Was Josh pulling some kind of stunt? Sometimes he fooled around with the unconnected telephone, pretending to call from the Antarctic or Mars, and you had to figure out where the call was coming from.

"It was Mrs. Twombly. Do you know her?"

Hal had never heard of Mrs. Twombly.

"She asked for you. When I said I was your father, she demanded that I come at once to take my cow out of her garden."

"What?" exclaimed Hal. "Where does she live?"

"Of course I told her I had no cow. She said the police had given her two numbers to call, and perhaps this one was incorrect and she'd try the other."

"What happened then?" asked Hal.

"She hung up. Presumably she called the other number."

"We thought it was just a funny mistake," said his mother. "At first."

"Then it began to sink in," his father went on. "Ducks, you know. Is it a Titcomb cow?"

Hal shook his head. "I was going to tell you."

"Tell us what?"

"That actually, in a way . . ." Hal gulped. "We kind of do have a cow." Rather rapidly he filled in, relying a lot on Chief Durand's support of the project.

Their heads began to shake in the slow, determined way he recognized as meaning the argument was hopeless. So he stopped and said simply, "It's not my cow. Only, considering that there are five people using one phone at the Thayer house, it seemed helpful to give the police a second number."

"It's out of the question," said his mother.

"An acceptance of liability," said his father.

Hal mumbled, "All right, then. Forget it. I'll tell the police. I'll tell Lew we can't be a part of saving this cow. And keeping it from hurting people too."

"If Lew Rifkin were a little older and wiser, I doubt he'd have anything to do with this wandering time-bomb."

"What's so great about being old?" retorted Hal, suddenly flaring up. "Look at those old Titcombs with their crazy ideas and stupid stories. If that's what happens to you when you grow old, I'd rather be like Lew or me. Or even Emily," he added as an afterthought.

He stormed down the hall to his room and slammed the door. He'd stay there till his parents went out. He could just hear them tonight: How's Hal? Oh, fine, fine. You know the age. Gets caught up in one craze after another. You'll never guess what happened today . . . And it would become another amusing anecdote. Fake, fake, fake.

77

But when his mother called him to supper, she sounded so normal he just naturally came out. His parents, dressed to go out, sat down with him while he picked off the crust of his leftover meat pie. The next thing he knew he was talking about the story and the Titcombs, and his parents were listening and not seeming in a hurry to go anywhere else.

"It's like when I stay home sometimes but I'm not awfully sick and you're both at work. Once in a while I start watching the tube."

"You'll probably survive it."

"The thing is, though, you can get hooked. When you get hooked, it's . . . well, first it's fun. Till you see they're having you on."

"Right." Hal's father paused before he spoke again. "Is anyone manipulating you?"

"I don't know. It's that story. See, I read the first part. I fell for it. The Titcombs' grandmother and the old curse and all that stuff."

"All that stuff brought to light some interesting history for you."

"I know." Hal shaled off a flake of crust. "Only I got dragged into the whole thing. I guess Miss Titcomb thinks she can tell me anything." He speared a lump of something in the gravy. "Me and my dumb project."

His mother said, "I can't believe she meant to deceive you. If her grandmother fantasized and based her fantasy on a made-up story, then Harriet and Harvey would have been taken in too. And there's always a possibility that the grandmother wrote the story as fiction, maybe to justify herself after Hannah left her, then later came to believe all of it. People do funny things with facts."

"The thing is, I believed. Especially after that letter of Hannah's. She was really someone in that letter." His voice fell. "I thought I was going to find out about her."

"It sounds to me," said his mother, getting up from the table, "as though you're spending too much time over at Candlewood. Maybe you need to get involved in some normal activities. I haven't seen Josh around here lately. What's he up to?"

"He's doing his project too."

"How about some new interest?"

"Like ducks and cows?"

His parents laughed and then said all right, maybe if Hal was only acting as a message service for Lew or the Thayer house crew, it might be all right for the time being.

"Anyhow," said Hal, as his parents got ready to go out, "there probably won't even be another call. Probably, the next thing we all know, the cow will be safe and sound next door."

10

The simple truth, though, was that it was getting harder for the cow to stay out of sight. This was perfectly evident to Lew and Hal by the time they finally caught the drake and took in the caged pair of ducks. Not only had more trees been cleared below the pond, but the cow was growing accustomed to attention. That is, to acceptable attention like corn. Any attempt to get near her with a rope was unacceptable to her. She seemed to be able to smell the rope even if it was behind Lew's back. He had only to approach that way, corn in hand, rope out of sight, and she would wheel and trot away.

The only temporary solution was to put hay out on the hill for her. When they went to the Titcombs to see if they could store a few bales in the calf barn, Hal brought along the magazines. He was polite, but he didn't say much.

"Now you know all there is to tell," Harriet stated. "A sorrowful story, isn't it?"

"Yes."

Harvey was nodding to Lew, telling him the calf barn was jammed, but there ought to be room for a little hay.

Harriet peered at Hal. "You read all three parts?"

He could tell she sensed something wrong. "I got the drift of them. I still have the book, if that's all right."

"You didn't have to return anything yet." When he made no response, she added curtly, "I'll just keep these down here for you. In case you want another look."

Even after it was all arranged about the hay, Harvey kept on nodding.

Hal couldn't wait to get out of the kitchen. He felt that at last his eyes were opened. What had seemed so comfortable here before looked just plain dingy now. He noticed that the floor by the sink had a dark stain of rot. Miss Titcomb smelled of mushrooms and Harvey was even worse.

After that, Hal and Lew established a feeding routine that seemed to work. Hal felt uneasy, though. Twice when he was carrying up some hay he had a sensation of being watched. Once, when he heard twigs breaking, he was sure he caught a glimpse of something passing through a pine grove. Not the cow. The cow was getting used to its hay and corn. Each time it came more readily. "My cow,"

Emily called it. Our cow, thought Hal, standing quietly till the cow thrust its broad, wet muzzle into his hands.

The Wednesday-afternoon visits to the back lot grew shorter. The evening would shut down like a shade drawn suddenly over the treetops. If Hal dug around in the dump, Emily tended to wander. One time when she returned to him with a report that the cow had visitors, Hal tensed up, only realizing afterward that this was more of Emily's private world.

She often pestered him to visit the Titcombs. He learned that he could distract her with promises of imported cheese and telephone games at his house. He taught her a secret telephone number which would always reach him. Actually it was just the Woodruff number and area code, but those three additional digits made it harder and more mysterious than her home one, which she had already memorized.

She rarely got the longer number right. When she did, he rewarded her with an answer. "This is Jack," he'd say. "I'm at the top of my beanstalk. Hal's sitting on my giant for me while I answer the phone. You want to speak to him? Just a minute; we have to trade places." Then Hal would speak in his ordinary voice: "Hi, Emily. What's up?" And there would be peals of laughter and more talk.

A lot better for her than sitting all afternoon in the Titcomb house, where there was nothing, just two really old people more dead than alive. Nothing but an attic full of things that crumbled when you touched them. And Harvey nodding like a puppet. What was the use of being so old you couldn't hear and you couldn't walk and you couldn't eat very well either? What was so wonderful about living to a ripe old age? People who said that couldn't know what ripeness meant.

The day came when Hal suddenly realized that he could stand at the dump and see all the way past the pond to the southeast lowland. He had carried up an armful of hay and was still there with it when he saw the cow completely exposed among the stumps of recently cut trees. She was using one giant oak trunk as a scratching post, switching from foot to foot as she wallowed in the ooze, her rump hard against the two-pronged section of what had been a huge twin oak. Even after she heard Hal call to her, she kept on rubbing for a bit, though she uttered the low-pitched moan that served as greeting.

After she had come to feed, Hal slithered down to inspect the newly cleared area. If this was to be the road, how would they manage to keep it from sinking? What would they do with all the heavy timber lying about? Probably they had left the six-foot lengths of oak here because the ground was too soft for the tractor to haul them off.

Perched precariously on a tussock, Hal pulled at the reddish hairs caught between the bark and the wood at the forked end of the trunk the cow had used. The bark was already so loose from the rubbing that he could raise it in one broad piece that spanned the crotch. He freed the tufts of cow hair and kept on lifting the bark. It was like the hide of some prehistoric beast.

He had an idea that if he could carry off this piece, he might experiment with it, make tanbark out of it for his project. But it was tough going. He'd have to bring a knife or a hatchet to cut the bark at the sides where it hadn't begun to separate from the wood. Meanwhile the cow could work on it some more.

He slid his hand under, trying to gauge the extent of the loosened area. It wasn't all smooth and rounded underneath. There was something with an edge, something flat. He reached back to the spine of the trunk section and hauled himself onto it. Now, leaning over the pronged end, he could pull up the bark and examine what his fingers had touched. It was hard and dark, like metal or stone, something jammed well under the bark. He swiveled, trying to get more light on the thing. Yes, it was stone, or slate, and something was written on it.

First he thought it was a sign for the chain-saw operator. He couldn't make out the words, though, not from this angle. He had to give up trying to stay out of the mud. Down he sank, gasping as the icy mud oozed up over his boots and around his knees. But at least he got the full light from above. He made out: "--ok -o- the co-." He tried to free the slab on which the words were scratched, but it was securely lodged, probably shoved in some more by the cow's rubbing. He made one last attempt to decipher the message. This time he read: "-ook -o- the cow."

He forgot about the cold mud. He remained knee deep, trying to gather his thoughts. Everything seemed to fit, the feeling of being watched, the hint of someone stalking, staying hidden. It had to be someone looking for the cow, as intent as Hal on saving it. That would explain why the person who scratched those words on the slate had shoved it into the cow's scratching post; that person knew that whoever was feeding the cow was likely to find it. But did that really make sense? Why wedge the slate in so deeply? Could the cow rubbing at it really have shoved it farther in?

Hal pulled himself out of the muck. Anyway, he decided, it had to be some kind of message for him. A warning?

Mulling this, he stumped up the hill. The mud in his

boots squelched with every step, announcing his approach to anyone lurking out of sight, as well as to the cow, which just glanced at him long enough to check him out—boy who brought feed and no rope—before she resumed her munching.

On his way past the cow Hal paused for a moment, awed by her bulk, amazed at her stolid acceptance of his gift of hay. He was tempted to stop in at the Titcombs', just in case they had seen someone around here, just in case there was a real urgency in that message he couldn't decipher.

But when he came down to their house, he saw a strange car parked outside. So he went on home.

All the way, he kept going over his discovery of the slate in the tree trunk. By the time he walked through his own door and breathed the essence of his own house, the only thing he was sure of was that he'd carried home a good deal of mud and a rather flimsy collection of assumptions about hidden messages. Like seeing a cow's face and declaring it a drake. That was the trouble with expectations, Lew had remarked. At least this time, thought Hal, he hadn't told anyone what he thought he'd seen.

And what had he actually seen? Could he even be sure of that? Maybe he hadn't read the scratched slate correctly. All he could recall were a few scattered letters and one entire word: cow. Or so he thought. Mud and outlandish notions were what he'd brought back with him, and they were out of place in the midst of newsprint and books, a bowl of fruit and a vase with dried sea lavender, a sleepy cat stretching and yawning on the hearth rug. Well, he'd have to go back and check more carefully. Only not now, not with his boots all gummed up and his feet freezing and the chill reaching up his back.

But he didn't get right back to the tree trunk, because he woke up the next morning with a sore throat and a fever. Lew was glad to take over all the feeding for a few days. He and Emily were going to be away visiting his parents in Florida at the beginning of vacation, and Hal would have to be responsible all that time.

Even though Hal was well enough to return to school on the last day before vacation, he was in no hurry to get out to the hill. It was bitterly cold, with snow in the air. Hal was quick to accept Bill's invitation to go Christmas shopping after school with his family and Josh.

Hal's parents didn't approve of bought presents; every year it got harder for Hal to think of something to make them. This year he bought leather remnants and waxed thread at a craft shop, figuring he could make a cover for a photo album or a telephone book. Everyone else took much longer with their shopping. They had pizza and ice-cream late in the afternoon, which was fine with Hal, who knew that his parents wouldn't be home until late.

That evening when the phone rang, all the parts of his Christmas present were spread out on the dining-room table.

"Mrs. Woodruff." The voice was brusque, indignant.

"She's not home. This is Hal Woodruff. May I take a message?"

"My wife spoke with her this morning. She understood the cow would be attended to. I've just returned home to find it trampling—"

"I'm sorry. I didn't know. I'll be after it first thing in the morning."

"Mrs. Woodruff assured my wife it would be gone before dark."

85

"I . . . I didn't get the message," Hal stammered.

"It looked in the window at her."

"It won't hurt her."

"Damn right it won't. Either you take it away or I'll get the police. It's eaten nearly all our salt-marsh hay and is now attacking the arbor vitae."

"Oh, no. Don't let it. Aren't the arbor-vitae berries poisonous?"

"Don't let it!" shrieked the man.

"Just shoo it away. I'll come right over. Tell me where you are."

The man told him. It was way down the Great Road, north of the Candlewood lot. That meant the cow was beginning to wander in a new direction.

Salt-marsh hay, thought Hal, looking for a flashlight, a bucket, plenty of corn. He opened a fresh box of oatmeal, which he laced with salt. He wondered whether Lew, who had left for Florida this afternoon, had remembered to feed the cow during these last few days. He wished he could call the guy who had scratched the message in the tree. Then they could meet and plan their strategy.

Hal even thought of detouring over to Reservoir Road to see if he could get Josh and Bill to come with him. But that would take even longer, and how would he explain everything fast enough? And convince their families that they should be allowed to go out in the dark to capture a wild cow? It was just beginning to snow too. Probably the bad weather made the cow restless.

All the houses along the Great Road were set back toward the woods. Hal trudged up one long driveway to a house with outdoor lights on, only to find that it was the wrong place. By the time he got to the right house, he had visions of the cow writhing in her death throes from the arbor vitae.

But there she was, looming larger somehow, maybe because of the landscaped setting. Her nose steamed in the night air. She was munching contentedly, switching her tail at the snow, shifting her weight from one foot to another.

He extended the bucket of corn. When she came to him, it was as though she had simply wandered too far and was eager to be found. He had a hard time getting the bucket out from under her. He shoved and wrenched. Everything he had brought would have to last for the long walk home.

When he started to look for a way into the woods at the back of the house, a voice shouted at him, "Not that way! Get that cow out of here!" Hal jumped, but the cow didn't seem to mind the unfriendly tone. She was probably used to it by now.

But when Hal changed his direction, the cow paused, not following. He retraced his steps. "Listen," he whispered, standing right in front of her, "you can't fool around here. This guy's really sore at us." He felt her tongue rasp his hand until every grain of salted oatmeal was cleaned from between his fingers. The cow's breath was rancid and hot in the snowy air. She let him rub the hard, hairy place between her ears. Then he set off slowly, the cow plodding after him.

The first car they encountered was coming toward them, so Hal had plenty of warning from the headlights. He dug into the precious salted oatmeal, switched on the flashlight and waved it at the approaching car. The car slowed; it veered out into the middle of the road. The cow was attending to the oatmeal and stood stock still.

The second car to come along whooshed past. Once

again Hal dug into the bucket and the cow licked up the salted oatmeal, but she turned her tail to the passing car and actually kicked out at it.

Hal walked on, keeping his manner brisk, but never letting too much distance come between him and the cow. The next car approached from behind. That was scary, because it did startle the cow. "Slow down!" Hal shouted as he dodged the oncoming cow. The car drew up. Hal turned, ready to shout some rebuke at the driver, and found that he was being paced by a patrol car.

"Everything all right?" asked the officer.

"If only I could get to Nutters Hill Road. The cars, they scare her, and . . ."

The flasher went on. The officer told Hal to take his time. He called to the station, then fell back just behind Hal and the cow, lighting their way beautifully and bringing every car that came along to a crawl before allowing it to pass.

The cow set an ambling pace that quickened once they turned the corner. Hal called out that he'd be fine now and thank you very much, but the police officer would not desert him until he was off the public roads.

It was the best feeling in the world walking along Nutters Hill Road with the sky a great black sieve and the fine granules of snow sifting out of it. The headlights turned the snow into silver sand; it gathered in creases on branches, but turned into shimmering droplets on the cow.

As soon as they turned into the Titcombs' driveway, Hal heard the police car speed up. In a moment it was gone. He switched on the flashlight, though he knew every step from here to the calf barn by heart. He noticed the strange car still parked beside the house, then realized it must be the nephew from California. He saw a rental label on the rear window. That was it, then—the nephew. He hoped the Titcombs wouldn't mind his interrupting the family reunion to run some water for the cow. If she got thirsty, she might wander off again. He dumped the remains of the oatmeal and corn for her and took the bucket to the house.

A strange woman answered the door, holding it open just a crack while he explained what he needed. Then she shut the door in his face. He was just starting down the steps when she opened the door again and beckoned him in. "You can't be too careful nowadays," she said. He stared at her and at the spare, wiry, gray-haired man beside her. It had never occurred to him that a nephew and his wife would be old and gray.

"A pail of water?" said Harriet Titcomb after she had introduced them. "You don't have to ask. You know that."

He felt badly then. It was a long time since he and Emily had sat talking with the Titcombs.

He ran warm water into the bucket, spilling some as he got it down from the sink. The Titcombs' nephew's wife clicked her tongue at that. Noticing how she was dressed, so trim and neat, Hal realized that another life style had come to Candlewood Farm. He murmured something about stopping by for a visit soon. Harriet told him he was always welcome, but in a tone that said to him his recent absence had not gone unmarked.

The cow stopped rubbing against the barn door to drink, at first with huge gulps, then slowly, swishing the water with her muzzle. Hal fetched more hay and led her up into the orchard. "Tomorrow," he told her. "I'll come tomorrow and every day now. So don't you go anywhere." He left her pawing at the hay.

When he got home, the first thing he did was forage in the refrigerator. Of course he saw his mother's scribbled note taped to the refrigerator door. It was all about getting the cow out of someone's salt-marsh hay on the Great Road. And "Be VERY careful," it concluded.

11

The cow had been at the forked section of the oak trunk and had trampled so much of the swamp around it she had somehow managed to roll it into the ditch she'd made. Most of the trunk section visible was covered with mud and leafmold. The crotch with its raised bark and wedged slate was buried in the slime.

So much for the message, thought Hal. If it was a message. He wondered if he'd ever get a chance to see it again, to confirm that he had read the one complete word accurately, or to discover that he had imagined "cow."

He came up by the meadow, which was grazed quite close; even the cat briars and blackberry canes had been eaten down. With the gaunt maples and oaks being felled below the pond, the entire hillside was beginning to look like a wasteland. Only the surrounding pines, thick and green, still provided shelter.

Glancing toward a nearby grove, Hal thought he saw a shifting in the dense darkness. He stared, and there was a sudden stillness like a suspension of motion, like someone watching. Then a breeze fretted the outermost needles. The pine boughs stirred and clasped the green-black emptiness.

Hal turned with resolution; he would believe only what he could see; he would resist the non-existent mystery.

On his way over the hill he came across neat clumps of hay, untouched, lying at the upper end of the orchard. When he saw that the nephew's rented car was not in the driveway, he decided it was a good moment to stop by. But then he noticed the partly open barn door. Had he forgotten to shut it last night?

Hal took a gingerly step inside. As soon as his eyes adjusted to the dimness, he could tell that the cow had forced her way in. Two barrels were tipped over. A hay bale was down and mangled. At the first partition a post was cracked and the partition wall was splintered.

His heart sinking, Hal tried to reconstruct the cow's course. She couldn't have come for hay because he had left plenty up in the orchard for her. No, she had come in because she wanted to, just the way they all said she would go out of any barn or through any fence if she wanted to. Then she must have changed her mind. But instead of backing out, she had lunged toward the window. Then what? Had she turned? Anyhow, she had made a very determined exit.

Hal couldn't budge the door, which rested on the sill. Maybe he could get Mac and Peggy to come and help lift it back into place. He wished Lew were home from Florida. As he cleaned up some of the mess, he was comforted by the thought that the Titcombs weren't likely to discover all of this for some time. What about the nephew, though? Hal couldn't be sure about him.

The first thing he did when he came into the house was ask Harriet Titcomb if she had seen anyone.

"Stamp your feet. Marjorie's terribly fussy about the

91

floor." Then Harriet shook her head. "Haven't seen a soul. I'll ask Carl when he gets back. He's gone off, him and Marjorie, with a load of stuff to some antique dealer."

Hal caught his breath. "From the dump?"

"From the attic and the cellar and everything between. We'll be stripped bare before we see this year out."

"But I was looking forward—" blurted Hal. "I mean, those are real things. . . ." He stumbled to a halt.

"Yes, well," Harriet remarked dryly, "they seem to have taken Gran's stories too."

"Why did you let them?" Then what she was telling him hit him. "But can't you stop them?"

"I'm alone." Her voice was constricted.

"What about Mr. Titcomb?"

Her eyes made him flinch. There was nothing in them but her helpless rage and the truth about her brother. She said, "Where have you been? All these days."

Hal shook his head. "How long are they staying?"

"Forever."

"But they live in California."

"Not if they can get us into a nursing home. The one over the town line. Rivercrest or something. Over where Cynkus had his piggery in the old days. Donatellis bought him out. Pigcrest!"

"Can't you just tell them to leave?"

She gave a thin smile.

Carl and Marjorie from California. Like terrorists in a beleaguered country. They had already infiltrated, all according to television formula. Hal had never thought of it happening to people he knew.

He sat down. The kettle on the stove began to steam. He

92

got up again, thankful for something to do. He brought cups and saucers to the table. He took the pot from Harriet, waiting for her nod of consent. "Any for him?" he asked, pouring the tea.

"He's sleeping. They've got him worn out."

Hal stirred his sugar. He stirred and stirred. Then he asked if she had a lawyer. She said, yes, for the real estate, for Candlewood Acres. He mentioned that his parents were lawyers. He'd never done anything like this before. He had a feeling his parents would be appalled if they knew that he was offering their services. But Harriet was so overwhelmed that she couldn't imagine any lawyer being able to help.

"They've never really cared for the farm," she told him. "Years ago they tried to get us to develop some of it. Now that we're doing it, now they drop from the sky like crows after the mower. To pick up the pieces."

They sipped their tea. The humming refrigerator clicked and went still. Harriet stretched out her hands and stared at her thin, crooked fingers. Hal guessed she was thinking that maybe her nephew and his wife were right. Maybe she was too old.

"Miss Titcomb," he said softly, "I'm going to tell my parents about this. Then they'll help you. They'll stop all of this."

They could hear a car driving up. Doors slammed.

Harriet fixed him with her eyes. She said, her voice level, "Maybe so. Maybe."

Feet stamped on the porch. The door opened. Carl and Marjorie were in the midst of an animated discussion about the price they had got for some object.

93

"You should hold out," insisted Marjorie.

"Every little bit," Carl answered, without finishing his sentence.

They set two shopping bags on the counter and took off their coats.

Carl rubbed his hands together. "Tea?" he asked. "I'll have coffee."

"Here's your apples, Aunt Harriet." Marjorie held up a plastic bag full of apples. "I hope these will do."

Harriet took one look and shook her head. "Mealy McIntosh."

Marjorie thumped the apples down. "They're top grade and all we could get. I don't know what you expect."

"Baldwins," Hal heard himself declare. "She wants good, hard apples like the kind they used to have."

"She's living in the past."

"You took the magazines. My grandmother's story."

Marjorie spoke up again. "Yes, they're big items, those kinds of things. Listen, Aunt Harriet, I know you think those stories are kind of family history, but if they were, wouldn't your grandmother have used the real names? Wouldn't she want to be sure that her own name was there for her sister to recognize?"

Harriet leaned forward, pressing the heels of her hands on the table. Slowly, unsteadily, she rose. Hal had to fight the impulse to help her up. He could tell she meant to stand alone.

But Carl, who wasn't looking at the set of her face, rushed to her aid.

"Now!" Her voice cut through his solicitude, but she couldn't straighten all the way. "Now *I'm* going to tell *you* something. I may not be able to read anymore, but I did

94

once. I was no fool then. What makes you think I have become one?"

Marjorie's eyes slid toward Carl, then toward the front room.

"Oh, yes," Harriet went on. "You're thinking of senility." For an instant she held her body erect. "You're not so young yourselves. Some people are born senile." Her body began to slump again, but her voice stayed firm. "My grandmother lived till she was in her middle nineties, and mostly she was as smart then as the child Emily will be when she's in *her* nineties."

"Emily?" Marjorie turned to Carl. "You hear that? I told you her mind's wandering."

"Oh, sit down, Marjorie. Stop driving that man." Marjorie swelled with indignation, but Harriet kept right on. "Where are the magazines? I suppose you realize there's three of them there together. Have you a receipt or something? I dare say I'll need a receipt to get them back."

"But you don't *need* them. You don't even have proof that your grandmother actually wrote them."

Harriet grunted. "I thought that was part of the trouble. You must think my Gran dim-witted to suspect her of making up a story about her own lost sister. Or embroidering the truth. Do you think she'd have risked driving Hannah farther from her? I *know*, because Gran told me, that the sole reason for writing that story was hope that somehow Hannah might come across it and realize it was meant for her."

Hal sat very still. He felt terrible. He guessed he was about to feel more terrible than he could bear.

Harriet sank back into her chair. "When the magazine first started, the mill girls signed their stories and poems

95

with made-up names. They all did. Gran chose 'Alice' because it was the nearest she could get to her own name. 'Alice' just missed being 'Eliza' back to front." Harriet's voice was fading. "Which is why she gave the older sister in the story that same name. For Hannah to read and understand how grieved her older sister was. For Hannah to forgive her and come back."

"Well," said Marjorie, "I'm sure I don't know what good can come from holding on to those magazines now. They're certainly not going to bring the lost girl home after all these years. Why hold on to magazines you can't read when they can bring more money than three grocery shoppings?"

"We're not that short of money," said Harriet.

"I . . . that is, Marjorie and I . . . we don't think you really know what state your finances are in. That's why we want to help, Aunt Harriet."

"Give Hal the receipt," said Harriet.

"This boy?"

"It's his. Also the apple scoop."

"What?"

"You had no right . . ." Harriet's mouth sagged. A little trickle of saliva ran down her chin.

Hal stood up. He was trembling. He knew perfectly well that she had guessed his doubts. Probably she had guessed more than that from the way he had recoiled from her before. He nodded to her. He said, "I'm sorry." He said, "I have to go now. Thank you for the tea. Thank you for . . . everything."

Marjorie handed him the receipts. She and Carl waved him off, but Harriet didn't even raise her head.

As soon as his parents came home, he informed them

96

of the Titcombs' predicament. They listened. Then they explained that lawyers can't barge into the midst of a family quarrel unless someone retains them as counsel. Besides, the Titcombs already had a real-estate lawyer and could seek help if they wanted it.

"Those people want to put Harvey and her in a nursing home," Hal retorted. "Do they have a right to do that?"

"Not against their will," said his mother cautiously, "unless . . ."

"Unless what?"

"A court would have to find them incapable of maintaining themselves."

Hal thought a moment. "How long would all that take? Because if it took a while, there might not be anything left for the Titcombs to maintain themselves with. Not if Carl and Marjorie go on cleaning out the attic that way."

"Don't you see, Hal," his father pointed out gently, "Carl and Marjorie might argue that when Miss Titcomb declared you the proper recipient of that scoop and that magazine, she was demonstrating her inability to make sound judgments about property?"

"But aren't those things hers to be kept or given away or anything else she decides?"

"It's possible all of this can be straightened out," said his mother, "with a little sympathy and understanding."

"Judy!" Hal's father spoke on a note of stern warning.

"You know what I mean. A neighborly call. A holiday visit. I'll bring her something for her Christmas table."

"Could you maybe find some Baldwin apples? And could I come too?"

Hal's mother smiled. "For the apples? Sure."

"I mean to the Titcombs'."

She shook her head.

"But you might never find out what's really going on."

His father laughed. "What a statement of faith."

His mother remarked that he had one or two things to learn about diplomacy.

Hal chafed all the next day. Every time he was on the verge of reminding her or prompting her, he managed to swallow his words. When his mother felt pushed, she became extremely methodical. Which is what she was this Saturday. She picked up dry cleaning. She sent Hal to the hardware store for duct tape and staples. When they finally met at the secondhand-book store, they were too late to retrieve the magazines. They would have to get in touch with the antiques dealer who had already purchased them.

Baldwin apples weren't all that easy to find either. After two farm-stand stops, Hal was ready to quit.

"You could bring her fruitcake or something."

"I think it would be nice to bring her what we know she likes."

Hal sighed. How much would it cost to buy back those magazines, and who would pay? How long would his mother stay interested?

The third farm stand had Baldwins. Dull apples, smaller than most of the others displayed, and hard.

"Come on, come on," muttered Hal while his mother stood chatting with the farmer.

In the car his mother said, "Hal, I don't think you were very polite."

Hal clamped his mouth shut.

But once she went, his mother stayed at the Titcombs' a long time. Hal and his father started supper. Then they started a fire. Outside it was snowing again.

"Just in time for Christmas," his mother announced, pausing before shutting the front door behind her.

Hal's father handed her a glass of sherry. She nibbled on the raw vegetables he had washed and scraped. Finally she began to talk about her visit.

"As far as the nephew and his wife are concerned, I don't think they're the scheming opportunists Hal made them out to be. Carl is really very fond of the old people. And Marjorie . . . Well, Marjorie's concerned about having to adjust to life in that house. And I must say, in its present state, I don't blame her."

"I knew it!" Hal shouted. "I knew they'd make you think that way."

"Now you listen." Hal's mother spoke in her low voice that meant business. "I went there because you wanted me to. I've done what I can so far, and I think I'm going to be able to do more, but I will not put up with any hysteria."

Hal subsided.

"The problem," she went on, "is ordinary domestic tension. Miss Titcomb's used to doing things her way, and I imagine her way has become progressively more slipshod over the years. The house is, frankly, awful. The floor's rotting under her feet. The living room smells like an unkempt sickroom, which—"

"But Harvey—"

"Which it is, because of Harvey's condition. It's obviously more than one old woman can handle." She paused. "Of course, that's what Carl sees. And Marjorie." She stretched her hands toward the fire. "He speaks of becoming Harvey's guardian, and conservator for Harriet."

"Is that warranted?" asked Hal's father.

"What's that *mean?*" blurted Hal.

"Possibly," Hal's mother answered her husband. Then she explained to Hal that the court could appoint a guardian for someone who was mentally incompetent, and a conservator to manage the affairs of someone who was competent but physically unable to manage her property.

"Did you get the feeling," asked Hal's father, "the nephew's using that prospect as a threat?"

She shook her head. "He has nothing to gain by pushing the old people around. No, I think he's honestly concerned for their sakes and for his own. As for Marjorie, she's just jumping the gun a little. Maybe she does want to make some money off that junk, but mostly she's just appalled at the prospect of living with it and the accumulated filth and rot."

"What about the way Miss Titcomb feels about *her?*" Hal demanded. "Did you ask her?"

"Oh, we got around to that." His mother smiled. "I'd hate to be on the wrong side of that woman. She's got a tongue like a knife."

"Sound?" asked Hal's father.

"Oh, yes. I think that's where we can apply pressure, if we need to."

"The will?"

Hal watched his mother nod curtly. This was lawyers' shorthand, and he couldn't follow what they were saying. "Will Marjorie be able to go on selling things?" he asked.

"I can't be sure of anything till I sit down alone with Miss Titcomb after Christmas. She's asked me to come back. To discuss some legal matters with her. All I did today was suggest to Marjorie that, while I sympathized with her, I wondered whether she wasn't being just a bit over-zealous about the mess in the house. I pointed out that all of that could seem pretty threatening to Miss Titcomb. I think Marjorie got the message."

"What about Harriet?" Hal pressed. "What did you say to *her?*"

"What did I say to her?"

"I mean, to make her feel better."

His mother smiled. "I told her, woman to woman, that it must be hell having someone else with different ideas move in and try to run your household. You know, Hal, even if Marjorie were an angel, I've a feeling that after three days that visit would have gone sour for Miss Titcomb."

"Well, what did she ask you to come back about?"

"Nothing was stated outright. But Miss Titcomb's obviously picked up a few little crumbs I dropped about wills and beneficiaries. Picked them up, turned them over, and tossed them right in front of Marjorie's eyes."

Hal's father began to laugh. Then he saw Hal's confusion and tried to explain. "A hint there. A suggestion that Miss Titcomb might consider changing her will. That the nephew and his wife better not take anything for granted."

"So you *don't* trust them!" Hal exclaimed.

"It isn't a question of trust," his mother said to him. "I imagine they're motivated by a restrained self-interest and—"

"Restrained!" Hal snorted. "Scaring Miss Titcomb with that nursing home?"

"That's not quite fair, Hal. The old man can't go on the way he is. It's really terrible there."

"I know. I know what it's like. But that's the way they want to handle it."

"How much longer can Miss Titcomb give her brother the care he needs?"

"Well, then they can get someone to come in. They'll have the money, with Candlewood Acres and all."

"That's true. But there remains the question of a workable solution for all, not just for one. If Carl stays east to oversee the development, it's only natural for him to live there."

"Not if Miss Titcomb doesn't want him!"

"Stop shouting."

"I'm not. I'm just trying to show you he has no right to take over. And Marjorie has no right to carry away the family treasures and sell them and—"

"All right, Hal. Calm down."

"What's the point?" he muttered. "What's the use of having a mother and father that are lawyers if they're not even interested in justice?"

There was a rather long silence. Then Hal's mother said carefully, "I'm seeing Miss Titcomb Christmas afternoon. I'm going as her lawyer. As is customary, I will not discuss the details of the situation with you, Hal, or with anyone else, except someone like your father in a professional capacity."

"*I* should get to hear about it too."

"That would be a breach of confidence."

"Well, what do I get out of this?" Hal demanded.

"A nice warm feeling," his father suggested. "Too warm, if you don't move away from the fire."

"They're my friends. I knew them first."

"True. And Miss Titcomb appreciates that. She wants you to get back her grandmother's articles. She says you're the first person she's ever met who's cared about her life and family. It means a lot to her."

Hal's eyes stung from the smoke. He stepped back from the hearth and turned to the vegetable plate. Maybe it was all right that his mother didn't pursue Truth and Justice with the fiery passion of a television lawyer. Maybe in her own way she would help to keep the Titcombs safe. He snapped a carrot stick.

"Oh, yes," his mother added. "She was so pleased with the Baldwins she's making us an apple pie for Christmas. I thought I'd never get away from there when she started in about old recipes and the lard they used from their own pigs." Hal's mother gave a huge sigh. "What a powerful little woman. I think, underneath, Marjorie's scared to death of her."

"Anyway," said Hal, "I hope they don't stay in Westwick."

"I think," replied his mother as she flashed him a conspirator's smile, "that's what Marjorie's beginning to hope too."

12

Hal spent Sunday with Josh. By the time he got home, it was too dark to carry hay out to the back woods. At least, that's what his parents said. Snow was falling again, softly, windlessly.

But at suppertime there was a call from Priscilla Sturgis:

a cow had broken into the pony's paddock and was eating its hay. The police said it was Hal's cow, so would he please come and take it away.

Hal's father drove him over, but by that time the cow was gone. Sam Sturgis showed the Woodruffs the broken rails of the paddock fence and said it would be nice to have help with repairs. After suitable apologies and promises, Hal and his father returned home to find that there had been a second call, this time from the police. Chief Durand felt that something more definite would have to be arranged about the cow.

It was an uncomfortable dinner that evening. The casserole was all dried out, and Hal's parents were all fed up. A bad combination, decided Hal, concentrating on chewing and swallowing lumps of leftover something or other.

Before the meal was over, the phone rang again. Hal's parents exchanged one of those instant eye signals.

"You'd better get it this time," his mother informed him.

He slid from his chair, feeling their eyes riveted on him, and caught the phone on its fifth ring.

"Hello?" Hal had to clear his throat. "Hello," he said more forcefully.

There was silence. With relief he was about to hang up, when he detected breathing.

"Hello, this is Hal Woodruff. Who's calling, please?"

"Hello," said a small voice.

"Emily? Emily! Where are you calling from?"

"What?"

"Are you home?"

"No, silly. I'm here."

"Are you calling all the way from Florida?"

He could hear Lew's voice approaching the phone.

"Emily," it said, "stop fooling around with that phone."

"I'm talking to someone."

"Oh, Lord! She's called somewhere. Probably Saskatchewan. Or Timbuktu."

The telephone slammed down at the other end of the line. Hal was left holding the receiver, grinning, and wondering who else Emily had managed to call before she was caught at it. Then he realized it was he who had taught her the area code, telling her it was their secret number. He turned back to the dining room. His parents were waiting, a bit uptight, he thought, obviously expecting some new cow trouble.

"It wasn't anything. A mistake. Some kid."

"Are you sure?"

"Really. Some kid playing with the phone. The father hung up."

In the morning the snow lay soft and vulnerable to the southerly wind. Hal scuffed what lay in his path as though he were kicking at dandelion fluff. Around the Titcombs' barn there were many footprints. Someone or -thing had been all over there. Seeing the ground so badly trampled, Hal started to worry. It was his fault the cow had been hungry enough to break into the Sturgis pony paddock. And now that she knew about forcing the barn door, she wasn't likely to wait for him if she wanted more hay.

When he shoved the door, it slid easily. That meant Carl must have set it up on its track again. Had he noticed the cracked post, the kicked-in partition? Maybe he didn't know what it had looked like before.

Hal gathered up a full armload of hay. He carried it some distance from the barn before dumping it on the ground and returning to drag the door closed. At least if the cow came to clean up the scraps of hay, she would not be led directly to the barn.

Then he started up the orchard. The closer trees looked veiled; the farther trees were practically invisible. He could feel his skin tighten with that sense of being watched. This time he was convinced it was more than the trees suggesting a shadowy presence. Groping for denials, he tried to tell himself that mist could produce visual distortions. Besides, he had this tendency to imagine, to jump to conclusions. What did he expect here: phantoms?

Then something was crashing through the brittle undergrowth of the lane. Something *was* there. "Cow?" he whispered, not out of timidity or fear, but because the mist that hugged the slope cast a hush over the land, over him. He clasped the hay to his chest, but his hands barely met. After a while he had to set down his load. Rising with a firmer grip on it, he looked up and saw a thing that was neither trees nor cow and that defied every reasonable expectation.

The shape emerged out of the haze. A second one appeared, then a third. Animals of some kind. Pigs! Three of them? No, here came some more of them trotting single file through the trees. Snouts low, each following the one before it, yet intent on something ahead, they veered off. Because Hal was there? Yet they gave no sign of alarm as they streamed down from the Candlewood lane, snuffling and grunting and hurrying on.

Where were they heading with such urgency? Not, it seemed, to the Titcombs' driveway, but around behind the barn, where the land dropped abruptly to the swamp between the Titcombs' and the Kleins'.

It was hard for Hal to accept what he saw. He cast back

to Emily's passing remark about the cow's visitors, and before that to her claim of seeing pigs. These were pigs, all right. Some were black and white, some splotched, others solid white or gray, and two of them were storybook pink. There was even one small black piglet, shaggy with a surprising coat of hair.

When they had all vanished into the low mist behind the barn, Hal headed for the walled lane they had just traveled. Turning to the house site, he dropped his load of hay. His arms ached, but he was satisfied with the amount he was leaving. It had to last at least a day.

Starting back, he moved more easily, breaking into a trot at the downhill slope. Like the pigs, he realized, and shivered at the thought of so many of them trampling along this path. He shivered first with the thrill of it, then with a sensation he couldn't understand. Except that there had been something about those pigs that had verged on muted frenzy. They had looked as though nothing could have stopped them, as if they would have gone right over or through anything in their way. No, they hadn't veered away because of him; they had known exactly where they were going, and he had been nothing to them.

Descending the slope, he returned to mist. But it seemed thinner now, more sun in it, the vapor tamed by the spring-like breeze and the mild, milky sky.

The next day, even though Lew and Emily were due home, Hal decided not to take any chances letting the cow get hungry. But when he reached the old farm site with his armload of hay, there was the pile from the previous morning. Untouched, not even pawed over.

Puzzled, uneasy, he stood for a moment pondering the

107

cow's possible whereabouts. Then from downhill he heard voices. Dumping the new hay beside the old, he started down to them. By now it was second nature to reach out where roots or saplings could be grabbed. Here was the milkweed, its brittle pod still intact, though long empty. There were the blackberry suckers with their vicious barbs. Avoiding these and breaking his fall with practiced caution, he skidded all the way down to the pond. It was black and silver, not one crack marring its slick, austere face.

The voices belonged to two men spraying orange paint on some of the trees. Behind them, parallel lines of orange stakes described a wide curve through the woods.

"That should do it," one of the men was saying as he rolled up a long tape-measure. They bent over a blueprint, then straightened, staring up past the pond. "Hello," they both said, seeing Hal.

"Hello." Hal stayed where he was. "What are you doing?" Not scratching messages on slates, that was for sure.

"Marking out a road. Before the frost strikes in hard."

"Did you see anyone here this morning?"

The men shook their heads.

"Also," Hal said, "a cow?"

They couldn't keep from grinning. Hal supposed it did sound kind of funny. He grinned too, and then they all three laughed. They promised to give him a call—Woodruff on Second Hill Road—if they came across a cow, a red-brown one with a white face.

Hal started back. He paused at the dump, where he uncovered a curved pump handle. He wondered what the road builders would do with the dump when they brought their machines in next spring.

He returned the way he had come, just in case the cow

had shown up in his absence. What he found on the crest of the hill was not the cow, but Bliss Atherton fuming about the orange spray paint.

"They're marking a road," said Hal.

"They're despoiling the countryside."

Hal said, "Have you seen a—"

"Plunderers! That's what they are."

It didn't seem useful to get involved with Mr. Atherton just now, so Hal nodded and hurried on down the orchard, past the Titcomb house, and then along to the Thayer house to see if Lew and Emily were home yet.

They were, Emily looking brown and ripe, Lew seeming distant or maybe just tired. Emily dragged Hal out to the chickens and ducks, to the goats, delighted to be reunited with her living possessions, which Hal figured probably included him.

"Aren't you glad to see them?"

The female call-duck gave her raucous greeting.

Hal said, "But I haven't been away."

"*I* have," Emily informed him. "Say you're glad."

Back inside the house Lew was making plans to go away again for a few days. Sherry wasn't sure she could cover for Emily the whole time. When Hal tried to bring Lew up to date on the Candlewood situation, Lew offered to drive Hall to the antiques dealer to retrieve the magazines. Hal supposed they could wait; he didn't think the cow could. Lew said he'd do his best, but he would have to be away and he might need help with Emily over Thursday night and Friday. He seemed to have his mind on that as they trooped back to the old farm site. Hal was bursting to tell Lew about the message in the tree trunk, about fetching the cow in the snowy night, about the pigs in the eerie mist of yesterday, but Lew was far away and Hal had no idea how to get through to him.

Emily wandered about, calling, "Cow! Cow!" in a voice as thin as the ice on the pond. Then she stomped back. "It forgot me. I stayed away too long."

"It wasn't that long," Hal told her, but he felt dishonest saying it.

Lew said no news was good news; at least there had been no more complaints.

"But if it's not eating our hay," Hal pointed out, "it's got to be eating someone else's."

"Then you'd better be home when the call comes."

Hal wanted to ask Lew what he planned to do, but it was as though Lew had his own orange stakes set all around him like a barrier.

Back at the Thayer house Sherry asked Lew if he was still planning to go after those magazines for Hal and if so would he do some house shopping. Hal opened his mouth to explain that they had decided to wait for the next phone call, but Lew nodded agreeably and said, sure, just give him a list. After that he stood in the middle of the kitchen, looking at nothing.

"Shall I go too?" Hal spoke to Sherry, not Lew.

She shrugged, and then Lew said Hal had better be home in case a call came.

You already said that, Hal thought, but he didn't speak. One thing was making itself amply clear: if anything was to be done, it was up to Hal to figure out what.

By the time Lew showed up with the magazines, it was late in the day and there had been no call about the cow. Lew hardly looked at the magazines as he handed them over. He only wanted to know when Hal's parents would be home so he could speak to them about Emily.

Hal waited until Lew was gone before glancing at the second issue. Now he scanned the titles, poems, advertisements. Lew had forked over the money, not questioning the price or bargaining or anything. Of course it was up to Carl and Marjorie to pay, but Hal hoped his parents would reimburse Lew until all that was worked out.

"I take up my story of the two sisters," read Hal. There followed a brief account of what had been written in the first installment. Alice, or Eliza, didn't fail to mention again that their father was "given to fanciful schemes," all of them failures. She also told about her own life in Lowell, not only about the mill work but about her evening classes in geography and physical science, about the Lyceum lectures the mill workers attended, and the circulating library, and something she joined called an Improvement Circle.

Then the main story resumed. "The sisters set out in the dark, traveling on a neighbor's cart toward the sunrise to Boston. Once on their way, Anna is amazed at the waking city. At the loading dock in Charlestown they board the *Governor Sullivan* for the thirteen-hour journey on the Middlesex Canal. It is a true adventure. After the bustle and crowds of the city, the boat glides into the quiet countryside. Alice sits in pleasant conversation with a fellow mill girl who has boarded at Somerville to return to the Corporation in Lowell. Anna discovers that she can disembark at one stopping point, run along the tow-path, then come aboard at the next stop. This frolic in the mild air makes Anna thirsty. Alice gives her a penny to purchase a glass of water when they stop at Woburn. There also a new kind of apple from the Baldwin orchard may be had, but that is too dear for the sisters.

"Anna watches every lock they pass through as if to learn some useful information from the machinery that raises the water level and lets the boat out higher than before. She is especially interested in the aqueducts that transport them way above the river, and in the floating tow-path upon the Concord millpond. It is only when the sun begins to sink, when the harvested fields they pass grow pink and orange, that she seems to realize that night will fall on her home without her.

" 'What of Brindle?' cries she. 'What of my ducks? They must be got in against the fox and weasel.' She recites a list of creatures in jeopardy because she will not be there to bed them in the coop or barn or fold. Alice strives to reassure her that faithful Fen will guard the fowl and kine. 'Fen!' exclaims the stricken child, bereft of the dog that has followed her everywhere on the farm.

"She runs no more about the boat. She does not disport herself as do the other children. She stands at the railing looking back as the night turns everything gray, then black."

Hal scarcely noticed that his parents had come in until they spoke to him for what was apparently not the first time.

"What's got into you?"

"Just a minute." Hal tried to finish reading about how Anna was brought shivering and silent into the Corporation boarding house, how the kind matron gave her tea and bread, cold meat and pie, and how Anna couldn't eat, but only sat in a daze until she was put to bed. It seemed incredible that early the following day she would begin her new life as a mill girl.

"Any messages, Hal?"

"Yes. Lew. Call him. Be right with you." He read, "For fourteen hours she carries off the full bobbins and fits back in the empty ones. Though she must race between the frames with her bobbin box so that the machine will not be stopped too long, between these tasks she may play with the other doffers or chat with the frame-tenders and look upon the verses these older girls have pasted to the wall beside their looms. But Anna, when she can, stands at the window overlooking the millrace. She watches the great wheel turn, gazes beyond to the riverbanks where Indians weave baskets beside their smoky fires, and looks farther still to the distant hills and forest."

"Hal, what is it, dear? You're hardly here."

"It's these. Miss Titcomb's grandmother's story. I'm reading it."

"So I can see."

Hal looked up. "Did you speak to Lew? Did he tell you how much he paid to get these back?"

"He told us. Also, he asked us to take Emily for a couple of days."

Hal's parents sounded strained. Was it because of the mark-up on the magazines, or was it the prospect of having Emily? Whatever the reason, the whole family seemed to be in a funny mood, not much in keeping with the night before Christmas Eve.

As soon as he could, Hal picked up his magazines and

113

retreated to his room. He was immediately caught up in the story again, with Anna as she was shaken out of bed each morning at five, as she gulped her breakfast in order to be ready when the bell clanged and she plunged out into the bitter dark for the mill. Still, she adjusted to her new life. Each week she sent a portion of her wages home to her mother and banked almost all the rest.

"Alice strives to encourage Anna in feminine tastes," he read, "but this child has too long played the man's part. She takes the hero's role when acting out one of Scott's romances, and she still declaims the robust orations in the old Reader more suited to a young man than to a girl soon to flower into womanhood." But Alice believed that when Anna went to school in the spring, she would learn new graces from the town girls.

Then Anna discovered that she wasn't going home for the spring plowing. Her mother's letters telling of the barter of laying hens for a bucket of maple sugar couldn't reassure Anna about the farm, where the seed must be sown for the next winter's fodder. "Nor is Anna comforted by news of the eleven thriving piglets and the four new lambs. She grows more fretful and quick-tempered and solitary.

"But while the scowl deepens on the once open visage of the younger sister, fortune smiles on the older with her renewed friendship with the young lawyer from last fall's husking bee. As he spends some time in Lowell on behalf of the law office with which he is associated, he regularly calls in the boarding house parlor on Saturday afternoons. Soon he has the confidence of the older sister and the wary regard of the younger.

"Attentive to both, he takes Anna to Merrimack Street

to purchase a ribbon for her bonnet, invites her to select a fruit for herself or a cinnamon candy stick or a fresh warm bun. She will not refuse, for he always brings word of doings from home. He has purchased a tract of land which joins the sisters' farm at its western border. There on the eastern slope he means to plant an orchard with that new variety of apple the sisters could not afford to buy. . . ."

The eastern slope, mused Hal, setting the magazine aside and getting into bed. The field behind the Titcombs' old dairy barn? Maybe Harriet would know if that orchard had been planted on that side. He was just drifting into sleep when he recalled her description of the hay wagon over there and the cows filing down to the barn.

Much later Hal started up. After a moment of dislocated numbness, he recognized his windows, gray rectangles in a black, blank wall. It was nearly morning. Christmas Eve. Whatever happened to all those delicious dreams you were supposed to have just before Christmas? His dream had been a grim procession of images. Images and voices. Bliss Atherton, in the sonorous tone of a narrator in a television docudrama: "Despoiling! Plunderers!" And the image of the beech tree falling in slow motion.

Had there been a girl's voice too? Crying out against the destruction of oak and maple? Anna's voice, only not Anna of the story but the real Hannah whose letter he'd read, whose very own writing he had touched when he taped the pieces of her letter onto a single sheet of paper.

He snapped on his lamp and turned to the third installment of Eliza's story. He was tempted to skip the beginning, which would be a rehash of the previous parts, but as he skimmed over the first paragraph, his eye was stopped by words like "inheritance" and "will and testament." This was something new.

He read on. It seemed that Alice had considered bringing her mother to Lowell too, until the young lawyer had persuaded her that all the family property would be at risk. Her father had arranged another of his schemes, this one called an Estate per Autre Vie, which provided that the son out west would hold the farm during the life of the widow. Only after she died would the daughters share in the estate; they would own the farm, with a third of its value going to the son. It was designed to pressure him into returning home and assuming responsibility at once, with a promise of freedom in the future.

The trouble with the arrangement, explained the young lawyer, was that with the son dead and the mother absent, anyone could move in and become "general occupant," pay up the back taxes, and become in effect owner of the property. "Later," wrote Eliza, "Alice discovered that Anna had absorbed much of this legal information. The fear of dispossession was to become fixed in Anna's mind.

"Then came terrible news. A fire had destroyed the farm. Their mother, stricken and exhausted, was taken to her sister in Vermont. The poor clumsy wretch who had probably started the fire was given another home. And what of the farm itself? All the outbuildings were afire before the nearest neighbors were aware of anything amiss. By the time the first appeared, the house was alight as well, the poor widow running hither and thither, the hens flying into trees that burst into flame, and the beasts screaming and galloping off. All was lost before the poor widow's eyes, after which she collapsed.

116

" 'Not all lost,' corrects Anna, 'for you have just said that many of the beasts fled. We must hurry home, for they will return and require feeding. Some may be suffering burns.'

" 'Home?' Alice weeps. 'Dearest Anna, there is no home.'

" 'We must go there anyhow. Father would want us to.'

" 'Mother is gone to Aunt Clara in Vermont.'

" 'That is why we must be home.'

"Alice tries to embrace her little sister, to comfort her, but Anna is cold as ice and speaks without feeling. 'How can you cry before we have done all we can to save what remains?'

"Alice can only run sobbing from the room, for with her mother's reason gone and this little sister beyond reasoning, Alice feels herself to be alone in the world. But she is not alone. The young lawyer draws ever closer, and he helps her look to a brighter future. In another year, when he has completed his apprenticeship, he will begin a new life, combining his apple growing and the practice of the law. Together he and Alice speak of the house he will build, joining the two properties and her family with him."

But Anna rejected his concern and promises. "Possibly," suggested Alice-Eliza, "her father's influence had twisted her mind. Now, with happiness and security promised, Anna charges her future brother-in-law, who stands to protect the farm from any outsider's claim, with plotting to become the general occupant himself. He bears these outrages with generous spirit, confident that in time he will gain the child's trust.

"Anna beseeches her sister to allow her to return to see for herself what is left. Once more Alice tells Anna that

117

nothing stands, nothing remains but the walls of stone. Anna grows thoughtful, shuttered and closed within herself. Then on an evening late in August when Alice is with her friends reading poems at a meeting of their Improvement Circle, Anna wraps a few belongings in her winter shawl and, leaving a note for Alice, steals away."

Hal rolled onto his back and lay with his arms supporting his head, gazing at the ceiling, at nothing. What struck him was that he actually knew a person who had heard this story from the person who had lived it. Yet there was nothing more to learn but the little that remained in this magazine. The time for questions was past.

He turned back to read of the frantic quest for the lost child. Alice visited the shops, the depot where the train of cars arrived and departed daily for Boston, the canal landing, and, finally, the bank, where she found that Anna had withdrawn all her savings. Finally a letter came. Alice read it again and again. *The* letter, thought Hal. The very letter he himself had taped together. Suddenly, vividly, he could see the Hannah of that letter hunting for her cow, never suspecting that long before the fire Brindle was supposed to have been sold. It was awful to think that Hannah was never to know. But then it must have been awful for Eliza too.

Hal read how the young lawyer aided in the search. He returned to Lowell with scraps of clues, telling Alice that Anna had visited the village shop to buy flint and tinder. She had called on the Tax Collector and the Selectman, who was also the Overseer of the Poor. The men were blunt about the impression Anna had made when she asked about the likelihood of the town selling the farm for taxes, and when she demanded to know the requirements for holding title for her mother.

" 'I regret,' declared the Selectman to Alice's betrothed, 'that I had to acknowledge the possibility that anyone setting out to usurp the rights would attempt some kind of occupancy. The child then sought to learn whether one family member residing or regularly visiting the property could so protect the title. When I perceived her argument, I felt constrained to warn her that if a child were found in solitary occupation, it would be placed in my charge as Overseer of the Poor. "Like the poor fellow lately in our care?" quoth she. "Like him," I responded. Then she turned to the Tax Collector, counted out twelve dollars, and proffered them. He informed her that another had recently paid a somewhat larger sum. She guessed at once who the benefactor was and commanded the Collector to return that payment. With that, she counted out two more dollars, and then, hesitating, drew them back into her sleeve and turned from my door. I never saw her again.' "

Hal paused. Knowing there could be no satisfying resolution, he was in no hurry to get to the end. He could almost see the conflict in Anna, her indecision over the amount to pay the Tax Collector and the amount to keep for her own use. He would never forget the tone of that letter he'd read, Hannah's indignation at being hunted, the harshness of her warning to her sister.

But it was hard to keep his eyes off the page. Glancing down, the words snagged him, and he found himself reading that as the months passed and Alice waited for word of her sister, the silence only deepened. "Alice's betrothed reported finding the poor simpleton upon the burned hilltop uttering inchoate phrases that included Anna's name. But that was all. After a while the neighbors began to tell each other that the child's wraith walked there at night, but of course they claimed that only the simple fellow could see such a thing.

"Who is to say whether Anna wanders still or seeks her fortune elsewhere? Next spring a new house will stand on the west slope, open to farmers and clients alike. There Alice will be married, and there a room made for her sad mother. Another room will be readied for the last daughter in hope of her return so that all these lives can begin anew.

"Only the poor fellow who labored for Anna may yet be seen stumbling over the rocks and charred remains of the old farm. He calls and calls, though the syllables are scarcely discernible. Those who are not acquainted with the history of that hillside would think him senseless in his simple grief.

"—ALICE."

14

Hal was so full of questions he couldn't bear to go off to feed the cow before his parents got up. In the kitchen he slammed the refrigerator door, banged a pot on the counter, and clattered a spoon. But no one stirred.

He listened hard. The refrigerator gulped and the oil burner started up like an animal yawning. When it stopped, he could hear the murmur of traffic from the Industrial Park and its main artery. Not individual cars, but a constant hum. It occurred to him that tomorrow would be different. Tomorrow, Christmas, he would go out and listen to the silence. Maybe then if he faced Candlewood and the wind was right, he would hear the cow chewing her cud or scratching against a tree.

He couldn't go on waiting, so he decided to find Lew. But the Thayer house was as still as his own. Only Emily was downstairs. She was pasting strips of colored paper together in a chain. Momentarily distracted, he dropped down beside her to show her how to make a lantern. Holding it up for her, he was back in the story of "The Last Daughter," thinking: flickering light, the barn lantern, the husking bee.

Emily got more milk for her sodden mush of granola. He watched her add brown sugar, then drink the liquid, spoonful by spoonful. He started to tell her about Anna, except that he used the proper name, Hannah.

"Aren't you going to eat that?" he asked her. His breakfast of cornflakes seemed flat and a long time ago.

Emily pulled the bowl close, away from Hal. "Go on about the girl," she told him.

"How late does your father sleep?"

"I don't know. You want some granola?"

He did. It was in a jar on the counter. He saw sunflower seeds and raisins and grains he couldn't identify. He thought of Hannah worrying over the sowing of winter fodder. He took his bowl to the table. "When you stay with us," he informed Emily, "I'm going to teach you a new trick about the telephone."

Emily brushed back her hair and licked the paste off her fingers. "Go on about Hannah."

"Does your father know you called me all the way from Florida?"

121

"It's a secret." Her fingers pressed her lips tight.

Hal scraped his bowl and took it to the sink. "Come on. Give me your dish. Let's go."

"Where?" She jumped up, wading through scraps of paper lying about like fall leaves.

"To feed the cow. Maybe we'll say hello to Miss Titcomb too."

Emily went to get her jacket and boots. He had to send her back twice to find a second mitten and to get her wool hat. God, he thought, how do parents go through all this with every kid?

Emily also insisted on feeding her ducks first. She needed hot water to melt the ice in their wading pan. Then she had to admire them as they flopped in, dowsing and preening, muttering and babbling.

On the way to Candlewood, Emily told Hal about Florida and about Christmas and Hanukah. She was half Jewish, which meant that she could have two birthdays. He tried to correct her, but she cut him off. She *knew*. It had all been explained in Florida.

"Why don't we get hay?" she wanted to know as he started up the orchard.

"First we have to see how much is left." But his legs wanted to take him to the barn. Almost involuntarily he stopped.

Already ahead, Emily called, "What's the matter?"

The matter was an uncomfortable conviction that if he didn't prove his faith by bringing a fresh supply of hay right now, then he'd be disappointed. It was dumb, of course; pure superstition. What he did at this moment couldn't alter what was already established. Anyhow, there was no cause for alarm; no one had called to complain

122

about a cow. "Can you see any hay there?" he asked. "Is it still there?"

She wheeled and clumped off as fast as her boots allowed. Waiting, he turned toward the Titcomb house, then looked past it across the road to the Sturgis place. Yellowed stubble poked up through the snow, giving an illusion of a net or web cast over the white field. He tried to picture apple trees standing in rows in that open expanse. But the orchard was here, not there.

"Hal, come!" Emily was back in sight.

He turned to her. "Did you see the cow?"

"I want to show you something. It's important."

He climbed the rest of the way and took the shortcut to the house site.

Emily, who had run ahead, planted herself firmly beside the scattered hay and pointed to the orange markers. "See? What are they?"

The stakes came all the way to the foundation stones, not straight from below, but curving in a double line that seemed to touch a corner of the meadow and cross the old stone-lined lane. They ended in a large double circle that included the dead standing beech. Hal's heart skipped. He hadn't realized the subdivision road would penetrate this far. For an instant he felt that he was Hannah glimpsing the hidden enemy who would steal the land.

Kicking aside the painted laurel leaves, he noticed that the foundation itself had been used as a marker. One stone was solid orange, with something shiny glinting in it. Thinking of precious junk, Hal bent down. It was the head of a steel spike set in the rock. The surveyors must have had to drill a hole for it. No wonder the cow hadn't shown up. Probably even her hay was contaminated.

Hal was turning away from the marker when his eyes fell on something else. The drilling had left a whitish powder and one larger stone split right across a hole. Examining it, Hal could see that the broken stone had fitted over the one in which the metal had been successfully driven. This lower stone, set deep in the ground, showed a clear, fresh face marred only by the glint of the spike and the orange paint, which, sprayed aslant, had left a spatter decoration that revealed two marks, two gray depressions. They were the letters H and W.

He squatted, stared, wanted to touch but didn't.

"What is it?" Emily's breath tickled his ear.

"Initials," he told her, adding, "The first letters of someone's name."

"Whose?"

Hal stood up. He reached with his foot, letting the toe of his boot graze the granite surface. Nothing smeared. Of course not. The spraying had been done yesterday and was dry.

"Mine." He swallowed. "Those are my initials. Someone . . . knows me. Someone was trying to tell me something." Or was he jumping to conclusions again? Now he did touch the stone. His finger came up with white stone dust on it. Whoever chipped those letters couldn't have done it till that other stone was split and shoved off this one. So the paint must have been sprayed afterward, hurriedly, the surveyors moving on without a backward glance, missing what they had revealed.

Emily said, "I'm cold."

Hal went to the hay and kicked it loose. He didn't know what to think. Maybe there was less of it now. Maybe the cow had fed there before the surveyors had come. Maybe there was someone out here after all, a guy who left messages in downed tree trunks, and maybe he had the cow safe somewhere else.

The more Hal kicked, the more hay there seemed to be. He was dreaming if he thought some had been eaten, just the way he was dreaming if he thought anyone would bother to chip his initials in stone and leave him secret messages on slate. He felt tight in his throat. He saw Emily waiting, blue-lipped and clenched with cold. "All right," he said. "We'll go."

Emily dashed ahead. Hal felt like a grownup. Here it was Christmas Eve and he wasn't especially excited about going out with his parents to find a small white pine in their back woods, usually the event of the season. As though everything normal was slightly out of kilter.

Emily came panting up to him again, saying, "I want to show you something."

"Not now." He supposed he was just uneasy about the damn cow. Maybe at this very minute someone was calling to complain about her, waking up his parents to tell them to get the cow off the tennis court or something.

"It's important," Emily insisted.

"You always say that." Then, "Did you see somebody, Emily? You know I'm looking for someone I thought might be hanging around here."

"I saw a pig."

"Yes, I know. I've seen pigs here too."

He let her drag him downhill, then realized she was following the route the pigs had traveled two mornings ago. Still, he went along with her, noting almost idly the absence of fresh hoofmarks, cow or pig. While he climbed over the old barbed wire, Emily squeezed between the strands. She was taking him the long way around the barn. No, she was stopping at the back. He stopped too. Stopped and gazed, as she did, at the huge carcass that hung from the eyebeam.

"What is it?" she asked him, her voice cutting through the fog in his mind, slicing through to clean air.

He began to breathe again. "I'm not . . . It isn't . . ." That was all he could register.

"What is it?" she repeated, clearing the way for him again.

"Beef," he said with his mouth, but not with his voice.

"What?"

"Oh, Jesus!" he yelled. "Can't you look and see?"

Emily did look. At him. Her eyes grew huge. He'd scared her. He had to get her away from there. Get himself away. He grabbed her shoulder and thrust her in front of him. But there was no way to go along the side of the barn. It was blocked by a cutter bar with its terrible teeth and some hulking barrels and the tractor skeleton. So he dragged her around to the barbed wire. They had to backtrack till they could come across through the gate of the orchard.

"But I want to visit," Emily protested as he swept her past the Titcombs'.

How could any kid be so dense? Hadn't she recognized the reddish-brown hair on what remained of the legs, where the skinning had stopped? Hadn't she seen pictures in advertisements or on the tube of sides of beef hanging in butchering plants? "Home first," he told her, meaning of course *her* home. He needed Lew to help him see what he had seen, and to fix it. To get whoever had killed his cow and then hung her up like that. Like meat.

126

But it wasn't that simple. Even with Lew doing most of the talking, it couldn't be made less ugly. The confrontation took place in the Titcomb kitchen, with Carl losing his temper.

"Well, of course it's meat," he snapped. "It was meat when it was bred, and it was meat when it was raised, and it was meat when it was lost off some truck or broke out of a field or something. What the hell else do you think it was?"

Lew drew a long breath before he replied. "That isn't the point. You knew we were feeding it. You didn't tell us what you planned, or even that you did it."

But that's not all, Hal screamed inside himself. That's not it. Only he couldn't utter a word. Harriet Titcomb kept glancing at him, then away, then back. Was she in on this too? Could she have done it behind Hal's back? He blurted, "It was *our* cow!"

They all turned to him.

"If it was anybody's," Carl retorted, "it was the people's whose land it was on. And whose barn it was wrecking."

Lew said, "But it was here because we were feeding it. *We* were, Hal and I. And had permission to store the hay."

"She was mine. Ours." Hal's face was burning. He felt hot all over. He could hardly get the words out. "She came here to be fed. Because we taught her. She trusted . . . because . . ."

"Still," said Harriet, "it couldn't work, what you wanted to do."

"That's true," Lew agreed. "We knew it wasn't working. The police knew."

Stung, Hal cried, "You weren't even here! She followed me all the way home!"

"They were going to have to destroy her, Hal. I asked for more time."

"Why didn't you tell me?"

"I didn't see you. I was going to. Look, it meant shooting her and then having the town dispose of the carcass at town expense, or else letting it happen some awful way, like a car running into her."

Hal couldn't fathom Lew's acceptance. He stalked into the front room, where Harvey was propped up in bed watching the tube. The sound was off. Harvey didn't seem to care. He greeted Hal with a nod. Hal sat next to him, trying to close his mind to the smell. He watched some people around a telephone. They held up a baby. He could hear Carl in the kitchen acknowledging that Hal and Lew deserved a share of the beef.

"How did you do it?" Lew was asking now. "How did you get her around back before killing her?"

Hal dove for the television, turning the volume way up.

"Reach out and touch someone," blared a singing voice, and there were grandparents at another phone, smiling, smiling.

Marjorie called from upstairs, "Is that you, Uncle Harvey? I'll be down in a moment."

The telephone faded and there was a still shot of a New England village church, white as the snow around it. Though carol-singing filled the room, Hal could hear the words, "dropped her with one shot, finished her with the second. . . . Would've had a hell of a time without the hoist. . . ." "On this day," sang invisible carolers, "earth shall ring with the song children sing. . . ."

Marjorie appeared, declaring as she came into the front

room that Christmas music always made her a little weepy but still all warm and— She broke off when she saw Hal; she smiled nervously. "Your mother with you?"

He shook his head.

She turned down the volume, but Hal could still hear the "in excelsis Deo" sounding like singing mice. "He doesn't need it that loud," Marjorie said. "He only looks, you know." Then she heard Lew's voice from the kitchen. Suddenly on her guard, she tugged at her dress, patted her hair, and headed that way.

Hal followed her. Harriet was pouring out tea as though nothing awful had happened. And Lew was taking a cup.

"Hal?" Harriet's teapot was poised over another cup.

He shook his head.

"Better have some to settle your stomach." She poured it out. "Go on. Put in plenty of sugar. It'll help."

Harriet's concern and the rising steam sent a wave of warmth up against him. He braced himself, withstood it.

"I'll let you take care of yourself," Harriet told Marjorie. "I can never do it right for you."

Marjorie helped herself to tea. There they stood, in a kind of circle, sipping, rattling cups against saucers, with nothing more to be said.

Hal looked at Harriet. She met his glance. "I told him to tell you folks," she declared briskly. "I'd have told you myself, only you didn't stop by since it happened."

"Did you know he was going to?"

"I told him to leave it for now. He had the gun ready, but I told him, leave it."

"You didn't see what it did to our barn, that's why," Carl broke in. "You'd have been right after me to—"

129

"*My* barn," Harriet corrected. "Harvey's and mine."

"You know what I mean," Carl muttered. "The family's."

"Mine," stated Harriet.

"Of course, Aunt Harriet. Carl knows that too." Marjorie smiled at Lew. "Honestly, these two, they're a pair of cards. Getting into these silly quarrels over nothing." Shaking her head, she signaled Carl. "Well, I just hope everything's cleared up now and that this young man will realize it's for the best."

Hal took his cup to the sink, then started for the door. Lew took more time. He washed his and Hal's cups. He said he'd take a look at the barn after he got back from where he was going for a couple of days and do something to fix it up. Carl said not to worry. He and Marjorie were going home to California to pack their things and sell their house. When they returned east, they'd have all the time in the world to set things to rights in the barn. They'd be back in two or three weeks, he told Lew. In time to cut up the beef and deal out fair portions.

"If those darn pigs don't get it first," Marjorie put in. "Carl says there was a whole pack of them out there when he was burying the entrails and the skin. They kept digging up all that stuff."

"I let them eat some of it," Carl said. "Made for less digging. Also thought about a couple of porkers to hang up beside the beef, but the ones that came right up close were too small."

"Yes, and you mind what Uncle Harvey said about those pigs. A whole lot like that, gone wild, they'd as soon take *you* as an old cow stomach."

"Hal," said Harriet, "this is your Christmas pie." The pie she held out to him was large and plump and crisp-looking. "Don't return the dish," she cautioned in a tremendous stage whisper, "until after they're gone. It's just one more thing for them to get their hands on. Nothing's safe, as you now know."

"Oh, Aunt Harriet, is that the kind of thanks we get supplying you with all this free beef?"

Ignoring her nephew, Harriet patted the edge of the pie crust crumbling in Hal's grip. "You take care now," she scolded, "or there won't be anything for your mother and father to enjoy tomorrow."

15

Emily gazed at the Woodruffs' Christmas tree while Lew and Hal's parents talked. Solemnly she touched a glass icicle. Was she comparing the glittering ornaments with her own homemade paper chains and strings of cranberries? Hal watched closely to see if she minded the talk about the cow.

His mother was saying, "That man is totally insensitive. He even offered me some of the liver."

Emily's fingers brushed a tiny candy cane, which spun on its slender thread, red and white blurring.

"Stood there," Hal's mother went on, "and tried to pawn off some of its liver on me."

"Maybe," suggested Lew, "he thinks sharing will put things to rights."

"At least he's not likely to be so high-handed anymore. Thanks to Judy."

"All I did was assure them that no court would find Miss Titcomb incapable or incompetent. And pointed out how easy it would be for her to alter her will. No, poor Carl may get to be conservator, but not without coming to Harriet's terms." She shook her head. "And each of them so single-minded. Carl bringing me this dish with a huge slab of liver, assuring me that it was the best I'd ever taste."

"It *was*, too," said Lew.

"What?"

"The liver. Delicious."

Hal and his parents gaped at Lew. Emily murmured to the ornaments. She rang a little ceramic bell; the clapper clinked like a single raindrop.

"You took some of that liver?"

Lew shrugged. "The animal's dead. I'm sorry we couldn't save it. I'm glad it was killed quickly."

"Are you going to accept some of the meat too?"

"Why not?"

"What about—" Hal's father nodded toward Emily, who was singing "Jingle Bells" in a breathy monotone.

"I'd rather feed her organic beef any day than what comes through a feedlot and into the supermarkets."

"But she *knew* that cow," Hal exclaimed. "She saw it first. She fed it."

Lew said, "If she's going to be a meat-eater, I'd like her to know what it is she's eating."

"God!" Hal stormed off to his room and slammed the door behind him. He was glad Christmas was over. Everything usually fun had stuck in his throat. He kept fighting images that leaped at him whenever he let his guard down. He would see the cow fall to its knees. He would see a faceless girl in a woolen shawl carrying a bag and running through the darkness. He would see throngs of pigs, silent and ghostly and onrushing with the scent of blood.

He couldn't grapple with Eliza's undigested story; questions about property and inheritance seemed so far-fetched. As for Lew, he could keep his history and his environment and his research.

Hal strode to his desk where the magazines lay, grabbed them, looked around for a big envelope to stick them in, and then started guiltily as the door opened.

Emily walked in. "What's that?"

"Articles."

"What's articles?"

"Remember the story I told you about Hannah?"

Emily nodded.

"It's in here." He flipped the magazines over.

She climbed onto his bed. "Read it to me."

"This stuff's too old for you. Besides, it's too long."

"Show me the new trick with the flower telephone."

So he brought the upright telephone over to the bed and had her practice making a collect call. He pretended to be the operator. He said, "What is your number?" and she said, "Five years old."

He flung the telephone aside.

She considered that gesture for all of a minute, then carefully, deliberately, reached for the phone again. She dialed correctly, first the operator O, then their area code, then his number. Then she waited.

Hal couldn't hold out against her. He picked up a flashlight and spoke into it. "May I help you?"

"Yes," said Emily.

"No, say, 'Collect.'" Like the Tax Collector, he thought,

133

bracing against the image of Hannah running from the mills. "Then you have to read the numbers on the phone you're calling from. Just get the first three right, and then you can make up anything you like."

She recited the first three numbers, but not in order, then repeated them, running them all together and scrambling her own and Hal's number.

"Listen," Hal informed her, "if you say too many, they'll know you're cheating and it won't work." Again he showed her how to place the call properly, which she then did. "All right. Now it's ringing." He picked up the flashlight. "'Hello?" he said.

"Hello," she answered.

"No, Emily, you have to wait for the operator to ask me to accept the call." He made his voice growl. "'Will you accept a call from— I forgot; you have to tell them your name."

"Emily," said Emily.

"Will you accept a call from Emily?" Hal paused. "I'd be glad to. Hello, Emily. How are you?"

"Fine," said Emily in a diminished voice.

"Did you have a nice Christmas?"

"Yes."

"Do you want to speak to someone else?"

"Yes."

"All right. Who do you want to speak to?"

Emily's voice came firm and loud: "Hannah."

Hal pulled back. "Hannah?" he repeated, stalling. "She's not here now."

"How do you know?" Emily demanded. "Maybe she is."

Hal slammed down the flashlight. "I won't play that."

134

Emily let the receiver droop, but she didn't hang up. "Why not?"

"Because Hannah lived before there were any phones, so you can't make her talk on them."

"Did she live here?"

Hal gestured with his chin. "The Candlewood place. Where we caught the ducks." He measured the next words, willing them to come out level and matter-of-fact. "Where we fed the cow."

"Oh. Is that who you were looking for there? Hannah?"

Hal pondered that. Maybe in a way that was who he had been seeking. Not some unknown guy who turned out to be Carl tricking him with phony messages.

"Let's go look for her now," suggested Emily. "For Hannah."

Hal wasn't sure he ever wanted to go there again.

"Or we could look for the cow," Emily went on. "Let's just go."

All Hal could think of was Lew and his down-to-earth principles about Emily understanding the meat she ate. He felt like laughing. Because Emily didn't understand anything at all. Not a thing. And Lew was so out of it he'd never even noticed.

Emily was off the bed now, the telephone lying on its side. "I'll wear my new scarf. We can visit *them*."

Hal couldn't tell whether she meant to visit Hannah or the cow or the Titcombs, but all of a sudden he felt like talking to Harriet. He didn't want legal explanations or history answers or anything like that. Just plain family stuff, like whether there were ever apple trees across the road. And what else Alice—no, Eliza—found started and

135

new when she finally came home to Candlewood.

When they reached the Titcomb house, the door opened almost at once. Marjorie was there, a Marjorie Hal barely recognized. Cordial. Sounding glad to see them.

Harriet sat at the kitchen table glowering. Maybe that accounted for Marjorie's welcome. Maybe Hal and Emily were breaking up another quarrel.

Emily said, "It's nice here. It smells like dessert."

Hal pulled up a chair, turned to Harriet, and asked whether there had ever been apple trees across the road behind the big barn.

"Why don't you ask Uncle Harvey?" Marjorie suggested as she set a dish of some kind of dark pudding in front of him. It smelled of raisins and spices. She poured custard sauce over it.

"All I can remember," said Harriet suddenly, "is when I was little, bringing the dinner to the men haying there. They'd rest in the shade along the edge of the field, and that was apple-tree shade. I do believe they were the old Baldwins. It was Father put the orchard in on this side."

The pudding made Hal thirsty. He was glad when Emily asked for milk. Marjorie poured a glass for him too. He scraped the dish.

"An old family recipe," Marjorie told him. "If you were a girl, you might collect some of these old farm recipes for your report."

He didn't bother to point out that a boy could do that as well. Anyhow, something else was nudging him, something he'd never considered before. "Your grandfather." He bent toward Harriet. "Eliza's husband. Right?"

"Naturally."

"The young lawyer in the story?"

"He was a lawyer, a state representative, and a farmer as well."

"Then his name must have been Titcomb," said Hal. "That means Hannah's was Hannah something else."

"Wray," Harriet told him.

"Ray?"

"That's what I said."

Hal sat lost in thought. He had been groping toward some kind of discovery when he asked that question. What was he looking for? He asked, "Was he . . . nice?"

"Nice!" Harriet drew back. "Grandfather *nice?* He was . . ." She stared down the years to her childhood. "He was like God or Adam."

Hal sighed. He was losing his direction. "What about your great-grandfather? Was he really the way your grandmother described him?"

"How should I know? It all comes from her." Harriet paused. "She always blamed him for making Hannah so headstrong, though she blamed herself as well for what happened."

"What *did* happen?" piped up Emily behind him.

"Oh, that's a long story," Harriet told her. "Long and sad. She was lost, poor little thing. Though my grandmother always felt she was still about here. Even when Gran was dying she still spoke as though she expected Hannah to be found. Of course her mind wandered a bit, the way Harvey's sometimes does now. But you want to mind them even so, because they may be trying to tell you something."

"What was your grandmother trying to tell you?" Hal asked her.

Harriet rubbed her stiff fingers. "To look out for Hannah."

"And do you?" pressed Emily. "Do you ever see her?"

"I see a picture of her sometimes," Harriet replied. "I don't know where that picture comes from."

"I do," said Marjorie. "From your imagination. You're filling this child's mind with nonsense."

"I see a picture of her too," Hal said. His eyes and Harriet's met. For an instant they shared perfect understanding.

"Speaking of ghosts," continued Marjorie briskly, "I believe Carl saw someone in the back lot this morning. Weren't you looking for someone in the woods a few days ago?"

Hal nodded. But what if it was Carl who left those messages? To trick Hal. To get the cow.

Marjorie got up to call Carl from the front room. Emily went to look for Harvey, passing through the doorway as Carl came out.

He nodded uncomfortably at Hal. The kitchen seemed clogged with his uneasiness and Hal's aversion, but Marjorie was determined to get them on speaking terms.

"That's right," Carl responded to her prompting. "When I called, they took off. Who were you looking for?"

Hal shrugged. "It doesn't matter anymore, especially if it was you trying to get me to keep the cow around here."

"I didn't do that."

"So you could kill it easily. Conveniently."

Carl shook his head. "All I did was take it before it got into more trouble. I'm sorry you set such store by it. But what I did was natural. And had to be done."

"Now," began Marjorie, "let's not—"

"You lured her. She came down to eat because she trusted me."

"Hell, I got her where I wanted her with headlights, salt, and molasses. Same as jacking a deer. Simple. Only afterwards was hard. Getting her up to bleed and all."

Emily, in the doorway, said, "Who's bleeding?"

"No one," Marjorie answered, adding, "dear."

"A deer?" said Emily.

"Carl was talking about something else."

Emily walked across the kitchen with her eyes fixed on Carl. They held a deep curiosity. She pulled her jacket from the chair, still staring at Carl.

"Don't forget your boots," said Hal. "Don't forget to say thank you."

"Aren't you coming?"

"In a minute. I'll be right out."

Marjorie ushered Emily out the door. Harriet, with closed eyes, was cat-napping, or else avoiding the confrontation between Carl and Hal.

"All I'm saying," Carl resumed, "is that I never even thought of tricking you."

"What about the messages, then?"

Carl looked mystified.

Marjorie broke in. "Sounds like a mix-up."

With her shut eyelids flickering, Harriet said, "Maybe it was *her*. Maybe Gran was right. And Nathaniel. Maybe she's gone and left you signs, Hal."

Marjorie hooted. "Oh, Aunt Harriet, what a card you are! Isn't she a sketch, Hal? You'd better go check out those signs again. I bet they'll turn out to be things you dreamed up."

Hal couldn't seem to clear his mind. Marjorie sounded so sane, so straightforward, while he was blabbering about messages he'd already decided might not exist. He couldn't

139

think straight. He wanted to get away from Carl and the sweet warmth of the kitchen, which was suddenly cloying and oppressive.

But as soon as he closed the door behind him, Emily planted herself in front of him and demanded he go her way.

"Where's that?"

"I want to show you something."

"You always do," he said, following till he realized she was turning off the orchard path to lead him toward the back of the barn. "No." He stopped in his tracks.

"Come on. You have to."

"No."

"I just want to show you—"

"No. You already did. I've seen it."

"What is that thing in there?" She tilted her face up to his.

He felt like shaking the stuffing out of her. "Didn't your father tell you?"

"No. I don't remember."

They glared at each other. Then he said, "You do so know."

"What?" she shouted. "Know what?"

"That it's the cow."

"It is not, stupid." She continued to challenge him. "What is it?"

He bent toward her. If Lew wanted her to know, then he might as well answer. But he would leave out the part about the pigs eating the insides of it. "The cow," he said softly. "Skinned. Dead."

Emily lowered her head and charged him. He was so taken by surprise he couldn't block the first blow. The one from her head nearly knocked the wind out of him. He raised his hand to ward off her fists, but she pelted him right in the stomach.

When he finally caught both her hands, she stood for a moment gasping, not trying to speak, completely dry-eyed. Then she gave him a vicious kick in the shins and broke away, stumbling and running through the trees, up the hill toward the old farm site.

He took his time going after her. He hurt so much there were tears in his eyes. He leaned against a trunk, then sank down, resting until the pain had eased. Imagine a kid that size making him so sore. He tried shallow breathing, then got slowly to his feet.

Plodding through the end of the lane, he looked all around; then, moving on, he nearly walked into her. She was down on her hands and knees in the scattered hay. As if she were looking for something. He stepped back out of her way before inquiring, casually, what she was doing.

"Eating my hay," she told him.

Hal tried a deeper breath. He still hurt. "Are you Brindle? I was wondering where you were."

"You shouldn't watch," she informed him. "I don't like to be seen. I like to surprise people."

Hal nodded and went down to the dump. But when he squatted on his haunches, the pain bit into his middle again. Anyway, it was too cold to sort and sift through the junk, too hard to separate things stuck together under the snow. He returned to Emily, but she wasn't in the hay anymore. His eyes swept the area. "Emily," he called. "Brindle."

She answered from somewhere near the pond.

"Stay off the ice," he shouted. "Come back."

141

After a moment he saw a gray blob emerge through the white tangle of leaves and brush. "Don't come this way," he warned. It's too dangerous. You can't see what's under the snow."

Emily stopped. She seemed to study the queer shapes lying between them in the dump. "I saw someone," she said.

"Come on around," he told her.

"I saw someone." She traversed the hill and made for the lane.

Hal met her there. He believed her this time. He had a feeling that he'd come to the end of all the wrong, embarrassing guesses. "Did you talk to him?"

"What?"

"Where was he? Did he see you?"

"No." She covered her ears with her mittened hands. "Not him. Her."

God, thought Hal, will I ever learn? He warmed her ears with his hands. He was a little wary of her, but she stood quietly to be warmed.

"I guess it was Hannah," she said.

"That's good. Because Hannah was probably looking for Brindle, you know."

"She called me Emily. Not Brindle."

"Well, that's all right too," Hal assured her. He pulled her hat down as far as it would go.

They started along the lane to the orchard. After a while Emily said, "Is it all right if I talk to her?"

"Who? Hannah? Sure, why not?"

"I just wondered. She's not a stranger, because she knows me."

Hal caught his breath in a tiny, painful spasm. "Did you

142

really see someone?" He tried to relax. "I mean really, Emily. Not pretend."

"Really," she said.

"And it was a girl? What did she look like?"

"Like a picture." Emily started to dance around him. "She had a long coat and a dress, not pants, and she was pretty as a picture." She started to laugh. "Like me, like me."

Hal broke into a grin. "And she spoke to you, right?"

"Right," Emily agreed, tearing down the Titcombs' driveway. "She knows me."

"Stop!" Hal called after her. "You're supposed to slow down when you come to the road."

"I was going to." She waited for him to catch up. "What was that stuff we had, Hal? That kind of cereal."

"Look both ways," he told her. "Now run."

"What was it?" she repeated, skipping in front of him.

"Ask them tomorrow," Hal suggested. "It's not cereal. It's an old family recipe."

"I hope they save some for Hannah," said Emily.

And Hal thought, Boy, she never lets go of a thing. Never.

They turned up Second Hill Road, into the wind, into fresh, fine snow they hadn't even noticed until now.

16

Having Emily overnight was different from having cousins or a friend like Josh. The difference, Hal decided, was due to his parents, who kept suggesting things to do. They seemed anxious to please Emily, as with supper.

"Do you like broiled chicken?"

Hal knew that at the Thayer house no one paid much attention to what Emily liked or didn't like. If there was something she couldn't stand, she ate more bread and honey or some granola.

"What do you have in there?" Emily pointed to the Woodruffs' refrigerator. "In case I don't like boiled chicken."

"Broiled," Hal corrected.

The door swung wide. Other people's refrigerators and cupboards were full of intriguing things, Hal knew. Maybe not quite as interesting as their trash, but pretty close.

"That," said Emily decisively, indicating a wooden cheese box. "I like that for my supper."

"That's Camembert," said Hal's mother. "You wouldn't like it."

"Let me see."

Obligingly, and without a word about keeping the refrigerator door open all this time, Hal's father took the box, opened it, unwrapped the smelly paper inside, and exposed the cheese with its oozing center and its orange-white rind. "Pretty ripe," he observed. "Fortunately, I like it that way."

Emily said, "So do I."

Hal's parents looked at each other over Emily's head. Hal's mother shrugged. "Let her try it."

They handed Emily a cracker with a small dollop of cheese on it and waited for the expected reaction.

"That's what I'll have for supper."

"It's not enough."

"Yes, it is."

144

"I mean, you only eat a tiny bit at a time on a cracker. It's not like—"

"It's like Brie," Emily informed Hal's father. "You put it on bread."

Hal's mother said, "Things are coming clear. I suspect she's been cultivating this taste on Wednesday afternoons."

"I was going to pay you back," Hal told her. "I thought of giving you some for Christmas, only it was too expensive."

"I know," said his mother with feeling.

"So is Camembert," declared his father, wincing as Emily spread the cheese like putty all over a large slice of bread. Hal's mother turned away to season the chicken, and Hal went to look for *Charlotte's Web,* because his parents wanted something really nice to read aloud to Emily before bedtime.

But after Hal's parents left for work the next morning, things got back to normal. Emily played with the cat, then spent an hour or so engrossed in old books of Hal's, waiting for him to read some more of *Charlotte's Web* to her.

Hal got on the real phone with Josh. They made plans to go cross-country skiing in the afternoon. Emily, overhearing this, announced that she would go with them, but Hal firmly refused to have her. Sherry would be home around noon and would then be in charge of Emily.

Emily said she might just go anyhow if she felt like it, all by herself. To distract her, Hal offered her another lesson on the telephone. That seemed to work. So did *Charlotte's Web.* Only he should have realized that once Emily sank her teeth into a thing, she was like a terrier or a bulldog.

She almost fell asleep while he read. Starting out on the

floor beside his bed, with her knees drawn up to her chin, gradually she pulled more and more of his quilt down to her face, then slipped sideways until she was partly rolled in it.

"Do you think?" she murmured drowsily, "that any of the pigs know Wilbur?"

"What pigs?" Hal didn't like to be interrupted.

"The pigs." She rubbed the corner of the quilt against her cheek.

"You mean those pigs in the woods?" He saw them in the mist, small but almost sinister, trotting through the orchard with their snouts thrust forward, lured by the smell of the slaughtered cow.

Emily opened her eyes wide. "We could call them up and ask them," she suggested. "Or call Wilbur."

"Wilbur's in a story. He isn't real."

Emily stared a moment, then threw off the quilt and sat up. "If he isn't, then what's the use? Don't read it." She reached for the book.

"Look," said Hal, "every story doesn't have to be true."

"Yes, it does!" Emily cried. "It does!"

"Okay, then. Believe in Wilbur and in Charlotte and all those animals. When I was little, I believed in a lot of my stories."

"Could you read when you were five?"

"I can't remember. It was a long time ago."

Emily considered this assertion. She asked, "Could you milk a goat when you were five?"

"There's probably a lot of things you can do that I can't." Quickly, before she could drag in the question of skiing, he stood up and suggested they go to her house and

146

check on the goats and chickens and ducks.

Emily jumped up. "I'll get my things."

"Not to stay. You can't stay till Sherry gets back."

There was a bite in the air, and no sun. He and Josh would have to keep moving this afternoon. Thank goodness they wouldn't have Emily tagging along with her runny nose and cold ears.

Emily pointed to Sherry's car in the driveway. They had got home just in time. It was clear that Emily had had enough of visiting. She was ready for her own house and her own room. Hal insisted that she make sure it was all right with Sherry; the arrangement had been that Sherry would call when she was ready for Emily. Probably she had just got home, was calling Hal this very minute.

Emily left Hal on the steps. She charged through the kitchen and disappeared around the corner to the stairs. After a few minutes she reappeared. It was okay, she told Hal. Sherry was just washing her hair.

So Hal hurried home to call Josh, and they agreed to meet at the crossroads in twenty minutes.

That afternoon the two boys hardly noticed the pall of gray. It was wonderful to get out, and they covered a lot of ground. They were amazed at how far they could get through woods and fields without seeing anyone, but the last bit on the road to Josh's was pretty bad. The commuters were returning from Boston; car after car whooshed by. The snow plows had left the usual piles, with no real shoulder, so Hal decided to leave his skis at the Rosinus house. They'd start out from there tomorrow morning for a full day, Bill included.

Mrs. Rosinus offered to drop Hal off on her way to the

147

train, and he arrived home just as his parents drove in. They walked to the door together until Hal, hearing the phone ring, dashed ahead.

It was Sherry, and she sounded upset. She had been calling all afternoon. He should have told her if he was going somewhere with Emily. Anyhow, would he bring her home now, please.

Hal tried to swallow a lump of uneasiness. It didn't go down. Hours ago, he tried to tell Sherry. He'd brought Emily home before noon. Then Sherry started talking too fast and he began to shake his head. His mother took the receiver from him.

It was strange. No one took any of their outdoor things off. No one sat down or moved into the living room. They just stood dripping on the floor and waiting for Sherry. Then they started at the beginning and went over the facts again. Hal told them about sending Emily to check with Sherry before he left her. And Sherry said yes, she'd come home early, and she had washed her hair, but she had gone out again and hadn't got back till nearly one o'clock. And she had called, gone to the Woodruff house, and then kept on calling.

"And you never saw Emily?" Hal's mother was incredulous.

"No. I'd no idea she'd come home."

Hal's father asked whether Emily had ever gone off before. Sherry shook her head.

"I know," Hal announced. "I bet she's gone to the Titcombs'."

"By herself?"

"It's where the school bus stops."

Hal's mother had to look up the number. Then she

148

dialed, waited, and began to speak. There were pleasantries. Then the question about Emily. "She did? Is she there now? When was that?"

Hal nodded. Of course. Everything was all right. Only his throat felt fuzzy and his mouth tasted queer. He wished his mother would hurry up and tell Harriet Titcomb that they'd be right over to get Emily.

But that's not what happened. After some more terse questions Hal's mother put down the phone and turned to Sherry. "I think," she said, "we'd better get in touch with Lew."

Sherry nodded miserably. She would have to go home to get the number of the place where Lew could be reached.

"And I'll call the police," Hal's mother went on.

"For all we know," said Hal's father, "the police are trying to reach someone about her right now. Let's not alarm Lew unnecessarily. She's probably been visiting somebody, or the police have her."

"Emily would call home," Sherry told him. "She knows where she is and who she is." With that, Sherry went out the door.

Hal listened to his mother speaking to the police. He marveled at her calm, careful way of handling essentials. He watched his father, who usually turned off every light the minute you moved from it, going around the house turning lights on. Why did he need all those lights? Hal wondered.

Hal went to his room. There was the quilt, half dragged to the floor, where Emily had wrapped herself. The cat was lying in it now. There was *Charlotte's Web*, open and face down on his unmade bed. There was the flower telephone, its receiver off the hook.

149

He knew that if Emily didn't show up pretty soon, he was going to have to sort out everything that they had done and said in order to figure out where she might have gone.

When he saw the lights from the police car on the wall opposite his window, he went back to the others. Sherry was there again. Chief Durand was talking on the telephone to the place in Vermont where Lew had said he would be staying. But it seemed Lew had been mistaken about having accommodations there. They remembered, because there had been a message for him to go on to some other place. They would try to find out where. They would call back. Chief Durand asked them to contact the Vermont State Police instead. "Now," he declared, turning to all of them, "let's start at the beginning."

Hal could hear Lew announcing, "First things first." As soon as Lew was reached, everything would be cleared up.

"Pay attention," his father said to him in a tight voice.

Hal looked at Chief Durand. He said, or tried to say, "I think we should look in the Candlewood lot."

"Speak up," said his father.

"What?" said Chief Durand.

"Please, Hal," begged Sherry, "try to think."

So Hal repeated himself, and this time the words came out. Some kind of words, because Chief Durand was issuing orders to a police officer and then speaking earnestly with Hal's parents.

Hal's father said, "You go along with the chief."

"Me too," said Sherry, sounding absurdly like Emily.

"No," Chief Durand told her. "You'll be more useful at your house. In case there's a call. Also, I'm sending someone to make a thorough search of the premises."

"But I've been all over the place. Indoors and out. She isn't anywhere."

Chief Durand propelled Hal toward the door. "I know," he said over his shoulder. "And chances are she'll turn up in some obvious place we'll all have thought we checked. Still . . ." Then he was slamming the cruiser door, backing up, and heading for the Titcombs'.

Hal said, "The cow's there, you know. They killed it."

Chief Durand said, "Had your supper?"

Hal said, "She wanted to follow me or find me."

"Anyone else she might have looked for?"

Hal's throat clamped down on the name Hannah. "Maybe the cow."

"I thought you said it was killed."

Hal nodded. "It's there, hanging in the barn."

Chief Durand shot a glance at him, reached somewhere, and pulled out a candy bar, of all things. A candy bar, thought Hal, as though I were just some little kid that needs to be bribed. But he found himself clawing the wrapper off and devouring the candy without even tasting it.

Another officer met them as they pulled up at the Titcombs'. There was talk about lights, about the snowfall, about the possibility or futility of looking for tracks. Some Highway Department vehicle was on its way to light up the woods by the eastern end of Nutters Hill Road. Chief Durand was concerned about tramping in the dark over possible footprints; but once they were actually up at the old farm site, it was obvious that as long as the snow kept coming like this, there would be nothing left to blot out.

"If she was going to teach you a lesson, really scare you," the chief asked Hal, "would she stay out this long?"

Hal didn't know. All of that about the skiing had been

151

hours ago. Besides, she knew enough to come in from the cold.

"Try calling her. Like you really believe she's out there."

"Emileeee!" Hal yelled. He cupped his hands to his mouth, swiveling so that his voice was directed down over the dump, swiveling again toward the pond, where high-beam lights could just be seen like candles fluttering in outer space. As he completed a half-circle in the direction of the meadow, the glare of a powerful flashlight blinded him for an instant. It was someone coming from the Titcombs' to report no sign of Emily in the barn. "Emily," Hal shouted, "you've got to cut this out and come home now! I'll take you with me tomorrow! Come on, Emily!"

They waited. Hal saw more flashlights coming from the orchard. Each light speared a hole through the darkness.

"Can you lead us to the places she might go to around here?"

He said they could start toward the meadow and work their way down. He wondered if he could find the cow's glade in the snow, in the dark, in the spinning lights.

They set off, a troop of searchers spread out behind Hal, their lights shattering like crystal ornaments against the solid trunks of trees and over the brittle underbrush. They lured him off the track and into a territory he was sure he had never seen before.

"Emily!" he called from time to time. Nothing seemed the same; nothing was familiar. If only, he thought, the snow would stop.

But it didn't. It kept falling all that night.

17

Because it was Saturday, the supply of searchers seemed inexhaustible. Only a few had any clear idea of whom they were looking for, but that didn't matter. In this weather, urgency dictated that all the woods be combed for the lost child. Any lost child would do, Hal guessed. But then he was beyond making sensible connections anymore.

At some point during the morning he went out again with one of the officers. They drove around and then they walked some. The idea was to recall whether this was territory familiar to Emily. Hal had no idea. But someone had reported seeing a child in the vicinity, and they couldn't afford to miss that lead. All Hal could do was follow the man, stop when he stopped, turn when he turned. By now it hardly took any time before Hal was shivering convulsively. The officer took him back to the Titcomb kitchen, where searchers warmed up with coffee or soup and exchanged news or, rather, no news.

To escape the heat and commotion and smells, Hal joined Harvey, who was in his wheelchair watching a sports program on television. Hal saw downhill skiers and a basketball dropping through a basket. He saw somebody knock out somebody else in a boxing ring, and a team of football players surge forward and bring down a player. Closing his eyes, Hal could feel himself sway. How could he possibly sleep with Emily still missing?

He opened his eyes. A huge man was flexing his knees, rubbing his hands, reaching for a weighted bar. Harvey muttered something and gestured toward a chair. Hal dragged it over beside the wheelchair and sat down. The man on the screen was making grotesque faces; he looked tortured. Bliss Atherton's modulated voice flowed from the kitchen into the front room, becoming for Hal the commentator for the television action.

"Perfectly avoidable," sportscaster Atherton pronounced, while the weight-lifter trembled, his knees straining, one foot shifting. "What kind of a father," demanded Bliss Atherton, addressing millions of viewers, "would try to raise . . ." The weight-lifter tried and did raise the bar, first to his chin, then, with another quick shift, still higher. "No responsibility . . . Properly raised . . ." The bar crashed silently to the ground.

Harvey grinned at Hal. "Like to put him to work around here in the old days. Worth three or four summer help, I expect."

Kitchen voices swelled in response to Atherton's last assertion. Hal watched another muscled strong man flex his knees and rub his hands. Where did they come from? Hal wondered. Had they ever been kids? He tried to imagine this giant, his face bulging, contorted, going to school with Bliss Atherton. Impossible!

The door burst open from the kitchen. Someone said, "There he is. Hal's in there."

"Where?"

"In there watching television."

"Oh, Hal," said his mother, advancing. She grabbed his shoulder. "How can you?" she whispered fiercely. "While everyone's out scouring the—"

"How about showing a little concern?" muttered his father.

Chief Durand pulled up some more chairs. He motioned

Hal to swivel around. Harvey was left in their midst, watching the silent show.

"Now," Chief Durand began, "Miss Titcomb tells us that there's been someone around here. That you knew about him."

Hal supposed Harriet was referring to the so-called messages.

"Speak up," his father prompted. "Was there or wasn't there someone?"

Hal shook his head. "I thought there was."

Harriet Titcomb interrupted. "I didn't say he *saw* anyone. *Emily* saw her."

"Her?"

Harriet nodded. "I expect Hal knows more than I do."

They all eyed Hal, who understood that he was to supply them with useful information about Emily's disappearance. He said, "Emily told me there was someone. She's always saying things like that."

"Then you don't think she actually saw anybody?"

Hal considered. Emily had seen the cow. She had seen the pigs. "I don't know. She's heard all this stuff about Candlewood being sort of haunted. She said she saw Hannah."

"Who's Hannah?"

Hal looked at Harriet.

"My great-aunt," she supplied.

"Oh, for God's sake!" Hal's father exploded.

Chief Durand raised a warning hand. "Let's just go on for a minute. What Emily thinks she saw could tell us something. Hal, did you see what Emily says she saw?"

Hal shook his head. Then, hastily, he added, "But I

thought I *almost* saw someone a few times. I was sure someone was around. Watching me."

His mother broke in. "That's ridiculous. The power of suggestion."

Hal kept still. He was thinking of the slate in the crotch of the tree trunk, the initials on the stone.

"No," said Chief Durand. "There's more to it. Isn't there, Hal?"

Hal covered his eyes with his hands, trying to rub some clarity into his sight. With his eyes still shielded, he told about the slate in the tree trunk, the initials on the stone.

In the kitchen Hal caught sight of Sherry and Peggy speaking with Mac. Someone had found Lew, and at last he was on his way home. Outdoors, the sun, which had broken through, was painful. Everything seemed rimmed in red, like a fire out of control. Bill and his brother were on their way to the Titcomb house for a hot drink. They greeted Hal with deference because he was walking between Chief Durand and another officer. Hal thought: That's Bill; we were going skiing today.

At the house site they cleared the area now defined by orange stakes, its previous borders obliterated by throngs of searchers.

Even the stone seemed different. The initials HW were clear enough, though they had lost their fresh look. Then Hal took the police to the tree trunk; only it wasn't there anymore. A backhoe and a small dozer had followed the surveyors and had already cleared the stumps from the staked area below the pond. There was a heap of debris like an elephant graveyard off to the east of the swamp. Somewhere in that pile of trunks and roots was the section of double oak with the slate, but it would take another

156

machine to spread the pile, and by then it might be crushed and crumbled.

"Do you believe me?" Hal asked Chief Durand.

"Why shouldn't I?"

Hal tried to collect his thoughts. "Even if there wasn't a message, there was something. . . . And someone who knew my initials. And knew Emily. Because the person called Emily by her name."

"But didn't you think Emily was making that up?"

"I . . . Yes, then. I don't know."

Back at the house the kitchen was thinning out. It was only an hour or so till sunset. Chief Durand beckoned Hal into the front room. Harriet was already there, busy with Harvey, who had had an accident. Harriet was mopping Harvey and the floor, attempting to straighten the bed and get Harvey into it.

Gertrude Atherton strode into their midst. She had a basin and a cloth. Kneeling at Harvey's feet, she swabbed, straightened, and altogether took over for Harriet. Hal's mother cast about the room, singling out the chief. "Maybe someplace else," she suggested.

There was a small, cold room beyond the front room, and they gathered there, like people waiting at a bus stop on a winter evening. Eventually Harriet joined them. Hal thought she looked awful. She hugged herself, her fingers seeking warmth under opposite arms.

Chief Durand asked her to tell everything that had happened when Emily dropped by the previous afternoon. Hal listened to the rise and fall of words. Emily had said she was on her way to meet Hal.

Once again Chief Durand tried to piece together Emily's probable route from there: uphill; out of habit to the

157

foundation where, he had just been informed, the initials on the stone were not recently carved but had been covered by another stone for a long, long time; on toward the pond perhaps. . . .

"But they're my initials," Hal broke in.

"Miss Titcomb says they're her great-aunt's."

Hal gazed from Harriet to Chief Durand. Bemused, he shook his head. "They can't be."

His mother said, "Hannah Wray. H.W. Same initials."

"Not Ray with an R?" Hal demanded. "Why didn't you tell me?"

"Why didn't *you* tell *me?*" Harriet snapped back. "You never mentioned they were there."

"I told you someone had written my . . ." He broke off.

"Hers," declared Harriet.

"Not . . . not for me?"

Harriet held his eyes. "I didn't say that."

"My God," groaned Hal's father. "We're trying to find a kid who's lost. Who may be—"

"All right," Chief Durand put in, "I'm getting the picture. Emily was full of quite a few notions about this place and about someone named Hannah. She told Hal she had seen Hannah."

"I knew this preoccupation was being overdone," Hal's mother burst out.

"Please." Chief Durand turned to Hal's parents. "I'd like a word or two alone with Hal and Miss Titcomb. Then I think the best thing would be to get Hal home to bed."

After Hal's parents had left, Chief Durand paced briefly, then faced Harriet and Hal. *"Was* there someone?" he asked abruptly.

158

Harriet said, "Some say there's always been."

"Did you yourself see anything, any sign of—"

"I told you. I hardly go out. In the past, though, yes. I have sometimes felt a presence there."

Chief Durand nodded. He was nodding respectfully, which gave Hal courage when it was his turn to answer.

"Things back there," he stated, "things that you think can't be, they turn out to be real. I don't know whether I was kidding along with Emily about Hannah or what. You see, now that I know those initials are hers, I—" He shook his head. What did he know? What was changed? "It couldn't be," he finished slowly. "Couldn't be Hannah, because she's been dead for years and years. And people can't . . . don't . . ." He stumbled to a halt.

Chief Durand said, "Emily, who was last seen heading for the woods, is not in those woods, nor in the pond or barn, nor, as far as we can tell, anywhere in the vicinity."

Was Chief Durand suggesting that she could have slipped into another time? Hal asked tentatively, "You think she's been taken . . . away?"

"It's a possibility. That's why it's so important to learn everything we can about this person Emily says she spoke to before."

Hal nodded. "When Lew gets back, he'll figure it out."

Chief Durand asked if there was anything else either of them recalled. Hal glanced at Harriet, who shook her head. "I intend to be careful," she declared. "I'm not going to say things Carl and Marjorie can use against me. To show some judge I'm not in my right mind. For all I know," she added, "those two could be responsible for this whole mess."

"What?"

159

"My mother can explain," Hal told the chief. He couldn't stand it if Harriet got all weird now. He was shivering again. Every muscle in his body ached because he was in the grip of the cold and of a baffling fear. If only Hannah, not the pigs, would be the answer to the chief's queries; if only Hannah had been there all along and had taken Emily away with her.

He was barely aware of waiting in the kitchen while his parents explained about Carl and Marjorie. He had to clench his chattering teeth to reinforce his refusal to swallow some lukewarm soup.

At home he still couldn't eat or drink. He tumbled onto his bed, burrowing deep, dragging the quilt from the floor where Emily had sat wrapped and snug and dreamy. And safe.

Then he was in a dream. He couldn't stop backing away, turning when he could to reach for roots and saplings, handholds on the steep hillside. The weight-lifter lurched after him, but Hal made it to the barn. Only there was the weight-lifter again; now he was hanging from the roof beam by his bulging legs. All that meat, thought Hal. He heard the pigs snuffling and snorting. He yelled, "Emileee!" The pigs closed in on him just as the weight-lifter reached down and grabbed him.

Hal blinked. His own breathing sounded harsh and quick. He stared into his father's face and at once started to explain that he hadn't wanted to watch that program; he hadn't even liked it.

His father said, "Forget about that. We were all just upset."

Hal said, "He's still there."

His father shook him again, though more gently. He

160

turned away, speaking to someone else. "Maybe some cocoa or something?"

Hal heard his mother respond, then another voice. He sat up. "Lew? Is it Lew?"

Lew appeared at the foot of his bed, saying, "I hate to wake you, but I thought between us we might put a few things together."

Hal nodded. His parents had withdrawn. The lights made his eyes ache. "I don't know what day this is," he whispered.

"It's all right," Lew told him, slumping on the bed, staring.

After a while Hal said, "Do you want to ask me about Hannah?"

Hal's father came in with two mugs. Hal gulped down his cocoa. Lew sipped, massaged his face, sipped some more.

"Did Emily describe her?"

"She said she was pretty. She asked if it was all right to talk to her. I thought she was pretending. Hannah was like . . . like someone on television you think you know. Do you believe a person can be in two different times?"

Lew cleared his throat. "I don't know what I believe. I think Emily's mother was here. Planned all of this. Has Emily."

"Your . . . Emily's mother?"

Lew nodded. "She called me when we were in Florida. Arranged for us to meet. She's just had a baby that didn't live. She wanted to see Emily, but she agreed to see me alone first. So I went to meet her, only it was a wild-goose chase. At the place, a message to go somewhere else. When I got there, no sign of her. I waited all night and day."

"And she never came?"

"I think she came here. With me out of the way."

"But like that? Why would she?"

Lew sighed. "She could still be . . . well, sick. Not responsible."

Relief warmed Hal. "So now you know what to do."

Lew slouched, more froglike than ever. "I may not be able to do anything. Tomorrow . . ." His voice fell away.

"The police will help you," Hal declared, and then heard himself appealing to Chief Durand: *Lew will figure it out.* Hal gazed at Lew. Why didn't he stand up and announce, "First things first," and set about the business of finding Emily? He said, "I suppose you need to sleep too."

Lew nodded bleakly. "You see . . ." Lew's words stumbled over his jagged thoughts. "I don't know . . . can't be sure she's all right."

"At least," thought Hal out loud, "we don't have to worry about the pigs. At least there's that."

"Pigs?"

Hal met Lew's baffled stare. "I mean," he amended, "we don't have to think of her out there in the cold somewhere."

Lew sat awhile longer without speaking. Eventually Hal's parents returned and Lew went away. And then Hal slept again, without dreaming, just slept and slept.

When he woke, it was afternoon, already growing dark, and the work of finding Emily was under way. His parents were organizing the legal side of things, and a detective had been hired to investigate the equally mysterious disappearance of Lew's ex-wife.

The next few days saw the outward resumption of normal living. Hal's parents returned to work, except for New

162

Year's Day. Lew went away to search out old acquaint-
ances who might have kept in touch with his ex-wife.
Christmas vacation would be over and school would begin
again. Hal wondered how Lew would manage that.

He tried spending a day with Josh and Bill, but it was
almost impossible to tell them about Candlewood and
Eliza's story. "Is this real?" Josh kept interrupting. "Is this
part from the magazine?" Or, "Are you talking about before
or now?" Hal wondered whether he himself had begun to
confuse the past with the present, the lost girl of 1840 and
the lost Emily of now. Josh, who read a lot of science fiction, saw no reason why the past and present couldn't get
tangled. Only he wanted to know exactly what Hal meant
when he said: "Hannah spoke to Emily"; when he said:
"She has never been found."

"I thought Lew found some people that knew the man
Emily's mother married."

Once again Hal had to shift from Hannah to Emily.
"Couldn't trace them, though."

"Don't you think," put in Bill, "he should've just let her
see the kid? Then she'd have left them alone."

It wasn't that simple, though. Hal had learned from
Peggy and the others that Linda had always been impulsive
and unpredictable. Like deciding to have a baby and then,
when it was too late, changing her mind. She'd married
Lew, since he wanted to take over as father, divorced him
right afterward, and never looked back till now that she'd
lost a new baby. You couldn't blame Lew for being
cautious.

"What if he finds her," asked Bill, "and it turns out she
doesn't have Emily?"

"Then," said Josh, "we'll know that Haunting Hannah

163

got her for company. If you ask me, that makes a lot more sense than having a crazy mother kidnap the kid."

"That means you believe in ghosts," said Bill.

"It means I believe that some people can be snatched away from their time into the future or the past. Probably you won't see any more messages from Hannah now, because she's got what she wants. See, if Hannah went on hiding and being miserable, then probably she went a bit crazy herself after a while. Probably grew into a lonely old woman. And along came Emily. Probably all those other people who thought they could feel her there weren't right for Hannah. They wouldn't come willingly. Only Emily would. See?"

Hal thought it was wonderful that Josh could be so clear-headed about what belonged to one time or another and still believe in time warps. For Hal nothing was clear. All he knew for sure was that Emily believed in Hannah just as she had believed in the cow. Only which cow had Emily believed in? The one she had fed, the one whose carcass now hung in the Titcomb barn? Or Hannah's cow, Brindle?

18

School began. The substitute teacher was all right, but she wasn't in touch with the kind of history they'd been studying. Anyhow, this was the worst time of the year, when mostly you waited for bad weather and school cancellations.

Hal dreaded the first Wednesday without Emily. He made plans to spend the half-day with Josh, but there was an ice storm Tuesday night. Hal woke up to the fire whistle shrieking its three blasts: NO SCHOOL. He didn't have to turn on the radio; he didn't even have to get up.

After his parents decided to risk the ice and set out for Boston, the very life of the house seemed quenched. Hal stared across the room at his unconnected telephone. He thought: That's me. I'm not connected.

Then the real telephone rang. Reluctantly Hal got up and shuffled across the hall to his parents' room. He stretched over the bed, reached for the receiver. "Hello." He hoped he sounded asleep. He hoped that whoever was calling would apologize for waking him up and go away.

But it was Peggy, and she was in a hurry and not the least bit apologetic. They had left the duck cage unlocked last night so the catch wouldn't be frozen in the morning. The wind must have blown the gate open, and now the drake was missing. They were worried about a fox getting it, or a dog, but they couldn't spend any more time looking. Hal understood. Since the ducks were Emily's, it was important to have them safe and waiting for her return.

After the Thayer house, the next obvious place to search was Candlewood, but Hal found it tough going over the ice-slick snow. When he reached the heights and looked down, he was surprised to find that even more of the lowland had been opened, directing the eye southeast to the point where the subdivision road would join Nutters Hill Road. It wasn't stumped out yet, all the cut trees standing about four feet high. They had the look of squat pillars, ruined columns leading to a stately mansion. Only there

165

was no mansion, just the surrounding woods and walls and meadow. The foundation stones, where Hal stood, were no longer the heart of the place.

Hal felt winded, as if he had come upon an alien landscape. Everything was vanishing so quickly. Not only Hannah, not simply Emily, not just the cow and now the drake, but the land itself disappearing before his eyes.

Something snapped behind him. He wheeled. It was only a chipmunk darting over the icy snow like a waterbug zigzagging on the surface of the pond. The pond, he thought. The first place to look for the drake. He started down, skidding, then changed his course, picking his way to the meadow and taking the more gradual slope.

But the pond was deserted. A muskrat hill collapsed underfoot, setting miniature ice floes sliding onto the pond. Somewhere between Candlewood and the main highway a car spun its wheels. Farther still, crows converged in raucous flight. Would they eat a duck? Probably. But Hal could never find those particular crows.

On his way back down through the orchard, his eyes slid sideways toward the barn. The cow carcass was like a magnet. How could something so horrible and repellent keep dragging him from his resolve to forget it? He stopped where Emily had charged him. He felt for the tender spot below his ribs. It was gone now, and with it the assurance that what he had felt then had been real.

Is it real, Josh had demanded, or is it that story?

He went on down, now abreast of the Titcomb house. And the door opened. Harriet called, "Yoohoo, Hal!" in a high, cracked voice. Real, said Hal to himself. Like an old movie, but real.

Real, too, the cornbread steaming on the stove, the

166

damp, sour smell of Harvey, the whiteness of his false teeth beside the yellow crumbs on the table.

Hal sat hunched in his jacket, his boots leaving prints on the floor, and began to choke out harsh, dry sobs. Harvey went on eating, slurping coffee and dribbling sodden bits of cornbread. Harriet rocked back and forth in a chair without rockers, her hands folded in her lap, her head nodding to the rhythm of a song only she could hear. Eventually Hal realized that the rhythm was set by his sobs. He stopped abruptly. Sure enough, she ceased rocking. They looked at each other.

"You'll have some cornbread now," she said after a moment.

He nodded. He was exhausted. He touched his middle again, wanting to feel that soreness. If he could recapture the pain, then there might be tears, and the end of tears.

"Is he back?" asked Harriet.

Hal shook his head. "He calls all the time. It's costing a lot—traveling, phone calls, the detective."

"The police don't cost."

"My mother and father say the police don't like interfering in a kidnapping by a parent."

"If it is," said Harriet.

Hal swallowed tea, but only looked at the cornbread. "I guess no one knows," he said.

Harvey said, "Find that duck, did you?"

"The drake? How did you know it was lost?"

"Came here during the storm. In the barn."

"I went out," Harriet supplied. "Late last night. In that wind I thought we'd lose the barn door. See, Carl left the back open because of the cow hanging there. In a norther, it picks the door right up."

"You should've called me. You might have slipped. I'd have come."

"Yes, well, when you're used to doing things for yourself . . ."

"And the drake was there? You shut him in?"

"Poor thing had feathers sticking out like a porcupine."

"Find the girl?" Harvey inquired. He clapped his teeth in and ran his finger around the false gum.

"No. That's why Lew's away. Looking for her."

Harriet shook her head. "Strikes me he's looking in the wrong place."

"But she couldn't still be here. It's been nearly two weeks. She'd be . . . She couldn't be."

Harriet shrugged. "Eat that cornbread. It's best hot."

Hal said, "If Emily was with . . . with Hannah . . ."

Harriet set her eyes square on him. "Well?"

"How," he blurted, "could we get her back?"

Harriet shrugged again. "They're smarter than we are. That's the trouble."

"They?"

"The girls."

"They're not the same, though." Hal struggled to get through to her, to himself. "Emily's just a little kid. Hannah went off on her own. Because she had to. Wanted to, I mean. And you don't know what happened to her. But Emily's . . . Emily. She's *now*."

"Came here, didn't she?"

"But not like Hannah. They're not the same. Anyhow, Hannah probably went somewhere to earn some money and never came back."

"She was here, all right. Nathaniel saw her. And you yourself saw the marks she left."

168

"Left, exactly. Probably because she was going away and wanted everyone to know that she had been here."

"What about Nathaniel?"

"He was crazy. I mean, retarded."

"Some people," said Harriet evenly, "say idiots see things others don't."

"Now you're talking about ghosts again. You're saying he saw Hannah's ghost. I don't believe in ghosts." Hal toyed with the cornbread, but without bringing it to his mouth. You could draw the line at ghosts. But that didn't rid you of more troubling habits of thinking, like blurring the past with the present. "Where did the cow come from?" he asked quietly.

"Off some farm, I'd guess. Some farm selling out."

"And the pigs?"

"Same. Though we've still got one piggery up by the turnpike. Yes, and the same for the little white call-ducks that've been here as long as anyone can remember. Now you've got the one back. Think you can carry it home safe, or do you want a sack?"

"A sack, I think, please. If I slip, I could lose it on the road."

Harriet nodded, rose, and went to the broom closet. Harvey jabbed his fork toward Hal's uneaten cornbread. Dutifully Hal took up a mouthful. He swallowed hard. It was funny how dried up he felt these days. The crumbly bread made him cough, and he gulped down the remains of his cold tea. No juice in me, he thought. Not even tears. And noted with a touch of envy the string of drool that formed at the corner of Harvey's slack lips.

So the drake got back, and then Lew was back too. Only Emily wasn't.

169

In school Lew tried to pick up and go on. He told the kids it was way past time to wrap up their projects. He wanted each of them to report on the most striking difference discovered between life in Westwick now and life in an earlier time.

Kim's hand waved. "Does it have to be about the place, or can it be about people?"

"Whatever strikes you."

"So I can use Mrs. Duncan? Someone else lives in her house now, the Moody house."

"How about something like lights?" asked Bill. "Like what you could see with."

Lew nodded.

"Even food?" demanded Bernie.

"Especially food."

Everyone laughed. The kids relished having Lew back, almost as if they'd forgotten why he had been away. Hal supposed it would be different if you didn't know Emily. Only Hal and his friends had been told that Lew's ex-wife, Linda, had finally called and apologized for running out. She'd simply panicked, she told Lew, and had been too ashamed to get in touch right away.

"Which means," Josh had figured, "she didn't take Emily after all."

Hal couldn't say. His mother insisted there was still a chance that Linda was covering, pretending. But Lew seemed convinced, and had nowhere else to look.

Here at school he made it easy for everyone to forget that he lived in a void, that Emily's disappearance left him floating, a man in space.

That's how Hal saw him, though. Saw him wafting through the unreal everyday world of school and home,

170

suspended, weightless. Lew looked changed too. Being thinner should have been an improvement, but all that loose skin had no place to go. It was as though the flesh had been eaten away beneath it.

Hal didn't like to think about that. It reminded him of the carcass, now mercifully gone, or anyway packed in freezers. Carl and Marjorie were back too, and life at Candlewood was already more ordered and orderly now that they had converted the small downstairs room into Harvey's special quarters and were restoring the front room for general use.

Hal seldom went there. He preferred being with Peggy and Sherry and Mac, who would talk freely about Emily and Lew. Anything, they kept telling each other, anything would be better than this not knowing. Peggy cried a lot, her face ugly and smudged with tears. Hal wanted to be near her and feel and hear that weeping, because he himself was hollow, still dried up and, these days, often cold.

But now with the assignment to wrap up their reports, Hal had to return to Candlewood. Lew had mentioned taking advantage of the January thaw to complete any unfinished outdoor research. There had been a few warm days, but soon it would be February, and everyone knew that winter would set in once more.

As Hal trudged up the Titcomb driveway, he opened his jacket and lifted his face to the sun. It made his skin feel clean, that was all. Inside he was frozen.

Carl was out polishing his car. He greeted Hal like an old friend and warned him to watch out for the bulldozer up back.

Hal slogged through the wet orchard and on toward the dump. The bulldozer had subdued the Candlewood low-

171

land. The grinding of earth, roots, and rocks, the squeal of the machine itself, and the roar of its motor filled the cavity that had once supported buttonbush and alder, gray birch and swamp maple, mountain ash and oak.

Hal was transfixed by the devastation. The yellow monster backed and filled; it pulled down a lump of the hillside and dragged it across the wasteland to a new hill. The machine was so enormous that one pass could wipe out an entire landmark. Hal watched it push back a pile of topsoil and swamp spoilage. He saw it gouge into the base of the hill, depositing blue-gray clay on a curving ridge of raw subsoil. Then back it lumbered, rooting like a giant pig.

It wasn't until Hal was halfway down the slope that he realized the pond was almost gone. He gazed at the yawning black basin. Where were the muskrat hills now? Where the egg sacs, next summer's frogs and tiny fish? All the reeds where the mallards and black duck would have nested in the spring were scraped away. Hal looked up at the sky, pale and empty, as if it too had been scoured by the blade of a huge machine. The blue was thin, watery, smoothed into blankness.

The machine halted, its blade poised. The driver waved to Hal, who continued on down.

The driver shouted up, "This your land?"

Hal shook his head.

"Thought it might be. The way you were looking."

Hal stared at him. How could you have a conversation with that engine roaring?

The driver jumped down and strode toward the edge of the woods. He raised a thermos to his mouth. "Coffee?" He extended the thermos toward Hal, who shook his head and asked the driver why he didn't shut off the dozer.

"Not worth it. Short break." The driver wiped his mouth. He had bright red curly hair and a reddish beard.

"Where did the pond go?"

"These road-makers can stamp out a pond, fill a marsh, even build a mountain before you can count to ten." He peered at Hal. "Not yours, huh?"

"I know the people, though. They made ice on the pond. In the olden days. It was bigger then, deeper."

"Nothing stays the same."

"Do you like running that thing?"

The man grinned. "It can do almost anything."

"It's so big," said Hal doubtfully. "So big you'd think it might make mistakes."

"If it does, they're mine. Come on, I'll show you."

Up close, the machine was gigantic. Hal couldn't figure how to get up onto it. The driver stepped from wheel to hub to a bar and heaved himself up. "Back there," he directed. "Give me your hand."

Hal found himself clambering up and hauled inside, towering over the land around him. The driver showed him the many gears, the bar at the driver's left that raised and lowered the blade, the steering levers, and the accelerator, which worked backward. With slow, precise maneuvers the driver shifted a boulder until the dozer had it squarely in its path. Then it thrust forward, and the boulder was torn from its bed and rolled toward the great mound of spoils. After that the driver stopped the dozer to let Hal off.

Hal staggered to a flatter spot where he could watch the work. Now that he knew what lever and which pedal controlled each action, he could see the skill of the operator as well as the power of the machine. Trees fell, boulders rolled, the woods collapsed and opened to the sun. You

173

could see the layers of the old, doomed hill, its black top-soil, the debris of rotting years, the peaty humus, the clay, and then the gravel. Roots protruded like splintered bones.

Shakily Hal climbed to the meadow, which was still intact. Though not for long, Hal supposed, for there were those orange stakes again. This time next year there would be houses and people and cars, cats and dogs and bikes, power lines and telephone poles. Not cows, nor pigs, nor ducks.

He wandered back through the orchard, his thoughts sliding from Hannah, and what she might have made of all this, to Emily. Hannah really had no right to expect things to stay the same for a hundred and fifty years, but Emily had only been away a few weeks. She was five years old and she was lost somewhere or taken, and even if she came back, she would not come back to what she'd known a little while ago, not here, not ever again here as it was.

This thought stuck to him as he entered the Titcomb kitchen and was urged by Marjorie into the newly renovated front room. "Where's Mr. Titcomb?" he asked pointedly. The room wasn't right without Harvey.

"Carl's out doing an errand."

Hal turned back to the kitchen, where Harriet sat. "Can I see Mr. Titcomb?"

"Oh, you mean Harvey," Marjorie answered for Harriet. "He's fine. Loves his new room."

"I can't find anything," Harriet stated grimly. "I can't even find Harvey."

"Now, Aunt Harriet, you're exaggerating," Marjorie chided. "I'll go get Uncle Harvey if it will make you feel better. Though why we can't let sleeping dogs lie . . ." She was on her way.

174

"Can't find any of my wooden spoons," Harriet muttered.

"I heard that," Marjorie called back. "You know I told you I'd get some new ones, colorful plastic ones. The old ones," she asserted, speaking, Hal supposed, for his benefit, "were gummy. Full of germs."

Harriet spoke to Hal. "Lots of doings up back."

"Yes," Hal agreed. "Lots." He told her about the bulldozer operator.

Harriet broke into a smile. "First time I ran the tractor, just before the war, it didn't hear a word I said to it." She chortled. "They were all laughing so hard they couldn't tell me how to stop her."

"How did you?"

"Ran her into the haystack."

Hal grinned. "I bet Harvey teased you."

Wheeling Harvey into the kitchen, Marjorie leaned over to shout in his ear, "They're talking about you, Uncle Harvey!"

Harriet told her brother what they were discussing, and his eyes glittered. "Her hands." He tried to demonstrate with his own. "See, she was looking for the reins to pull on, and hollering, 'Whoa!' "

"He's in good spirits," Marjorie declared. "I wish your mother could see how he's thriving with all the care he's getting now." Her declaration shut down Harvey's reminiscences. After a pause she shouted to him about the work being done in the back lot. If the thaw held another week, they'd be able to lay the road in March. "I guess we won't be seeing much of you then," she said to Hal.

He didn't know how to respond, so he said, "I'm supposed to finish my report."

"I imagine you'll tell all about the old place."

175

"What I know," he answered guardedly.

"The family ghost and that." There was a note of condescension or amusement or both.

"I don't know," Hal told her. "You see, my teacher's . . . Well, right now with Emily missing . . ."

"Missing?" said Harvey. "Talking about the girl?" He turned to Harriet. "Didn't Gran say she must be hereabouts?"

"We're talking about the little girl," Marjorie corrected.

Harvey nodded agreeably. "There's places that don't let go. You can feel them." His last remark was punctuated by the crash of a giant steel blade striking rock not very far off.

That machine could cover a lot of ground, Hal thought. This time tomorrow the remains of the old house would probably be gone.

19

Hal's father was mixing salad dressing. His finger and thumb were green from the herbs.

"They're digging for the road," Hal told him. "At Candlewood."

"Progress," Hal's mother responded, pulling up her chair.

Hal said, "We're supposed to finish our projects."

"Good. I do think Lew went a bit overboard with this."

Hal sighed. He was getting farther away from what he wanted to talk about. "Do you think Lew's a good father?"

Both parents set down forks and stared at him. "Have we led you to think we don't?" Hal's father sounded a little huffy.

"Mr. Atherton said . . . sounded like he thought it was Lew's fault."

"Bliss isn't aware of the whole situation."

Hal wanted to ask: But how can you tell what's good? If you can't judge for the present, how can you decide for the past? He said, "I was thinking about the Titcombs' great-grandfather. Eliza's and Hannah's father."

"What about him?"

"He set things up to keep Candlewood in the family, but it all depended on the son that didn't care about the farm. Why didn't he leave it to the wife and daughters that were willing to work for the place?"

"In those days not many women handled property."

"In Lowell, Hannah had her own bank account."

"Well, I don't know," his mother answered. "And I don't know the terms of the will."

"It was called an Estate per Autre Vie."

Hal's parents were visibly impressed. "How did you pick up a thing like that?" his father wanted to know.

"It's in Eliza's story. I don't really understand it, though."

"It's an old-fashioned arrangement. Peculiar. Leaves the property for the benefit of one person during the life of another."

"The older brother," Hal supplied. "The brother for the life of his mother. Only he was killed before he got home."

"I see. Then everything would just go along while the mother lived until—"

"But there was this fire. The mother had to go away to Vermont."

177

"I see," Hal's mother repeated. "An unoccupied estate. A mess."

"Yes, because Hannah thought the man who was marrying Eliza would take over the property. Which I guess he did. Hannah," he finished flatly, "tried to stop it. She thought her father would have wanted her to, no matter what. To keep the farm in the family. So," demanded Hal, "was he a bad father?"

Hal's parents shook their heads. How could one judge?

"But he taught Hannah all that about the farm, and yet he made it impossible for her to save it."

"He couldn't know his son would be killed," Hal's father pointed out.

"And most women weren't expected to assume material responsibility," Hal's mother added.

"Hannah was responsible," Hal countered. "She believed in him."

"Then," Hal's father told him, "at least *she* must have considered him a good father."

Hal digested that a moment. "Eliza didn't, though."

Hal's father grinned. "You can't win if you're a parent." He looked at his watch. "Judy, if we're going to make that meeting—"

"Please," Hal begged. "I don't understand."

Hal's mother gathered up the leftovers. "If this is for your report, why don't you pick something a little less subjective?"

"Like what?"

"Like comparing the old walled lane with the road that's going in there. Or the water table."

"I want to do Hannah and her father. People are always

178

saying someone's a good parent or a bad one, that a relationship is good or bad. Like with Lew."

"I am sure," Hal's mother stated firmly, "that you should leave this issue alone. It's too emotionally charged. I don't think you're even making a distinction between Hannah's father, who's been dead nearly a century and a half, and Lew, who's alive and perfectly capable of defending himself."

"But he's not!" Hal shouted at her as she went into the hall to put on her coat. "He doesn't think that way. He would never bother to explain."

"I tell you what." Hal's father emerged from the bathroom. "If you hold off till the weekend, I'll sit down with you and some library books and see if we can get some hard facts about differences in the value of money."

"I already know that," Hal declared emptily. "I know what Hannah was earning in 1839. And how much she paid to the Corporation boarding house. And that she had to pay for a glass of water when the canal boat stopped. And what the circulating library charged. I already know that when I took care of Emily on Wednesday afternoons I earned as much as Hannah did in a week working as a bobbin girl fourteen hours a day."

The next day in class Hal found himself surrounded by kids who had a firm grip on straightforward comparisons, of clothing or transportation, fuel or lighting, medicine or manufacture. So when it was his turn to say what he would report on, he mumbled, "Communication," and no one questioned what he meant by that.

When the school secretary rushed breathlessly into the classroom with a whispered message for Lew, everyone fell

179

silent. Lew's face closed, turned blank. He cleared his throat. "Sorry, I . . . I'm—"

"I'll take over," said the secretary, but as soon as the door shut behind him, the class was in an uproar. Bill flew to the window in time to see Lew stepping into a police car, which sped away. With only a few minutes left in the period, the secretary gave up. Kids rushed out, clotted into groups, streamed on.

Hal borrowed some change from Kim and went straight to the pay phone to call his mother. He wanted permission to go home.

"But there's no bus in the middle of the day."

"I'll walk. I'll—" He stopped himself from saying "hitch" just in time. "I'll go to the police station, see if anyone's going that way." He argued, pleaded, argued again. When his mother grew alarmed by his intensity, he gave in abruptly, forgetting even to say goodbye before he hung up. Then he walked out of the school.

At the police station he asked for Chief Durand and was told he was out. He reminded the dispatcher that he was the sitter for the missing Rifkin child.

"Aren't you supposed to be in school?"

"It's all right. I just called my mother."

"Well, they're over where the development's going in. Digger uncovered something."

"Something? You mean like a jacket? Mittens?"

"Can't say."

"I should've gone with Lew."

"Just a minute." The dispatcher called another officer from the back room. The officer, who recognized Hal, said he'd run him up to the corner of Nutters Hill.

180

"Oh, thank you," said Hal. "Thanks."

Hal ran all the way from the corner to the Titcomb driveway, only to find it blocked. The man on duty didn't know him and had orders to let no one through. Hal turned back to the road and headed for the newly graded entrance to the backland a half-mile on. Here again he was stopped. The officer there did know him, but wouldn't answer any questions.

Why? Hal wondered. What was he trying to hide? Cars drove up. People disappeared up the roughly leveled roadway that had been part of the woodland such a short time ago.

Hal retraced his steps till he was almost directly below the meadow. At least here there would be no road block, since there was no road. He started up, keeping close to the white pines that could conceal a cow, pigs, a stranger, anything. He got close enough to see the bulldozer, shut down and silent, the driver leaning up against it lighting a cigarette.

Cautiously Hal approached. "Hey," he called softly.

The driver looked around.

"Here," called Hal in an undertone. "Over here."

The driver saw him, beckoned him forward.

Hal said, "They won't let me near. I'm trying to find a guy named Lew Rifkin. Have you seen him?"

"I don't know who I've seen. All I can get out of anybody is that I'm supposed to hang around in case they need more digging."

"What for?"

The driver shrugged. "I'm not sure. First off, I thought I was into an old graveyard. You know, for cows and stuff.

181

But then I saw this . . . well, some guy said it's a child. The coroner, I think. Anyhow, they've got people falling all over themselves up there."

Hal said, "Could you go and ask Chief Durand if I can come? He'll understand."

The driver looked doubtful, but he headed up toward the northern ridge where the dump bulged out of the hill.

Hal heard voices, but couldn't decipher a word. He caught sight of more people, but no one he recognized. What else would he see when he went up? What could he bear to see?

The driver came striding down again. "Sorry, no luck. Chief's gone. They told me I could leave too. Someone from the state's there now."

"Did they say . . ." Hal couldn't speak the words. "Do they know who it is?"

"You mean the remains?"

Hal nodded.

"Something about a missing kid. I better get going."

Hal turned back toward the road. He couldn't run anymore, only put one foot in front of the other. Just off the shoulder, chickadees and nuthatches clustered around a doughnut bag and crumbs. A little farther on Hal saw a dented beer can and the plastic container for a six-pack. Stooping to pick it up before some hapless bird got caught the way the duck had, he tugged at the stretchy plastic, making red welts on his hands, but unable to tear the thing apart. When a car came around the curve and had to swerve to clear him, words erupted in a rush of anger: "Look out, can't you? Want to kill . . . kill someone?"

He expected the driver to be some guy drinking booze,

flinging beer bottles from his window, but as the startled driver passed him, he saw it was only a harassed-looking mother with a car full of little kids. And the kids, he was sure, gazing at the rear of the disappearing car, were all Emily's age. Each and every one of them an Emily, and yet none of them her, because there was only one five-year-old person who could be Emily, and she was gone. She was what the bulldozer man called remains, like this misshapen plastic container that someone had left lying half buried in the leaves and melting snow.

That evening Lew sat hunched with his knees splayed, his hands dropped between. His face was a wasteland, a ravaged plain with creases like erosion ribs.

Hal's mother knelt in front of him, placed a drink in his hands. He just held it. He said, "I tell you, Judy, I was so relieved that afterwards it hit me like the first time. Like hearing she was missing all over again. How could they have thought . . . ?"

Hal's father reminded him that Chief Durand had realized the error as soon as he learned it was only bones.

And what did *I* feel? wondered Hal. What can I feel, not knowing anything more than I did before?

Harriet, who had heard only that the bulldozer had exposed some animal bones, some notebooks and old artifacts, and the skeleton of a child, had nodded calmly. "At last. We'll bury Hannah beside Gran. We'll have Emily back now."

"How can you be sure it's Hannah?" Hal wanted to know.

Harriet had snapped at him, "You know it is."

But all they really knew so far was that the bones were

183

those of a female human about twelve years old. Thinking that now, he blurted, "How could she get there? Someone must have put her under all that stuff."

Lew said, "Maybe she was there first."

"Then how could they? How could anyone put junk like that . . . ?"

"Maybe they had no idea she was there. Maybe those notebooks will tell us something," Lew suggested. "Or whatever they are."

The notebooks, as Lew called them, were two stacks of loosely bound papers packed in a tin box found with the child's bones. The State Historical Commission had taken them to send to a museum that had techniques for freezing and separating the pages and then preserving them. They also had the other bones and things found with the child's remains.

Remains. A terrible word. Hal would never say it, not about a person who had lived. Bones was a better word. It made you think about what was solid inside yourself. He said aloud, "Miss Titcomb knows in her bones that it's Hannah," and instantly sensed his parents' wariness.

His father frowned. His mother got up to pass some cheese to Lew and Peggy. The doorbell interrupted her, and she went to the door with the cheese still in her hands.

"Oh, Bliss," they heard her say.

"Forgive my barging in like this, but I just heard the most extraordinary thing. Miss Titcomb. I was over there."

Everyone in the living room was perfectly still as Hal's mother led Bliss Atherton in. He nodded a greeting to Lew and Peggy, but he addressed Hal's mother and father. "Simply extraordinary. Miss Titcomb informed me that you, Judy, represent her. I couldn't believe my ears."

184

"I've been counseling Harriet Titcomb in some estate and domestic matters," said Hal's mother. "That's all."

"Not with Candlewood Acres?"

"Don't you think I'd have mentioned it when we were trying to save the land?"

"Well . . . yes, of course. But I was dumfounded. Look here, Judy, it means the old lady trusts you. It's just the break we've needed, especially since the bones and things will halt the work for now. I've a friend on the Commission for Conservation Archeology who says there's an automatic restraining order. He was out there, says some of the things from that site are remarkably intact. He mentioned an old footstove. Of course, the bulldozer charging in probably obliterated—"

"He's very good, the bulldozer operator," Hal heard himself declare. "He stopped as soon as he saw the bones of the cow or whatever it was. So maybe he didn't smash anything."

Bliss Atherton sighed with impatience. "You can't expect a bulldozer operator to care or be careful, or he wouldn't have that kind of job."

Hal opened his mouth to retort, but his mother announced that it was much too late to argue the merits of that occupation tonight.

"It *will* be too late," Bliss Atherton pursued doggedly, "if we don't act now. What about getting to work on Miss Titcomb?"

"I work *for* her, Bliss, not *on* her."

"Of course. But you know what I mean. Let me know as soon as . . . if there's anything I can do." He was on his way to the door.

The others stood without speaking until they heard his

185

car drive away. Peggy got her jacket and Lew's.

Hal's mother put her arms around Lew. His baggy jacket made him look like a pillow she was dumping into its case. "Don't give up," she said.

Lew mumbled something Hal couldn't hear.

"This thing today," she said, "has nothing to do with getting Emily back. The two aren't connected. Remember that."

Hal was wrapped in wonder. Because, no matter what his mother said or his father believed, Harriet Titcomb *knew*. And soon now they'd bury Hannah, give her her death and her resting place.

20

The car with the television equipment was parked outside the cemetery. "Let them come," Marjorie had implored as Harriet snapped, "None of that here!"

"It's historic, Aunt Harriet. It'll be recorded for posterity."

Harriet stamped one foot, then the other. "The Woodruffs will see to them."

The cold had descended over New England like a lid on a cauldron. All the juices and aromas coaxed into the air by the January thaw were stopped and sealed. Marjorie and Carl had fretted and fumed because the road work could not be resumed. The great yellow machine would not return before mid-March.

As soon as Hal's parents rejoined the group, everyone

gathered around the small box containing the bones of twelve-year-old Hannah Wray, which had been measured, labeled, and photographed. Bliss Atherton, through his friend on the Historical Commission, had seen with his own eyes where the skull had been broken by the cave-in. He told this to everyone, and Harriet queried sharply, "Who invited this person?"

"Now may the Lord bless you and keep you . . . ," the minister intoned. Hal stared at the stone marked ELIZA WRAY TITCOMB *1821–1916* that stood next to Hannah's grave. A blue jay raked the icy stillness, and then Sadie Duncan moved closer. A thin, stringy voice came out of her. "O God, our help in ages past," the words unwound. "Our shelter from the stormy blast . . ." The minister joined in and Bliss Atherton's rich voice swelled the sound: "and our eternal home." Harriet listened open-mouthed but silent. The cold afternoon dimmed; voices dropped away till there were only Sadie Duncan's and Marjorie's and the minister's singing, "Time, like an ever-rolling stream, / Bears all its sons away; / They fly forgotten as a dream / Dies at the opening day." When the hymn ended, Hal could hear the television crew talking out on the road.

While everyone was going to their cars and being invited by Marjorie to the Titcombs', a strange man fell into step beside Hal. Hal looked at him. He was the television guy that his parents had kept from the burial service.

"Mind if I ask you a question? You a relative?"

Hal shook his head. "A friend."

The man looked down the row of cars. "Whose?"

Hal nearly said, "Hannah's," but he answered, "The family's."

"I suppose this is pretty unusual for you," said the man.

187

What could anyone say to that?

"I suppose," the man tried again, "I suppose it makes you wonder what happened and all. What kind of girl she was."

Hal faced him, saw two of his crew right behind him. "I know what she was. She was a doffer. She changed the bobbins in the spinning frames. She came home to . . . to hold the land, to keep the animals, to save . . ."

The man gaped at Hal, then wheeled like a flash. "Get that?" he demanded of the man holding the camera. "Were you rolling? Oh, Christ!"

Hal watched the one man giving the other one hell. So much for what Marjorie called posterity.

"Hey, kid, you want to run through that again?"

Hal shook his head and went off to the car.

Back at the Titcombs', in the newly decorated front room Marjorie served hot spiced cider.

"Let's go out," Lew suggested. He led the way up through the orchard. In wordless agreement they stopped above the cleared dump. Hal could see the slabs that formed the opposite walls of the stone cellar that had been carved out of the hillside long before it had been buried under junk. Everything, even the debris, had been carried off to be inventoried and examined. Hal touched the stone that had roofed the child and then killed her. Part of a broken beam still protruded, its rotten end thrust skyward, its butt lodged in the hill.

He started down toward the place where the ducks had splashed and fed, where the cow had gone to drink, where they had endlessly worried lest Emily come to harm there. Would strangers in another generation find what was left of

188

Emily? Hannah, at least, had been able to account for herself a little. She had left marks, a message, her letter, and probably much more in her notebooks or journals. Her very presence haunted this wood. But Emily could scarcely write more than her own name.

Hal turned to Lew. "I . . . I have to go home. Need to."

Lew came back from his own distant thoughts. "Your parents—"

"No, right away." He couldn't tell why. He knew only that he had to be home.

"Okay, I'll take you."

As the car slowed at the driveway, Hal tensed. "Just drop me," he said, opening the door.

"I'll run you all the way," Lew offered.

"No!" Hal was off, tearing down the hard driveway. His legs jarred as he pounded the rocklike surface. Just as he reached the door, he heard the telephone ring. Keep on ringing, he willed it, dashing in. Don't stop.

"Hello!" he gasped. "Hello!" he shouted.

"I have a call from Emily," the operator said. "Will you accept the charges?"

"Yes, yes."

"Go ahead."

"Emily! Oh, Emily, are you there?"

"Hal?"

"Yes."

"I was afraid I'd be wrong again. There's so many numbers."

"No, you're right. It's me. Are you all right? Where are you?"

"The burger place."

Hal sagged against the counter. "Yeah, okay," he said. "Which one? Where?"

"I don't know. The same one. I want my daddy."

Hal suddenly understood how tenuous this connection really was. He pulled the telephone close. "Listen, Emily, you've got to find out where you are. Can you ask someone?"

"I don't know. She won't let me talk to anyone."

"Where is she now?"

"Bathroom."

"Okay, just ask someone. Don't hang up." Hal tried to sound calm and commanding. "Just ask and come right back and tell me."

There was silence. Had she gone already? "Emily?"

"What?"

"Do what I said."

"I want my daddy."

"Yes, yes. Find out where you are, Emily. You have to do it before she comes looking for you."

"Wait. I'm dropping my french fries."

"Ask the person nearest you. Never mind about the french fries."

"Will you wait?"

"Of course. Hurry up and do what I said."

"Okay."

There was silence again. Hal strained to catch some words in the general hum of voices he could hear through the receiver. While he listened with all his might, he could almost feel the hand that reached out and set the receiver, with a click, back in place. The line was dead.

Hal's first impulse was to call Lew. But what if Emily

was dialing again this very minute? What if some stranger had hung up, not the person who had Emily? What if Emily was trying to get through to him before *she* came looking for her?

The thing, Hal told himself, was to decide exactly what to say next time. Every word might count. If only he could tell Emily how to call Lew without confusing her.

He checked the time on the kitchen clock. Nearly six o'clock. They must be having supper. But what if they were far away, in a different time zone? Oh, why hadn't he made her read off the numbers on the telephone? Well, he could do that first thing when she called back.

But the phone did not ring. Hal waited nearly half an hour. When he saw the headlights of his parents' car, he dashed to the door. He was already yelling out the news as they pulled up.

"What on earth . . .?" his mother exclaimed.

Hal was incoherent. He grabbed them, railed at them for taking so long.

"Emily?" His father scowled. "Hal, pull yourself together."

"You wait in case she calls again. I'll go and tell Lew." Hal raced out, with his mother calling after him to zip up his jacket. He banged into the Thayer house, startling Sherry and Peggy, already babbling about Emily's call.

Lew appeared in the doorway. "What's up?"

"Oh, Lew." Peggy burst into sobs. "Oh, God, it's Emily. She's all right."

All through Hal's account Lew stood immobile. Afterward he stepped sideways and slumped against the wall. "Hamburger place." He gazed vacantly, not at anyone. "She could be anywhere."

"But she's all right," Hal said to him. "Aren't you glad?"

"Glad?" Lew gave Hal a queer sort of smile. "Jesus." He dropped his face in his hands, but his fingers stayed clenched into fists. Hal saw the knuckles whiten. Then he saw tears wet them.

Peggy's sobs became snuffles. She blew her nose.

"Can we call the police now?" Hal ventured. "They might be able to trace the call. It was collect."

"If it was collect," Lew returned, his voice a trace more gravelly than usual, "it'll be on their computer." A lopsided grin broke through the creases and tears. "Collect, huh? You taught her that?" He lurched forward and caught Hal up in a great, clumsy hug. "Collect! How do you like that?"

Even after Chief Durand met them at the Woodruffs, and sounded a note of caution, their elation couldn't be quelled.

"Sooner or later she'll call again," Peggy maintained.

"And we'll get the detective going," Hal's mother put in.

"Once we get that call located," Hal's father added, "we may get some help from the courts."

Chief Durand turned to Hal. "You're certain Emily said 'she'?"

Hal said he was, though he felt funny about what he couldn't say.

"Is there something else?" Chief Durand spoke in a soft, insistent voice. "Something else you want to tell us?"

Hal shook his head. How could Harriet Titcomb's pronouncement about Hannah have any bearing on Emily's real whereabouts? Harriet was a very old woman with a lot of peculiar notions. "No," he said. "I told you exactly what happened."

192

Then Chief Durand did a strange thing. He caught Hal by the shoulder and very deliberately turned him so that they were eye to eye. "Is there any chance that Miss Titcomb might know something?"

Hal gasped. He couldn't speak, couldn't even blink.

"Is there a chance Emily might try to reach her?"

"She couldn't."

At this moment the phone rang, and everyone whipped around. Hal's father answered, but the call was for the chief from the telephone company. Hal stayed long enough to be sure that nothing specific was being communicated. Then he slipped away from the others. He went to his room and closed the door.

His glance fell on the telephone. No wonder Emily saw it as a daffodil; it seemed to nod at him. But it was the old Reader that brought him across the room. Taking it, he sat down on his bed with Lesson 149 open beside him. His fingers spread out, gathering in the texture of the yellow paper, its small, thick black print. Hannah must have felt it too, and after her Eliza straining against the emptiness to find some echo of Hannah's recitation, binding all who looked on and felt and smelled these pages.

He needed to feel with his mind as well as with his fingers. A page was a thing; it was Hannah's self he reached toward. His eyes picked out the phrase "a hundred years hence." Backing up, he read, "The hours of this day are rapidly flying, and this occasion will soon be passed. Neither we nor our children can expect to behold its return. . . ."

Yet in a way Hannah had returned. Was Emily a part of that returning?

He shut his eyes and imagined Harriet Titcomb with her

eyes shut too. Harriet would not be surprised to learn that Emily had called. Perhaps she already knew.

It wasn't until the next day that Hal found out where Emily had called from. St. Louis! He couldn't even place Missouri, which prompted his father to mutter something about what they ought to be teaching in school, including major rivers and state capitals.

"Lew says we can look up things like that."

To Hal's surprise, his mother agreed. All Lew needed to do was call airline reservations and let *them* worry about how to get him to St. Louis.

His father pursed his lips, and there was a brief, rather heavy silence. Then Hal asked whether Lew was there already and when they might hear from him.

"There may be nothing to report. It may take a long time." His mother went on to say that in all the excitement she had forgotten to tell him that a large portion of the journal had been readied for transcription, though the museum was still working on the damaged part. "Anyway," she told Hal, "they've confirmed that it's Hannah's."

"It had to be," Hal answered. "The thing about Hannah is that she sticks to . . . She said she'd keep a journal. I just don't understand how Harriet knew . . ." His voice trailed away.

"Knew what?"

He couldn't come right out about Harriet's certainty that Emily would show up as soon as Hannah was buried. "Knew that Emily . . ."

"You mean with respect to Hannah?"

He nodded.

"Oh, Hal, if Hannah's burial were today instead of yesterday, do you think that phone would not have rung with

194

Emily at the other end of it all the way from St. Louis?"

Hal drew a long breath. "I only know it did happen that way. Not any other way."

Hal's mother picked up her coffee and then set it down again, dabbing irritably at what sloshed over the rim. "Fond as I am of Lew, I've strong reservations about the way he's got you thinking."

Hal's father grunted and gave her an I-told-you-so look.

Later on in Social Studies class, while the substitute teacher announced that Bernie was going to report on the ropewalk, Hal whispered to Josh, "They don't believe Hannah has anything to do with Emily calling."

"Thought they loved the past and all."

"In its place," Hal responded. "I think they want it to stay put."

"Hal," asked the teacher, "is that a contribution to this discussion?"

All day Hal chafed to get home. By bus time it was snowing hard. The wind bit into faces as though it meant business.

At home the phone was ringing. Why did he always have to answer it on the run? He kicked the front door closed and grabbed the phone. It was Sherry. Could he go and feed the goats and ducks and hens, please? It looked like a long time before anyone would make it home.

Outside again, the wind lifted him, pushed him along. "Everything's going to be all right," he told the ducks as they gobbled their cracked corn. The chores done, Hal had to fight against the storm. He was so sure the phone would be ringing that when it wasn't he was brought up short. He waited in the stinging wind, then dragged out his last steps to the door.

When the phone did finally ring, he was already settled in the kitchen with cookies and milk.

"Hello?"

"Hi, dear. Looks like we won't be home for a while. Don't wait for us if you get hungry. You could heat up some—"

"Did you hear from Lew?"

"Several times. It's pretty discouraging. I'll tell you when I see you." She sounded tired and depressed. "All right?"

"All right."

"And the tuna—"

"I'm fine. I'm eating now." Hal hung up. He flipped open his math book, then slammed it shut. He turned on the television, but it was that awful children's-hour stuff, so he turned it off again. Back to math.

The phone rang, and he thought, Saved by the bell. "Woodruff residence," he declared with phony elegance.

"I have a call—" the operator began, and before she could finish, Hal was shouting, "Yes, yes! I accept, yes!"

"Hal?"

"Emily!"

"I did it again." She giggled. "I didn't think it would work. I'm standing on some telephone books."

"Your father's looking for you. He's—"

"We're at the airport. She's in the bathroom. She's throwing up. She thinks I'm in there too."

"All right. Now listen carefully. Are you listening to me?"

There was no answer.

"Emily!" he screamed.

"What?"

How could he do this right? If he panicked, he'd lose

her again. "Listen." He was hardly aware of what he was saying. "Go right back to that toilet. Where you were. As fast as you can. Talk to her, so she knows you're there, and take off all your clothes. Do you hear me?"

"Why?"

"Do it!" he yelled. "Everything! Stuff it all in the toilet. So it's wet, Emily. Everything."

Emily giggled again.

"Don't tell her what you're doing. Get out of that bathroom before anyone can stop you. Run where there's lots of people. Okay? Someone will come. A policeman or something."

"She'll come. She won't let me near any policeman. She says they're bad."

"Emily, listen. As soon as there's someone like a policeman, start yelling. Tell him to call the chief of police in Westwick, Massachusetts. You can remember that, can't you?"

"What about my clothes?"

Hal was sweating so hard he had to tighten his grip on the receiver to keep it from slipping. "Never mind the clothes. See, she can't take you anywhere with no clothes on. So do everything I said, and—"

"She'll be mad."

"Emily, please. Hurry. Remember, the chief of police. Say the Westwick police are looking for you. Quick, now."

As soon as she was off the line, he realized he didn't even know if she was still in St. Louis. And he didn't know whether the bags were checked. If Emily were caught before she got out of the bathroom, she still had a chance if there were no fresh clothes for her to wear.

Shaking, he dialed the Westwick police number. He

197

spoke in spurts, repeating himself, stumbling over his own words. They understood, though, were ready for the call that might come in at any moment from an airport somewhere in North America.

"Will it . . . will you let me know?" he stammered.

"Hold on, son. You just sit tight."

That's what Hal did. He barely breathed. He kept thinking of what he might have done or said; he kept shaking his head. If it doesn't work, he thought, it will be my fault. Not Lew's, not Harriet's or Hannah's; only mine.

He went over the conversation again. Had Emily really understood? Everything depended on timing, getting to the john, getting out again ahead of her kidnapper. Just far enough ahead to cause a stir. Those airport security people or the police would be around. Then it wouldn't matter what the kidnapper said. Even if she said she could prove she was Emily's mother, there would be this naked child screaming about the chief of police in Westwick, Mass. And they would have to check.

Hal glanced at the clock. It was nearly fifteen minutes since Emily's call. Too long. Something had gone wrong. And if Emily had tried and failed, she wasn't likely to get another chance.

He waited five more minutes before lifting the receiver and calling the police again.

"I'm sorry," he began. "It's Hal Woodruff. Did they call?"

"Yes. We'll get back to you."

"But is it all right? Where was she?"

"Buffalo," the dispatcher replied. "Going to Canada."

Canada, thought Hal. Then she would have been out of the country: Gone. He let that sink in for a while. Next he tried to get used to the idea that it was over, that Emily would be home. He found himself grinning at the thought of her, stark naked, hurling herself into the midst of tired passengers and harassed flight personnel, like a force of nature that no one could possibly ignore. I bet they got a blanket or something to wrap her in, Hal told himself. He laughed aloud.

21

Even during the first thrill of Emily's return, with Lew overjoyed and everyone congratulating Hal on his quick thinking, Hal could feel a letdown. His parents must have noticed, because they pointed out that Emily might not be herself for a while. She could regress and become babyish, even destructive. It was to be expected, they said.

But nothing prepared him for Emily's stridency, for the taut expression of calculation that made her look prematurely old. Lew didn't help. He indulged her in everything except her compulsion to brag about her adventure. Peggy told Hal that Emily's kidnapper had doped her, probably to keep her quiet. No doubt she had· encouraged Emily to call her Hannah for the same reason.

No one at the airport had actually identified the kidnapper before Emily was in the hands of the authorities. The woman had just melted away in the crowd.

The first Wednesday afternoon that Hal had Emily, she kept pestering him for attention, until finally he blurted, "You know what, Emily? You're spoiled."

"Well, are you going to read all that while I'm here?"
He dragged himself up out of the typescript of Hannah's journal. "Later on I'll play fish with you."

"What'll I do now?"

"Oh, Emily."

She met his gaze with her own sullen, wounded stare.

"Go watch television. You keep telling me your . . . the woman let you watch it whenever you wanted. Well, you can watch it now."

"Why do you say 'woman'?"

"Why do *you* say 'Hannah'? Hannah's dead and buried."

"I thought Hannah was lost. Like me."

"Well, now she's found, like you. Only she's dead."

Emily pulled her knees to her chin. "What happened to her?"

"If you let me read this, maybe I'll find out."

"Read it to *me*. Come on, Hal. I know her too."

"Later. Go watch television."

Emily marched out of the room muttering, "It's no fun anymore."

Shrill, manic television voices filled the house. God, she was watching one of those game shows. A woman squealed, and a man bellowed to the audience, which cheered and stomped.

"Emily!" Hal shouted. "Emileee!" He got up and went to the door.

"What?"

"Turn that down."

"It *is* down. I can't hear when it's down."

From opposite ends of the hall they glared at each other.

"All right." He sighed. "I'll read this to you."

Emily started toward him.

"Go back and turn off the tube," he ordered.

She skipped back in time to a brassy fanfare and an announcement that Hilda DeVoe had won a trip for two to the fabulous— Hal never got to hear where the fabulous place was.

"I love you," sang Emily as she flung herself onto Hal's bed. She grabbed the quilt. "This is my best time."

He said, "Well, don't expect me to start all over."

"How will I know what's happened?"

"Nothing's really happened. It's not a story, Emily. So far it's just about how she came from Lowell and found that John Titcomb had already started to pay off the taxes. So she thought she had to stay at Candlewood, but without being found out."

"Why?"

"Because she'd be taken away."

"Like me?"

"No, by the Overseer of the Poor. It was the way the town used to take care of people."

"Why didn't she want to be taken care of?"

Hal said, "Because she had to save the land, save Candlewood. Emily, why don't you just let me read?"

Emily straightened. "But why?"

"It was how she felt." How could he explain about Hannah? "It was her home. She knew every stone and every tree. She knew all the shortcuts, like where the cows went to keep cool and the sheep to get away from the flies."

"How do you know that?"

"She says so."

"I want to know what she says."

"Well, you will from here on. Listen. 'September. Third Sabbath.'"

201

"What does that mean?"

Hal exploded. "I'm not going to read."

"Hal!" wailed Emily.

"Then shut up. It means the third Sunday in September." He would leave out things like dates and words that could only lead to interruptions.

" 'I have cleaned the cellar shelves. I found the barrel of soft soap newly made this summer and have scrubbed everything. All that remains is the floor, which is still littered. There is enough sand in the corners for a proper sanding once I've cleared it out.

" 'It rained for two days since last I wrote. I began to feel quite sorry for myself. Nothing would dry out. The friction matches from Lowell would not strike, but I have my flint and tinder, and now the footstove is working. Each day I find more to comfort and sustain me. There is some tallow, so I shall gather rushes as long as they remain green, and of course cut candlewood. How glad I am to have the old rushlight holder.' "

"What's a rushlight holder?"

"It holds the sticks that burn. I'm not exactly sure how. Let me read. You can ask your father later on."

Emily sighed deeply, but Hal ignored her and went on with Hannah's journal:

" 'I never thought to bless the tangled weeds, but they have kept the squash and pumpkins hidden. I came upon them while gathering grapes, and now must set myself the task of clearing the field before frost. I can wait to pull the turnips, for they will bear much cold.

" 'Is it not a sign of Providence that all lies ready about me? Truly Grandfather named this cellar well when he dwelt within it before our house was raised. It will be a

202

keeping-room once more and not just a cellar in the hill to store things in.

" 'A while ago I heard the bell in the village call folk to meeting. How I longed to join them. Still, I will sing a hymn of praise as I go to find a sharpening stone along the brook. I shall sing Mr. Watts' verse: From all that dwell below the skies, Let the Creator's praise arise; Let the Redeemer's name be sung, Through every land and every tongue.' "

"Go on," murmured Emily.

"That's all for that day."

"Then what?"

Hal turned the page. The typescript left a space after each entry.

" 'Wednesday,' " Hal read. " 'I could not wait for Sunday to write my news. This morning three sheep returned, the ram and one ewe with lamb at side. Now I have four hens in trees, the rooster that joins me in my doorway, the five call-ducks on the pond, and the three sheep. To celebrate, I pulled a few turnips, some to store and some to let them nibble as a treat. Shall I have enough to keep them through the winter? What if Brindle returns or one of the other cows? The ewe knows me and comes right up. Soon I shall have gentled her half-grown lamb.'

"September. Fourth Sabbath," Hal read to himself. Then, aloud, " 'The cellar is ready. I even have a proper bed of corn husks which I have covered with sweet grass. My shawl will be my coverlet. Soon I shall pluck some wool to bind round my legs. Perhaps later I shall devise a spindle and knitting needles and make real winter hose from the yarn. But for now, the apples must be turned and dried, nuts gathered, and wood piled.

" 'The days are still and warm. At times I hear voices clear across the valley. I hear the Moodys' cows lowing. I light only the smallest of fires, for the smoke could bring someone. How glad I am that the trees beyond the pond were spared and keep me hidden. The beech is only scorched and is backed by a line of hickories and oaks to the north.

" 'October. First Sabbath. The days grow shorter. At twilight the scarlet maples stand out like flames behind the burnt tree trunks. The ducks are quarrelsome, as if they sense that when the fire dies, winter will glaze their home. The sheep are fat on acorns and meadowgrass. I have found one rusty scythe that Nathaniel must have dropped and forgot about. I sand and sharpen it as best I can, but when I go forth to cut the yellow grass, most of it bends before the blade and I pull the mangled hay by its roots. I have begun one stack in a blackberry thicket. The other is my very roof, and will serve two purposes, sheltering my keeping-room and providing fodder for my beasts when the snows are deep. I have tried to bring the roof out from the cross-beam, though I lose much light in this way. I believe that when my grandfather lived here he kept an opening in the thatch behind the roof slab. I shall try to find timber the proper length for support. If I could have one tool now, it would be an axe. Instead I must forage for my wood. There is little white wood left among the charred timbers of the barn and house, but I have not yet finished digging through the ashes.' "

Hal glanced at Emily, who was nearly asleep.

"Go on," she murmured, but couldn't suppress an enormous yawn.

Hal read on, certain that soon he could lapse into silent reading. " 'It is hot work pulling grass and building the stack. I cool off at the pond, then hurry back to work, knowing how swiftly the weather can change. The grass itself is poor, overgrown with weeds and headed off. As I return to my small keeping-room, I think of coming home from the field to Mother's cool water sweetened with molasses.

" 'I can't help thinking as well of the lemons we bought for last July 4th, Eliza, Dorcas, Minnie, Lucy and I. I recall how the taste of the countryside on that picnic and the scents of the grass and wildflowers made me yearn for Candlewood and hay-making. How displeased Eliza was at my moping. So here I am now, and thinking of Lowell. Shall I always think of the place I am not in? Truly I have no longing for the chattering girls nor the mill itself and the way it made my ears throb with the din of machinery long after I lay abed.

" 'Here each sound comes at night as a single voice. I realize now that I grew accustomed to work and read and think with the constant clamor in the background. Now I hear owls and the cries of animals and the brook. Oak leaves make one sound, maples another. The sheep chew their cud in rhythm, then all cease at one instant, alert to something away in the darkness, while the ducks are murring and muttering in their sleep. Off across the valley there are cows and horses and people speaking among themselves, each to its kind. A dog barks, and another answers from the other side of Candlewood. I am alone and not alone. Eliza, I say. I say, Mother. Nathaniel. I speak his name with that command that would bring him to his poor clumsy feet. Though no one answers, I feel them here with me. And then I say, very softly, Father. Father, I whisper. Father.' "

For Hal, Hannah was no longer a ghost conjured out of her sister's account, out of a couple of letters with their convincing voices falling silent at the end of a page. At some point he had given up reading out loud to Emily, who was sound asleep. He was barely aware of reading at all, for now Hannah simply existed. Not in his time, but not out of it either.

He turned another page of the journal transcript, his mind traveling faster than his eyes, until he caught a single line: "Fen has come! He was here this morning. It was as though he had returned from a night's wandering, heard me calling, and come home. He looks well and cared for. I must be grateful to some kind neighbor. I hugged him and laughed and cried for joy.

"October. Third Sabbath. I fear that Fen may bring someone here, for he comes and goes. With the leaves gone, I feel less protected than before. Yet not one person has come, though I have twice heard voices, both times from the west face of the hill. I am certain that at least once it was John Titcomb.

"October. Fourth Sabbath. Now I know how Fen has managed to come and go and that my anxiety was well founded. On Friday last in the blue cold light of a harvest moon, Fen dashed out, tail a-wagging. I believed that all was over, that it must be Mr. Hinckley come to fetch me away or John Titcomb himself. I huddled in the darkest recess of my abode. Yet Fen never barked. Then I heard the mutterings that I knew so well. Nathaniel.

"I determined to remain hidden. Every time I thought myself safe, I would again perceive his clumsy footsteps stumbling through brambles and sticks of branches I had gathered. When he commenced to weep, his crying drew me out of this darkness.

" 'Now then, Nathaniel,' I addressed him. 'What is this grief?'

"The poor fellow ceased lamenting at once, but for a long while uttered not a sound, only stared.

"I wondered that I could speak so sharply to this pitiful youth. I had kept myself from flinging my arms about him in such greeting as I gave Fen.

"Finally he told me what he could of himself. He resides now in the barn of the Widow Gooding, Fen with him. He has but one cow to milk and the wood to chop and split. Time falls heavily on his broad shoulders. I suppose it gives him fancies that cause him to babble like a true idiot.

"He drew me with him to the charred remains of the barn and made as though to lift something from an imaginary wall. It might have seemed the antic of a demented soul, but I could tell he meant to show himself carrying the lantern from its peg. Down he crouched, I with him, just as when we struggled to save Brindle from the bloat after she ate the withered cherry leaves. So there must have been a stricken cow thrashing out as they do, and she must have kicked over the lantern. Nathaniel flung himself back, then, wailing, pulled me from the place. He beat his head against the elm stump. I tried to quiet him. He rocked, I with him, as when I rocked my rag babies in their basket by our hearth. I told him everything was not lost, else I would not be here, nor the keeping-room with its good things and its hope for the future. Though I doubt he understood much of what I said, he grew still at last and slept.

"While he slept, I repaired to my keeping-room and tore a precious leaf from my copybook. I wrote a modest request for tinder, a small quantity of flour and meal and salt, and a length of rope, all items the Widow Gooding might demand. As I laid aside my quill, I thought to add a sweet for Nathaniel. Then why not two? My mouth watered at the prospect of Turkish delight. Then I counted out money enough to pay for these items and went to wake Nathaniel."

Hal read on. After carrying out his errand, Nathaniel returned to Hannah more often than she thought wise, but she made good use of him for heavy work, like carrying a stone already shaped for holding oil-soaked pine splints that made up her candlewood. He also dug potatoes, and with them Indian arrowheads which became invaluable tools.

Meanwhile Hannah rummaged in the ashes of her home, finding nails, a pot, and a fireplace crane. In the fields and woods they found more precious objects: a gunny sack, two wooden spouts and a trencher that Nathaniel had carelessly left among the sugar maples, and a tapping iron, which made a fine chopper. Hannah used it to concoct a kind of molasses out of the pulp of beets and squash. This she added to the nuts and acorns she mashed together. With a frost-specked apple chopped in, it could have been a Thanksgiving pudding except for the bitter aftertaste from the acorns. Nothing, though, compared with the feast she made with the cornmeal: a delicious johnnycake which she couldn't keep from gobbling all at once.

Using her best arrowheads to peel the slivers of wood, she intensified her preparation of rushes and candlewood until she ran out of the yellow lard oil in which she soaked them. She saved enough maple bark and butternut shells to set some ink, though she lacked sufficient filings and vinegar to finish it properly. As for writing implements, she had goose quills enough to spoil several before she cut a perfect center slit. She kept her writing things with her copybooks in her mother's airtight cake tin.

One night Nathaniel brought her a headless hen. She made every attempt to determine whether it was the Widow Gooding's, then eventually made a fire, scalded and plucked the bird, and boiled it with turnips and potatoes, well salted, as it was already high. She shared the meal with Nathaniel, and then informed him that his visits must end.

"He became so agitated I feared trouble. I promised that if he did my bidding now, in the spring when Mother returned to Westwick and I came forth from my hiding he could be with us again. But if his visits gave away my hiding place, he would spend the rest of his days in the Widow Gooding's barn.

"He came no more. I was relieved, yet more lonely than ever." And winter set in. Hannah counted her shelves of roots, the apples in their nests of dried weeds, her nuts, her remaining ink, her candlewood tapers and bundled rushes, her dwindling supplies of untried lard and tinder. Wasn't this after all, she asked herself, the way her grandfather, Elijah Wray, had provided for his first winter here?

"Sabbath. After Thanksgiving. I have been unwell. I was cold and could not catch my breath. I longed for water. I had many summer dreams, of hay-making and cider, sweetened lemonade, and the beans to be weeded and fresh-baked pies. But I am not hungry. I need to wash myself and my clothing. I dread the darkness, but fear to spend my rushlights and candlewood. Even bundled, the rushes burn so quickly. It is too dim to read inside, too cold out. I sleep much.

"December. First Sabbath? A momentous week. Now I am about again, I have commenced feeding the animals, pine boughs for the sheep and seed cases for the fowl. There is still one open spot on the pond for the ducks. I recollect Father telling me he caught pickerel there when he was a boy. When the ice thickens, I shall try to fish from that spot if it stays open.

"The splendid event was finding hoof prints by the pine boughs. My first joyful thought was of Brindle, but there came Bestor. He stood to have his broad face stroked and his neck rubbed. He looks thin, his brown eyes standing out, his shoulders sharp, so he must have been away from his new home for some time. I know I cannot winter an ox with what I have stored, but I will use him while I can and let him feed on the frosted pumpkins.

"December. Second Sabbath. Even without a yoke, Bestor has hauled much wood. Should I have another spell of fever, I shall not lack fuel. I know it is a risk to surround my keeping-room this way, but I have made small piles to have them less noticeable. Bestor has a sore on his neck from the rope. Even with the gunny sack wrapped round, it cuts him.

"A duck was killed last night. It is too bad. Father said they were too small to eat and were only to lure other ducks for shooting, but I believe he would have kept them for their beauty if they had called no wild ducks. The one that was killed never uttered a sound, but the others raised a terrible fuss. I see afresh how no creature may depend on life. Since that small death, I have begun to

210

chip my initials into the door sill of our house. I am using an Indian flint. Now if I sicken again and do not recover, there will be proof of my occupation of Candlewood. After the letters, I shall gouge the month and year.

"December. Third Sabbath. More snow. John Titcomb was here. He was so amazed to find Bestor he scarce looked about him. The sheep were away along the brook. He had a companion to whom he mentioned Eliza and her anguish over me. I could almost smell her scorchy apron and never came so close to giving myself up.

"He stood not six rods from my roof, looked about him, and, seeing nothing, remarked that the ox must be claimed. Then he marched away. The snow had covered the most obvious signs of my presence. Yet he was blind to all around him.

"I made haste to cover my initials. Bestor hauled with all his might till he dragged the northwest cornerstone onto the sill. The stones are nearly matched, each cleanly dressed. With brush piled around them, I think they will soon seem as one. When Mother returns and I can reveal myself, I shall oppose any claim of John Titcomb with that carved stone, even though I did not finish with the month and year.

"I pulled a great wad of wool from the ewe. It is thick with grease and I have applied it to Bestor's wound. At sunset he put his nose inside the doorway, shifting from one foot to the other, until I fed him two turnips. The ram is greedy and must be beaten off to let the ewe and shearling at their portions. It is nearly Christmas, and it felt right to share my stores with these homing beasts.

"New Year's Day, I think. Bestor is gone. They came for him. Not John Titcomb, but others at his bidding. I

211

heard them coming and sent Bestor down toward them so they would not come this far. He was unwilling to leave me. I followed, waving a stick and hissing. I struck him such hard blows on his flank that he leaped forward and trotted down toward his captors. I hastened back to conceal myself. He will always have this remembrance of me whipping him, sending him away.

"It is very cold. I let the lamb and ewe inside, but must tie them near the door to prevent them taking roots stored at the back. Though they dirty the keeping-room, they also warm it, and that limbers my fingers to write.

"I have lived here four months and am halfway through my vigil. I have lost one duck and still have three sheep, the hens and rooster, and, rarely now, dear Fen. I wonder where they have taken Bestor. I think he will not be driven to Brighton for meat, for he is too thin. By the time he is fattened, his willing nature may save him.

"If I must work in the mill again, I will first start the spring planting. I wonder if there will be the money to bring Bestor home. And Brindle too, wherever she is. Someone will surely know. Mother will tell me. And she and Nathaniel will manage during mid-summer, when a new house may be started. I wish I had listened more to Father's schemes for borrowing. How clearly I recall his dying words instructing me on the seed-grain to procure for the next season, but with no provision to pay for it.

"My mind dwells on coming here, how I followed the river as it flowed away from Lowell, how overjoyed I was to leave those high brick walls, to find at dawn farmhouses and barns, gardens and orchards, fields and grasslands and potato plats, the herds of neat cattle and the flocks of sheep. I recall that kindly lock-tender, and the two men in

212

their queer boat. How unhurried they were, those two, while I could scarce stand still. One of them had a way of measuring with his eye all manner of things, a lily pad, a dragonfly, the far horizon. Our paths crossed by chance, he journeying upriver, I fleeing down. I cannot help but feel that if he had stood above my keeping-room instead of John Titcomb, not one thing would have passed his notice.

"My next entry will begin my second copybook. If only I could tell Mother and Eliza that I am not lost, but safe and keeping."

As soon as Hal slapped the folder shut, Emily started, then sat up. "What happened? You stopped reading."

"You fell asleep," he countered.

"I don't remember." Her voice trailed off, then returned, charged. "You can tell me, though. Tell me everything."

"Those ducks." The thought slowly deepened into conviction that Emily's pair from Candlewood pond must be direct descendants of Hannah's. "Your ducks, Emily. Hannah had ones like them. Hers must have been the great-great-great-grandparents."

Emily started laughing. "No one has that many greats."

"Ask your father."

She grew thoughtful. "Father," she repeated softly, as if tasting the sound on her tongue.

Hal supposed she was trying out a replacement for "Daddy," but to him her whisper seemed like an echo of Hannah's muted call.

Emily jumped up. "Daddy!" she proclaimed. "We'll ask my daddy!"

22

Lew allowed Hal to postpone his report until the second journal was transcribed. So Hal listened to everyone else in class. Brenda said wearing a bonnet must have been the pits, but going barefoot super. Amy said teeth were the worst, and smells. Bill said being out of school and learning a trade at fourteen beat anything he could think of today, but the wages were crummy. When someone started in about pollution and what a tannery in the center of town must have been like, Kim maintained that a tannery made sense because Westwick had plenty of uncleared land supplying tanbark. Bernie argued that Concord must have had lots of woodland too back then, because that was how come Thoreau could go and live by himself at Walden Pond and build a little house in the woods without bothering anyone. Then all the kids launched into the pros and cons of wilderness and farming, whole grains and processed foods, energy and conservation, and pretty soon it was a free-for-all.

Lew let them unwind. They even made johnnycake and old-fashioned mincemeat to celebrate the end of the project. They planned to see how long the leftovers could be stored without refrigeration, but the leftovers mysteriously disappeared overnight.

It made Hal wonder whether there could have been any signs of the remaining food that Hannah had stored. He asked Lew about it, but all Lew could suggest was that with the ox there the decay must have been excessive. As soon as Hal tried to imagine what it must have been like, all he could think of was Hannah not being found. He asked Lew why someone, Eliza's husband-to-be, for instance, hadn't suspected something was wrong there. Lew thought John Titcomb would have stayed clear of the stink except when he had his own refuse to dump.

"But then he'd have *seen*," Hal insisted.

"He'd have seen the ox, not the child. She was under the roof, completely buried. He'd have been hauling stuff from the present Titcomb house that he was building then, and he'd have just thrown his junk over the hill."

Hal wanted to consider other possibilities, but Lew was involved in his new class project, which focused on immigration and ethnic diversity, and he didn't want to dwell on the Candlewood situation.

But for Hal the questions about Hannah were still hanging.

"Why bother about it?" his father asked. "You'll soon have the second journal."

"It's over," his mother reminded him. "She can't benefit now from your getting hooked on her. Listen, Hal, a sense of history is a fine thing. But if it gets out of hand, if it comes to mean more than your present life, that's a kind of retreat or escape. This preoccupation pulls you away from the real world. Which you have to live in."

"Look," said his father, "we don't want to get in a hassle with you. We just—"

"Why not?" Hal suddenly flared up.

"Because it would be counterproductive," his father told him.

"Counterproductive," said Hal. He hated words like that. Why didn't his parents ever just yell like Bill's mother? "You know what I think?" His voice was constricted with helplessness. "I think maybe you're like other people's parents that don't approve of the guys they're hanging out with, that's all. You don't approve of Hannah because she did this weird thing, and it looks like suicide, and you think she's a dangerous example."

The next day, on the way home from school, Hal asked Josh what happened when his family talked things out. Josh supposed it ended up with majority opinions. Or who was loudest.

"Not in mine," Hal reflected. "It's the quiet ones that win."

Josh asked, "Is it Haunting Hannah?"

Hal nodded.

"If I were you," Josh advised, "I'd just shut up about her. Anyhow, now that we know the kidnapper was Emily's mother, that finishes the time slip."

"I hope it *is* finished. You know she took off as soon as she saw Emily being listened to. I just hope she stays away."

"Don't you ever wonder how he could have married someone like that?"

"He only did because she was pregnant. She thought she wanted the baby, then changed her mind."

They bounced along, staring straight ahead, not talking. Then Josh looked out. "Hey!" He stood up. "Missed my stop."

"Come on home with me, then."

They got off across from the Titcomb driveway.

"Maybe she wasn't even his kid," mused Josh. "Wouldn't that be something? I mean, after all of this?"

Hal was staggered. The idea hadn't once occurred to him.

Josh suggested looking for things the frost might have heaved up since the archeologists were at Candlewood.

216

When they got to the hillside, they found nothing.

Josh jumped down into the cleft in the rock. "Do you think you could have lived here through the last storm? With what she had, I mean."

"The cold was worse than the snow," Hal answered. "And being alone."

Josh shook his head. "I guess they had weirdos then too."

Hal knew that sooner or later he would have to respond, to speak for Hannah. The way he would for Josh if Josh needed him. The way he had for Harriet Titcomb when Carl and Marjorie were pushing her around. You did that for someone who was helpless or absent. Or lost, like Emily. You didn't just forget them or let them be forgotten.

But he didn't have the words for what he had to say, so he took Josh to the Titcomb house, only to find Harriet in a sour mood, carping about everything Marjorie did. The kitchen smelled of disinfectant, not of ginger and apple.

As the boys were leaving, Marjorie mentioned that she wanted to speak to Hal's mother about some new plans. "We think it might be a good idea to have a local lawyer speak to the Board of Appeals and the Planning Board for us."

That evening, when Hal delivered Marjorie's message, Hal's father said, "Bliss's hand, I think. He's been after them to set aside that one area for conservation," and Hal's mother said, "She ought to know I represent Harriet and Harvey, not her. I'll have to make sure she understands." A moment later she asked, "Did you just happen to meet Marjorie, or were you at the house?"

"We stopped in for a minute," Hal answered.

"We?"

217

"Josh. He came home with me this afternoon."

"Oh, good!" Hal's mother exclaimed. "Oh, Hal, I'm so glad to hear that."

On the verge of explaining, Hal thought better of it. Better to take Josh's advice and just shut up.

Before Hal's mother got back to Marjorie, Harriet Titcomb fell and broke her hip. The Woodruffs planned to visit her in the hospital on the weekend, but on Saturday a late March snowstorm swept the Boston area, dumping over a foot of heavy, wet snow. The radio reported power lines down and extensive tree damage; the public was urged to stay off the roads.

In the middle of the morning Bliss Atherton showed up looking like an abominable snowman. He had just talked Carl and Marjorie into setting aside a conservation area and he was so elated he had to tell the Woodruffs. "Of course it'll give them more clustered house lots, but it's worth it, isn't it?"

Hal's mother was surprised that they could make decisions like that with Harriet away in the hospital. Bliss Atherton said they seemed to be taking her absence very much in stride. Carrying on.

I'll bet they are, thought Hal.

After Bliss Atherton left, Hal's mother observed that it was time to have her talk with Marjorie. She started dressing for the storm, and Hal ran to get his things. They went out into a wilderness. The light had a greenish cast, tinging the misshapen trees with the eerie look of tropical forests. Some branches seemed to have doubled over; one limb almost blocked the driveway. The snow underfoot was dense and slippery. There wasn't a single car on the road

218

between their house and the Titcombs'.

Wasn't it awful, Marjorie clucked, what the weather was up to these days . . . ?

Hal went through to Harvey's room. The television blinked blue light across the old man's sleeping face. Back in the kitchen Marjorie and Carl were talking a mile a minute about their new plans.

"Something like a shrine for that poor little girl," Marjorie was explaining. "To commemorate her sad story."

"Some television station wants to dramatize it," Carl confided. "Called it a genuine piece of Americana. Didn't he, Marjorie?"

She nodded. "About human endurance and tenacity."

Hal's mother looked from one to the other. She managed to say nothing.

"And we thought," Marjorie went on, "not a shrine exactly, but more like a restoration, like Thoreau's cabin. Something tasteful." She paused expectantly.

"I see," Hal's mother said presently.

In the silence that followed, Hal asked if Harvey knew.

"He doesn't even know about that poor child's bones."

"Yes, he does. Because of what Miss Titcomb said. Because Emily came home." He refused to meet his mother's eyes, but Marjorie picked up her disapproval and quickly assured her they had no intention of playing up silly superstitions. They were going to be strictly historical, with authentic reproductions, like a little museum.

As soon as he could, Hal tried again. "I mean, does he know about Miss Titcomb being in the hospital?"

Marjorie laid her head to one side like a hen contemplating an egg-gatherer. "What good would that do him?"

219

"Doesn't he miss her?"

Marjorie smiled. "He has no idea of time, so it doesn't make any difference."

"Wouldn't it be better for him to know the truth?" Hal's mother objected. "She's his own sister."

"Look," said Marjorie, "I take good care of him. You won't find him soiled now, at least not for long. I can tell what he needs and what he needs to know. So why rile him?"

Hal went back to Harvey, who was awake now and looking out the window. He told Hal about a blizzard long ago when the snow came all the way up to the second floor and the cows went two days without milking and the bull was buried alive. Hal shivered. How long did it take to find the bull? Harvey wasn't clear about that, but the bull was good as new anyhow. They brought hay to him because the snow built up like walls and it was weeks before he could be got out. And not one cow in the whole herd developed mastitis, not one.

By Sunday afternoon the Woodruffs were able to drive to the hospital, but the visit was a dismal failure. Harriet Titcomb clutched the sheet to her throat and glared at her visitors. "It's not right," she charged. She seemed confused too. She called Hal, Abel. Why wasn't he home cleaning out the chicken house like she said? Hal's mother sent him out to wait in the corridor.

Later she came and told him to go in to say goodbye. Hal sidled up to the bed, trying to avert his eyes from the wisps of hair and the blue skin and the terrible, bruised-looking eyes.

"Stand where I can see you," Harriet ordered. "Look at me."

220

Hal stepped closer.

"You're not Abel. You're nothing like Abel. Why didn't you say so?"

Hal said, "Who's Abel?"

"Never mind," she snapped. Then, crossly, she commanded him to leave Hannah's second journal alone. "You're not to read it first. Don't even touch it."

Hal understood. She didn't want him to find out anything ahead of her. "I'll wait," he promised. "When you come home, I'll read it to you."

"That's right. Now go."

As he started to leave, she called after him, "Hal, if you read ahead, I'll know. I'll *know*. Do you understand?"

"I won't," Hal assured her. He couldn't help adding, "I wasn't even thinking of it. I only came here to tell you I was sorry."

She bristled. "Sorry for what?"

Oh, Lord, thought Hal. You couldn't even tell her you were sorry she'd broken her hip without risking insult. She was impossible. Instead of trying to answer her, he said, "I'll tell Harvey I saw you."

She rose up on one elbow, grabbed for the sheet, and flopped back. "Tell him," she said, "tell him . . ."

Hal waited for the message.

"Tell him this is a terrible place. Tell him, whatever happens, to stay put. You hear?"

Hal said he heard. He said he would deliver her message. He said he hoped to see her soon, which was a lie, except that it would mean reading the rest of Hannah's journal. Except for that.

At home Hal's mother commented on how hard it was for elderly people to adjust to infirmity and to changes in

221

their living arrangements. Hal's father grunted an assent. But when she mentioned that it must be just as rough on Marjorie and Carl, Hal retorted, "They're the reason she's in such a rotten mood. Are you going to let them turn the keeping-room into a shrine?"

His father started up from his newspaper trance. "A what? Judy, what's he talking about?"

Hal's mother said evenly, "A kind of museum to go with selling antiques. A retirement business for them. I didn't mention it because it won't happen."

"Bliss never said anything about—"

"I doubt anyone confided in him."

Hal's father threw back his head and roared.

"What's so funny?" Hal demanded.

"Wait till Bliss discovers he saved the old Candlewood farm site for soft ice cream and pizza."

Hal's mother was laughing too, but she said, "You know, they mean well, and I can't let them go on believing it can work out that way."

"How *will* it work out?" Hal asked stiffly. He still didn't see what was so funny.

His parents couldn't spell that out for him. Like all these things, they supposed, it would probably end in some kind of compromise.

23

Two weeks later Hal was able to visit Harriet Titcomb at home.

"Can you carry up some ginger ale?" Marjorie asked him. "She's supposed to drink a lot."

Hal traipsed upstairs with a glass for Harriet and one for himself. He called ahead so that she wouldn't be caught unaware. He found her listless, with a kind of sadness he'd never seen before. She gestured toward the bureau, and he saw the transcript of Hannah's second journal.

"The glass is too full." She spoke faintly, not querulously. "Marjorie never remembers I can't hold it that heavy."

"I'll get another glass."

"No. Read now. When you've drunk some of yours, I'll have the rest."

Hal looked around the room. It faced east over the orchard; very little afternoon light entered the window. The peach-colored wallpaper made you think of a nursery, but the bed was dark and heavy, the lampshade scorched, the bedspread patched.

Harriet seemed to have shrunk. She sat propped by several pillows. She wore a small knitted cape around her bony shoulders. Her elbows stuck out from it, and they looked raw and swollen.

Hal gulped down enough ginger ale to let Harriet handle the glass, and then he opened the folder. " 'January,' " he read. " 'What a long month. I sleep much, or rather keep to my bed for warmth. But this morning, when I woke to the clang of a bell, all befogged I thought myself too late for breakfast, that I must rush to the mill before the gates were shut. Then I realized my confusion. I thought of Lowell and the throng of us at Mrs. Keeler's table, how we barely swallowed the last morsel before the bell sent us to the yard. Back and forth and forth and back, the bell summoning us, the bell dismissing us. I minded those long winter days in the mill, but minded most the bell which drove us. Yet how ready I was to spring up this morning, and with scant hope of sustenance.

" 'It was the Meeting bell that woke me. I think of visiting the village at the next Sabbath. The idea warms and cheers me more than my one daily hot meal. I am not rushed at my eating as when I ran obedient to the Corporation bell. I savor every bite to tell myself I am fully satisfied at the end of the meal. Some days it is very hard to set aside some of the cooked turnip and potato to eat cold in the evening.

" 'January. Sabbath. A bitter week. The fowl huddle, all puffed out, feet tucked up beneath. Fen came one night, curling beside me and warming me through, but I was not sorry when he left next day, for Nathaniel may have greater need of him than I. A hen is failing and I think of killing it. I am so taken with the thought of eating that chicken that I hardly trust myself.

" 'This week I pulled wool from the sheep and made leggings. Spinning is out of the question, for even if I had a spindle my fingers would be too cold to handle it.

" 'January. Sabbath. Last week I lost courage, it being so cold, but today I went to Meeting. Several carts passed me, but no one paid much heed to this bundled walker. Only at the village center did I hang back, waiting through the first verse of the hymn, singing under my breath. It was one of my favorites, O God Our Help in Ages Past.

I wanted to stay and sing on, but after one glance through the window I took myself off while I might still go unseen.

" 'On the way home, knowing all were at Meeting, I stopped at Mrs. Moody's. The dog barked, then wagged its tail when I spoke it down. I looked into the kitchen, then entered. The heat and aromas brought tears to my eyes. I don't know what devil possessed me, but I reached up and plucked a shiny onion from the beam. Clutching it, I ran away, heedless of footprints, but fortunate that the light snow continued to fall. That onion is here now. I know Mrs. Moody would gladly give me it, yet I am uneasy. I slip its clean shell. Will I eat it? I don't know. But returning it is out of the question.

" 'Mother would press her lips and Eliza speak of right and wrong, but I do not think it clear what is right, what wrong, what good and what bad. For I have wronged Eliza while acting in good faith according to Father's most fervent desire. I suspect that Father would laugh at this theft and then bestow some extravagant gift upon Mrs. Moody. O God our help in ages past, I sing to myself. I do love a good strong hymn. It thrusts away confusion!' "

Harriet said, "She must have liked that at her burial. And it was Sadie Duncan, old Moody's great-grandchild, that sang for her. Read on."

The next entry began with a vow to write less and make the paper last till spring. " 'I killed and cooked the chicken with turnips and the stolen onion. I could not stop myself eating every last morsel. True, there is not that much meat on a famished bird, but I would have done well to save some. As it was, I suffered a terrible cramp. I know someone like Mrs. Sherwood would find justice in my suffering after eating of stolen food.' "

"Rubbish," commented Harriet. "You must tell her, Hal. Tell Sadie."

What was he supposed to tell her? he wondered. "Don't you see Mrs. Duncan now that you're home?"

Wearily Harriet shook her head. "Too hard."

"But you should have a telephone up here. You could talk to her." He would speak to his mother about Harriet all alone in this dim room.

"Will you go on?"

" 'February,' " read Hal. " 'First Sabbath, I believe. A terrible week. I tried to fish without a proper hook at the open hole above the spring. I had my catch all but cooked in my imagination. At length I gave up, but my sitting there must have warmed and weakened the ice, for when the ram later went to drink, the ice gave way.

" 'I heard the cracks like lightning shafts. I ran for rope and did what I could to save the poor creature, but he thrashed so I could not tie the rope securely. At last, his wool soaked and heavy, he drowned. The pond was like a broken looking glass, all slivers and peaks, sharp and cruel. My legs and hands were badly cut, but I could not feel them then. Afterwards I took the ewe and lamb with me into the keeping-room, lit my footstove, and huddled between the woolly creatures. I shivered all the night, not only from cold, but with the horror of that death.

" 'The next morning I hauled the ram to the bank. I cut some of the wool, which came in stiff wads. I thought of how he had leaned against me as though I were a scratching tree when I had pulled the fleece for my leggings. It was only after I bared a patch of skin that I thought of the mutton. By the time I commenced cutting, it was growing dark. I could not bleed the animal nor gut him. The wind grew bitter and he was frozen stiff. With some meat from the brisket, I resolved to complete my work in the morning.

" 'But a bobcat's awful screeching woke me during the night. The ewe and lamb were inside with me. I thought of my ducks and hens. For three nights the bobcat returned to tear away at my ram. Foxes came too. I could hear them battle over the carcass. Lastly crows dropped from the sky, till the bloodied mess was shrouded in black feathers. I have tried to smoke some strips of the mutton, but the fire is too small, the smoke too dangerous. So I have eaten heavily again.

" 'February. Second Sabbath. No momentous event this past week. Yet I must confess my growing fear for this place and these creatures should I meet a fate like that of our ram.

" 'February. Third Sabbath. Having finished the mutton, I take stock of myself. If an accident should happen to me, the sheep might browse awhile and find their way to a barnyard. But what of Candlewood? How could I prove my occupancy? If I die, will not the bobcat find me too? Five days after the ram drowned, nothing was left but some wool which fringed the edge of the pond and clung to the brush the carcass was dragged through. By spring the birds will have gathered that fleece for their nests. There will be no trace of him left.

"February. Fourth Sabbath. The cold continues. My fingers will not bend. I tried to spin from a stick and weight, but the thread was lumpy and broke. Weakness shows in all I attempt. I think of going to the Moodys', perhaps to Nathaniel, but cannot imagine the consequences. I imagine little but the sheep waiting for fodder and the ducks and hens at my empty doorway.

" 'March. First Sabbath. The light stays longer, but I am colder. I have cut my meals. I wrote a message on the slate my mother kept to mark the levels of the kegs. I scratched as hard as I might, so a passerby could not fail to see it. I took it to the double oak, the one Caleb and I called brother and sister after ourselves. Before he sickened, it was our secret home where we were safe and sound. After Caleb died I kept my rag babies there in the crotch of the tree while I worked with Father, and later on I left things there for Nathaniel. If something happens to me, might not Nathaniel look there and take the slate to show someone? I dared not take the time to finish all I meant to write, but set the slate with its unfinished message that called on its finder to look for the cows.

" 'Why do I think of Lowell now, of camphene lamps and hot bread and sheets, of books and lectures and school? If I went back now, I might someday become a teacher and have scholars of my own. Am I wedging myself as tight as that slate into this place? I wonder if it matters whether the message I scratched is finished or not. It may never be found. It could lie there for years with the bark growing over it. If it is found, it may seem the scrawl of a child leaving clues in a game of hunt the treasure. Only someone like Caleb would take up its challenge. I need a friend, a sister or brother, who will know that someone meant them to stop and look. Perhaps some person I do not now know will read it and seek Brindle for me.' "

Here Hal broke off. Harriet nodded in silence. After a while she spoke.

"Well, Hal. So you came. Finally. A friend, a brother."

Hal said nothing. He was filled with a sadness that was like loss.

Harriet asked, "Is there more?"

Hal nodded. He didn't want to reach the end.

"How much more?"

He riffled through the typescript. "It's almost over," he said.

" 'March. Third Sabbath. Heavy rains. The keeping-room is muddied and full of filth. It reminds me of the hovel we passed one Saturday afternoon on the road outside Lowell. It was a dwelling of mud and grass for a poor Irish family, children in hideous rags, an infant with sores all over its face. Dorcas said the Irish bring disease and unthriftiness. Eliza said they will work for nearly nothing and therefore bring down all our wages. We hurried from the stench of them and the look of them. I kept thinking, They are people, they are like me. But I could not imagine myself living that way, except in my dreams.

" 'Perhaps I am dreaming now. Perhaps I will wake up dry and warm and clean. To run to the window, looking for the sun and apple blossoms and Fen driving the hens from the garden.

" 'March. Fourth Sabbath. It is snowing. It is as though I fell asleep and missed summer and fall. Yesterday spring seemed here. The red-tipped oaks and the lacy white shad were well along. The ducks had begun nesting. Like the wild fowl, they vanish for a spell. That is when many fall prey, for they will not stir and so are plucked right up and eaten. The survivors lead their babies home, tiny creatures no bigger than dandelion heads marching out of the woods. Every creature of sky and water and earth will feed on them, yet they cannot be kept like the barnyard fowl. So we cherished them all the more and looked to their return each spring, and they so small and quarrelsome

229

and proud, with nothing to give us but their bright beauty.

"'Of course the scraggly hens come scolding to my door as soon as the weather worsens. Now they have settled in at the far end of the keeping-room. The sheep lie here facing the storm. Then Bestor reappeared, I know not where from. He pressed his dear face toward me as though he too would share this shelter. Glad as I was to see him, I had to push him off, for his shoulders squeezed against the jambs and I could hear the roof creak. Snow and straw fell from the lintel.

"'I have just been out to view the storm. All is overcast with a shadowy green. Bestor makes a path for me through the drift that builds against my hill. The wind howls. All within my keeping-room are quiet. Do they fear this storm? I am uneasy because it rages out of season, but the ewe chews her cud and is calm.

"'I have many pages left, but I think not many days before I may show myself. I feel restless, anxious to be out and free. Here the moisture beads the walls and I can scarcely write without blurring. The candlewood smokes and sputters. I bring my tin box to the writing-stone, so that if the candlewood fails I can set my journal in its place and keep it dry.

"'I think of Nathaniel, who is so alone. We must care for him always. Nathaniel is like Bestor and Fen and the sheep and hens and ducks. Only the ducks cannot be safe. Out in the storm they huddle on their nests, each alone in the green whirl. Will branches weighted with snow bury them? It would be terrible to find them blotted out by the snow, and all their eggs with them. I will not allow such thoughts. Winter is behind us. We are safe and— I had to

230

stop just now, because Bestor stirred and sucked the light right out. I slept awhile. I cannot tell what time of day it is, but I woke as Bestor settled at the doorway again. Quickly I struck a light. Now Bestor lies with his head inside, his eyes shut, his great mouth grinding.

" 'Now, without haste, I will put away my journal, cover it tightly, and write a list of things to procure at the shop when soon I come forth. I shall start with soap. No, bread. Only I see the confectionary shop window in Lowell, and the bakery with its aroma escaping into the street. I hear nothing. Perhaps the storm is already over. I will finish my list while the light lasts.' "

Hal and Harriet sat without speaking. Gradually the room darkened. Still they sat. They could hear, as from another season, a car drive up. A door slammed. Strident voices broke through the eternity of Hannah's final words.

Then someone came stomping up the stairs. "Harriet? Where's the light? Harriet? Hal?"

Hal recognized Gertrude Atherton's voice. He jumped up to switch on the light.

"Don't leave me," Harriet said to him.

He turned to her. "I'll have to go home soon."

"I should have died when I fell."

"No!"

"Harriet? Oh, there you are." Gertrude Atherton filled the doorway, bringing with her fresh, crisp air and a huge spray of forced forsythia.

Hal said, "You had to know."

Gertrude said, "Well, how are you feeling?"

Hal said, "You needed to know."

Gertrude Atherton took his place beside Harriet's bed.

231

He said, past her, "I'll keep coming. I'll bring Emily."

"Will you visit Harvey?" Harriet demanded. "Will you take messages to him for me?"

"Of course," Hal told her.

Gertrude Atherton said, "Don't you have a telephone up here? How can you stay here all alone without some way of getting in touch with people?"

"Who would I call?"

"Me," declared Gertrude Atherton.

"Me too," said Hal.

"You mustn't cut yourself off," Gertrude Atherton continued, "and I for one won't let you."

Leaving them, Hal had a very good feeling about bossy Gertrude Atherton. There were forsythia petals all over the place and a feeling of open windows and scatter. It was almost as if Harriet were about to discover, because she had no way of avoiding it, that she and Gertrude Atherton had something in common, if only the way they went at things head on and with all the force of their definite personalities.

24

"Put the whole thing behind you." That's what Hal's mother told him after she arranged for Harriet's telephone, letting Marjorie think it was her idea. "Now you can finish your project and put the whole thing behind you." Hal had looked at the frozen brown-and-serve rolls waiting to go into the oven and thought of Hannah's memory of the bakery aroma escaping into the streets of Lowell.

At his desk later he swiveled in his chair. His room was as cluttered as Harriet's was bare. He liked his things. He liked knowing that even his old ant farm was buried back there somewhere.

"Can't get started?" His father was in the doorway.

Hal said, "I keep starting with the end."

His father walked into the room. "You're thinking how awful it was the way it happened."

Hal could feel his face going hot. He turned away.

"It had to be instantaneous."

"How do you know? You just want me to feel—"

"Listen, Hal, it had to be. Because of the ox. The ox wouldn't have been found right there. It would have pulled away. Don't you see? The whole roof must have collapsed so suddenly it got him too."

"Bestor," said Hal.

"What?"

"The ox." He looked at his father. He spoke carefully, choosing his tone as well as his words. "Does Mother have to work?"

His father looked stumped.

"Do we need the money? Is that why she works?"

"We could live without it. Not the same way, though. But that's not the only reason she works. Are you saying you wish she didn't?"

Hal thought that what his mother did, say with Harriet, was wonderful. Or with Lew. She could really help people. "She's not like some of my friends' mothers," Hal answered. "Not like Bill's."

His father nodded guardedly.

"So why does she want *me* to be like . . . like Bill? Why can't I be different too?"

Hal's father opened his mouth, then shut it again. A moment later he said, "We just hope we haven't cut you off too much, living the way we do."

Suddenly restless, Hal got up, wandered around the room, then stopped and picked up the telephone.

"Feel like getting it installed?" asked his father.

"Could I give it to Miss Titcomb?"

"Oh, Hal."

"She'd like it because it's old-fashioned."

"Well, it's yours to do what you like with."

"I want to give it to Miss Titcomb."

Hal's father, on his way out, asked, "Want me to tell your mother?"

"Oh, would you? Thanks." Parents could surprise you sometimes.

After his father had gone, Hal sat down and began to write: "Candlewood Farm. Until this year, the changes at Candlewood were mostly due to road building and the disruption of Ragged Brook and the swamp growing and the pond getting smaller, and also second-growth woods in place of cornfields and grazing land. . . ." He described the walls and the meadow and the standing beech tree, and all the rest.

Then he came to the second part of his report. "Communication. Westwick had its first postal service in 1825." He thought how Hannah could hear the church bell, the cow in the barnyard across the valley, a dog answering a more distant dog. The screech owls and the hooting owls, the crows in January, the ducks murring in February, the

234

peepers in March. Each season had its callers, its listeners. But was this communication?

"Today," wrote Hal, "we can call the fire department or police or doctor. Back in the nineteenth century a house could burn down before anyone knew there was a fire. That happened at Candlewood." But didn't it still happen right in the middle of the city with people all around? "There has to be someone there to hear the call, to answer."

What was he trying to say? Weren't there telephone numbers you could call for certain messages? Dial-a-Prayer or Dial-a-Joke. And there would be a recording. Was this communication? He scratched what he had just written, and began instead with, "A telephone call can save a lost child. . . ."

He shoved his chair back. It was no good. He couldn't write about the wonders of instant communication. He knew that without that telephone Emily could not have reached home, that Harriet would be cut off and feel herself a captive. But what had this to do with Hannah? The stone she chipped her initials into and then had the ox cover; the slate with its message jammed in the oak; the journals. These were her telephones. Even so, Hannah could remain alone and lost, because no operator would ever ring and inquire: "Will you accept a call from Hannah Wray?" Nearly a hundred and fifty years ago Hannah had made the call with all the equipment at hand—stone and flint, slate and stylus, copybook and goose quill and butternut ink.

"It depends," wrote Hal, "who picks up the phone. Someone has to answer, or the phone leads to nothing but a machine repeating a prayer or a joke or a busy signal."

His hand was shaking. Maybe he should change his

235

topic. Maybe he could do canals instead. Only, wouldn't that be like refusing the call?

He turned back to his messy paper and wrote, "Some very old people don't like the telephone because they grew up not used to it." He scratched that too. He went over to his shelf and picked out Pierpont's Reader. Opening it to the Daniel Webster address, he read, "The hours of this day are rapidly flying, and this occasion will soon be passed. Neither we nor our children can expect to behold its return."

Candlewood had its orange stakes and yellow bulldozer, the filled pond, the road. Webster was right. You could not return to what was.

He began to copy for his report the part of the speech addressed to "those who shall stand here a hundred years hence . . . to survey . . . the progress of their country during the lapse of a century." He skipped to the section Hannah had loved: "And when, from the long distance of a hundred years, they shall look back upon us, they shall know, at least, that we possessed affections, which, running backward, and warming with gratitude for what our ancestors have done for our happiness, run forward also to our posterity, and meet them with cordial salutation, ere yet they have arrived on the shore of Being."

Hal could hear some wise guy like Bernie Gower asking, "What's the connection? Get it? Connection." Hal wasn't about to stand up in front of the class and assert that there was this ghost named Hannah with a message from Daniel Webster. He wrote, "Hannah Wray was a caller. Nathaniel couldn't carry the message, though a hint of it came through his grief, enough to haunt Eliza and make her children's children believe in Hannah's presence."

236

What did it have to do with what people called communication? Nothing Hal could put into words. Except this: that maybe ghosts were what people dreamed up to remember something they were afraid of forgetting, something that needed to be passed on from one person to another, from one time to another.

Hal jumped up. Whom could he talk to about this? It would just upset his parents. Lew would be troubled too, because he wanted Emily to forget Hannah. That left Josh, who'd always liked the idea of Haunting Hannah.

Hal started down the hall, then stopped short. You couldn't just call up someone with an idea like that. They might be in the middle of a game or an argument or a television program and not really listening to you.

He went back to his room and brought the unconnected telephone over to his desk. A daffodil? Why not paint it like one? He could even give it a green stem. Harriet's room would never be the same!

The very next day, Sunday, Hal used Peggy's acrylic paints on the telephone. It was a gray, drippy day. Inside the Thayer house kitchen something delicious bubbled on the stove. Lew and Peggy took turns lifting the lid, adding herbs, throwing in more diced onion.

Emily, stretched out on the table, inspected the flower head. "Now is it my turn?"

"Not till I get to the stem."

"But I want to do the yellow. I don't like green."

Peggy said, "Get some eggs, Emily. You could paint them for Miss Titcomb."

"Can I take duck eggs?"

"Only if they're not under the duck."

Emily ran out, returning a few minutes later with a

237

small egg in each hand. Hal looked up. The eggs had a translucent look, off-white with a greenish tint. Like the snow, he thought, Hannah's last snow.

Lew helped Emily spread newspaper and find her own brush. Outside, the fitful spitting turned to a drumming rain. Emily finished her garish eggs and set them on a plastic freezer cover to dry. Hal put a few last touches to the receiver.

Lew and Peggy began to set the table around the spread newspaper. They asked Hal if they should set a place for him. Lew was thickening the pot-roast gravy when Mac and Sherry came in. "Pot roast?" Mac inhaled. "Let's open a jar of applesauce."

Cleaning up at the sink, it came to Hal that this pot roast was the cow. He could feel his throat close. He continued washing, shaking out the brushes. He hadn't said he was staying; he could just go quietly away.

"Here." Peggy handed him a bunch of celery. "Stick this under the faucet, will you?"

Hannah had spoken of the meat of the ram as mutton. This was beef. It hadn't been a cow for a long time. It was pot roast of beef with carrots and potatoes and homemade applesauce on the side. Hal brought the celery to the table and helped himself to a slice of Sherry's oatmeal bread. By the time he had eaten half of it, a full plate was in front of him and he dug in.

At school on Monday when Hal gave his report, he mentioned the two call-ducks from Candlewood pond and how there had been ducks of that kind breeding there since at least the early nineteenth century.

"Not anymore," Lew broke in.

"Well, no, they're in a cage now, and the pond's—"

238

"Not anymore," said Lew. "I was going to tell you."

Hal stared at him.

"Gone. As of this morning. Someone left the cage open. Must have been a raccoon got them."

Hal remembered Emily, an egg in each hand.

After school Hal went directly to the Thayer house. No one was home. He walked through to the back, to the duck cage. White feathers, some bloodied, were strewn everywhere. The cage smelled rancid. He saw one bright orange duck foot stuck in the wire mesh. That was all.

He was staring at the webbed foot when out in front a car door banged. He felt someone come up behind him. It was Emily, who looked pinched and miserable.

He started to speak, but she spun away from him.

"Don't you say anything," she railed. "Don't talk to me." She ran, not back to the house, but over to the goat pen.

He found her plucking burrs from a dead burdock beside a pile of sawdust and manure. One by one she stuck the burrs to her sweater. When they failed to hold, she pulverized them.

Hal wanted to say that it wasn't her fault, that anyone could have left the door open, but the look on her face kept him from speaking.

She said, "I wish I had some of that medicine. No one here takes care of me like she did."

"It wasn't good for you. You weren't sick."

"It was so. So was the french fries and candy. It was good, and you don't know anything about it."

"How can I if you don't tell me?"

"I'm not supposed to talk about it. About *her.*"

Lew came out with a manure fork and basket. Without

239

even glancing their way, he began to clean out the duck pen. Emily went over to watch him. She watched in silence, then walked away. That left Hal. And Lew.

"Why don't you let her talk about what happened when she was away?"

Lew raked dank straw. "I just don't want her turning the Hannah thing into a myth."

Hal said, "I don't know what that means." Lew sounded like his parents.

"She can't handle the real truth yet."

"How do you know what's real for Emily?"

"Well, I can't have her believing Hannah's her mother."

"But you don't even know she believes that. You're not listening to her."

Lew shook out the fork. The stench of slimy bedding rose between them. "Right," he said after a moment. "All right." His eyes met Hal's. "What did you say to her?"

"Nothing. Nothing any good."

"All right," said Lew again. He went to look for Emily.

Hal took up the manure fork. The orange foot was gone now, so it wasn't too bad. It felt good doing something. It must be awful to be Emily and too little to be useful.

The following weekend, after the telephone extension was installed, Lew wired up the painted telephone, and Hal's mother drove Hal and Emily to the Titcombs' for the presentation.

Marjorie was in fine fettle, surrounded by a number of priceless antiques recovered from Hannah's cellar hole. She also had the original journals, now back from the museum and packaged in plastic.

Hal clutched them to his chest, the telephone in his fingers, the receiver dangling. Up he went, Emily behind him with her basket and the two painted call-duck eggs. His mother stayed behind for a word with Marjorie.

"What's this?" Harriet, in bed, picked one egg out of the basket that Emily proffered. "What's this?" she exclaimed, setting it down and taking the other. "Such spiffy eggs. Really and truly."

Emily grinned. She pressed up against Harriet, whispering, "One is for Harvey."

"Of course," Harriet retorted. "We always share. Are you going to take it to him now?"

Emily scooted off, and Hal came forward, slipping the journals onto the bed and presenting the telephone, which Harriet eyed warily. Hal's mother walked into the room, but Harriet had eyes only for the yellow daffodil head, the green stem in her hands. She stroked the mouthpiece. Real mouthpiece or real flower? How do you know what's real?

Hal held his breath. Harriet began to laugh. He had never heard such laughter. It seemed to come from a time long before she had become old. Soon Hal and his mother were laughing too.

Then Harriet fell back against the pillow. She pulled a handkerchief from under her sleeve and wiped her eyes. She looked at Hal and spread her arms wide. "It's splendid," she told him. "Splendid."

Then she poked at the bound journals. "Go ahead. Look inside."

He turned back the plastic cover and saw Hannah's writing, the faint brown scrawl on almost equally brown paper with ragged edges and some wormholes visible. Some pages were so torn they were stitched into fresh paper margins like picture frames. Hal turned page after page. He felt his mother leaning close, looking. All of a sudden he knew he was coming to the end, and it was real, with blots where the quill had split and smudges from condensation. On the last page with writing there was more blurring, some of the words smeared and indistinct. Then came a blank space. There were five empty pages in all.

His mother reached over his shoulder. "It's not the same," she murmured. "Not like the typescript." Her fingers rested on the spotty brown paper with nothing on it but the marks of its age and condition.

Harriet nodded. "They will be yours, Hal."

Hal's mother drew back. "Oh, no."

"They will. Hal is the closest to her." She smiled. "He even has the right initials. My grandmother named her son Howard and insisted that all his children's names begin with H. So there you are. I want it in my will."

"But Carl's your closest relative. And these journals must be valuable."

"Carl and Marjorie would use them."

"Why not? They belong to our local history."

"Not like that." Harriet spoke with a firmness that put an end to argument. Then she added, looking directly at Hal's mother, "Hal will know what to do with them."

On their way downstairs Hal's mother said, "Marjorie and Carl were telling me some of their plans. I suspect they have a real flair for this sort of thing. Of course the Board of Appeals won't let them run hog-wild—"

"Did you say something about the hogs?" Carl broke in, coming from Harvey's room with an empty plate. "They're all over the place these days. Keep running into them along Nutters Hill Road."

"Someone actually will hit one if the town doesn't do anything about them," chimed in Marjorie. "What will

242

people think, coming to look at Candlewood Acres and finding pigs?"

"Maybe when the building starts," said Hal's mother, "the pigs will go elsewhere."

And what happens, Hal wondered, when they run out of elsewhere?

"Is it time to go?" asked Emily. She handed Harvey's mug to Marjorie, then turned to scrutinize the things from the cellar hole lined up on the counter.

Hal's mother started for the door. "Coming, Emily?"

Emily reached up and pressed the jaw of the rushlight holder, which opened.

"I bet you're wondering what that funny thing is for," Marjorie declared.

Emily let the iron jaw snap closed. "It's for holding the candle sticks," she said. "They burn at one end. You have to keep moving them."

"You're clever to know all that." Marjorie didn't sound too pleased. "Who told you?"

Emily regarded Marjorie with her dark, solemn eyes. "Hannah used it," she said. "I know about it because I asked."

None of the adults said a word. Hal shot Emily a look of triumph, but she seemed unaware of having created any kind of stir.

25

They were up extra early because it was such a gorgeous morning, but only Hal was dressed. Here it was, nearly the middle of May, and they hadn't even got the peas and spinach in. But finally this weekend they were going to start their vegetable garden.

When the phone rang, they all three groaned. After a delay Hal's father went to answer it. He returned saying, "Harriet Titcomb. Some garbled message for Hal."

Hal slathered butter on his English muffin. "What?"

"Nothing, really. About dandelions. I said I'd tell you."

"Tell me what?"

Hal's father shrugged. "That's it. 'Tell him the dandelions have come.' " Hal's father drained what was left of his coffee. "I suppose that's what you can expect when you give an old woman a flower to talk into."

Hal smiled at the image of Harriet speaking through her daffodil. Why not dandelions? *Dandelions!* Hal leaped to his feet. "What did she say?"

"Stop shouting. She said—"

"—the dandelions have come!" Hal finished for him. "Call Lew. Tell him. Tell him to bring the duck cage."

"Where?" Hal's father called after him. "Listen, Hal, it's garden day."

"Get Lew!" Hal yelled. "I'll be back!" He waved at his father standing in rumpled pajamas, squinting in the sun-filled doorway. "I'll be back," he promised, and ran.

He found all four Titcombs out on the porch, Harvey in his wheelchair draped in a blanket, and Harriet supported between Marjorie and Carl.

"Now, Aunt Harriet," Marjorie was scolding, "I told you to let us get a place ready for you before we brought you down."

"Anyway," Carl protested, "I don't see a thing. Oh, Hal, could you drag up that chair?"

Marjorie fussed as they seated the old woman. "You can't see anything that small. It's your imagination again."

"I didn't see," snapped Harriet. "I heard. Over the hill and complaining every step of the way. Just like all those other springs."

Lew's car turned into the drive, but stopped near the road. The duck could be heard from somewhere in the orchard, that same raucous fanfare, only more severe, more wild. Emily came padding up in her nightgown. Lew followed, puffing; Hal could see that he'd just thrown on a shirt and climbed into his jeans. Straight out of bed, Hal guessed.

"There!" Carl pointed. "There she is."

At first they could see only the small white duck, with her bright orange bill going a mile a minute, whipping the world into line, screaming behind her, screaming before her, and announcing herself to those assembled by the house. Hal stared past the green-black trunks, still drenched from the heavy dew. Blossoms curled in deep pink buds; a woodpecker, alarmed, took flight. Then, out of the long orchard grass they came. Yellow fluffheads in a line, peeping dandelions scurrying to keep up, faltering, hastening, marching downhill until they were in full view.

"My ducks!" cried Emily. "Not eaten. Are they mine?"

Lew nodded, but remarked in an undertone that the drake was eaten, all but his one foot.

245

Emily ignored him. "Are they?" she demanded.

"One of them is yours," Harriet told her. "And one is Hannah's. And one Hal's. And—"

"How many?" wondered Lew. "I counted six, but now I get seven."

The duck gathered in the stragglers, some of them so exhausted they pitched forward and crumpled about her.

Carl walked around behind them, found a hub cap lying beside the barn, and turned on the hose to wash it out and fill it. The ducklings gravitated toward the overflow.

"A punishing trek," Harriet commented. "All the way up the hill from the pond. I wonder how many she lost."

Marjorie said, "There is no pond."

"Tell that to the duck. There's supposed to be."

"I told you, Aunt Harriet, there will be. A little one."

"We should get them in the barn," Lew told Hal. "Give them a rest before caging them. I'll go home for some mash."

Carl and Marjorie and Lew and Hal and Emily formed a semicircle around the duck and her ducklings. The duck screamed, but allowed herself and her babies to be driven into the barn. Hal stayed long enough to see the ducklings beginning to revive and feed on bugs in the rotten flooring.

Back outside he heard Harriet shouting at her brother, telling him the ducks were back.

Harvey looked her up and down, then called toward the house, "Harriet, Harriet! Gran's out here!"

"Old fool," Harriet grumbled. "Suit yourself." Seeing Hal taking this all in, she grinned. "I'll keep him company till he comes to his senses, but I need another chair for my leg."

Hal said he'd get it and ran into the kitchen, where he

246

found the things from Hannah's keeping-room still arrayed on the counter like trophies. Hal opened the second journal and turned the pages till he reached the end. He carried it to the other counter, where telephone and message pad and a felt-tipped pen were neatly set out.

He had the pen open and poised over the blank page when he realized he couldn't make one blue mark in Hannah's copybook. Instead he tore off a sheet from the pad beside the telephone. At the top it said, "While you were out . . . . called." He turned the sheet over to its blank side and wrote: "May. Second Sabbath. This morning the ducklings came. They are tiny and yellow, like dandelions. The mother duck was looking for the pond, which is gone, but she came anyway, because she knew this was where she belonged. So the ducks are not lost. We will take care of them and keep them safe and sound. H.W."

He slipped the telephone message sheet into Hannah's copybook and set it, closed, beside the other one on the counter. Then he picked a chair with a pad on the seat for Harriet's leg and carried it out to the porch.